D1542126

LUDINGTON PUBLIC LIBRARY
BRYN MAWR & LANCASTER AVENUES
BRYN MAWR, PA 19010-3471

A HENRY HOLT MYSTERY

LIGHTNING

JOHN LUTZ

HENRY HOLT AND COMPANY
NEW YORK

Henry Holt and Company, Inc.
Publishers since 1866
115 West 18th Street
New York, New York 10011

Henry Holt® is a registered
trademark of Henry Holt and Company, Inc.

Copyright © 1996 by John Lutz
All rights reserved.
Published in Canada by Fitzhenry & Whiteside Ltd.,
195 Allstate Parkway, Markham, Ontario L3R 4T8.

Library of Congress Cataloging-in-Publication Data
Lutz, John, 1939–
Lightning/John Lutz. —1st ed.
p.   cm — (Henry Holt mystery)
I. Title. II Series.
PS3562.U854L54   1996
813'.54—dc20   95–43273
CIP
ISBN 0-8050-4379-9

*Henry Holt books are available for special promotions and
premiums. For details contact: Director, Special Markets.*

First Edition—1996

DESIGNED BY LUCY ALBANESE

Printed in the United States of America
All first editions are printed on acid-free paper.∞

1 3 5 7 9 10 8 6 4 2

FOR BOB AND MARTHAYN
Thanks for livening up
the old home turf

307195729

The winds grow high;
Impending tempests charge the sky;
The lightning flies, the thunder roars;
and big waves lash the frightened shores.

—PRIOR, *THE LADY'S LOOKING GLASS*

1

BETH TOLD him not to be so gentle. Which surprised Carver as he made love to her in the beach cottage with the surf whispering outside in the night.

It was cool for a summer evening, and a soft breeze was pressing through the screened window along with bright moonlight. Laura, Carver's former wife and the mother of his children, had during the early months of both of her pregnancies reassured him that he wasn't going to injure her or the fetus during sex. In passion she'd urged him not to be tentative; she was pregnant, not breakable. Still, Carver had been careful.

Beth was careful, too.

She'd been pregnant once before and it hadn't turned out well. The baby had been stillborn after strangling on the umbilical cord.

Since her pregnancy their lovemaking had been unlike its usual desperate pleasure driven by lust as well as love. Love had become ascendant.

Carver felt her long body become rigid and arc beneath him. Her stomach muscles tensed and rippled, and he became still for a moment. Then, propped on knees and elbows so his weight wasn't bearing down so heavily, his bad leg slightly to the side, he resumed thrusting into her. Her moans merged with the sighs of the surf and were like the low keening of powerful breakers turning deep water as they rolled toward shore.

Then they were both still. A single bead of perspiration dropped from the point of his chin and landed near her left ear, then tracked glistening along her neck in the moonlight before disappearing in shadow.

He kissed her lips as he withdrew from her. For a while he lay beside her, one of her long dark legs flung sideways across his, and listened to the sounds of their breathing even out. The scent of their sex still lingered, but the ocean breeze was fast chasing it from the room. The currents of cool air felt good as they played over his perspiring chest and stomach.

He was going to be a father again. He hardly ever saw his daughter Ann, who lived with Laura and her third husband in Saint Louis. And Chip, his son, had been a murder victim four years ago here in Florida, burned to death by another doomed son whom Carver eventually had come to pity. During that time he'd almost made the mistake of trying to reunite with Laura. Moth to flame.

"What are you thinking, lying over there so quietly?" Beth asked beside him.

That doomed sons keep me in business. "About marriage," he said.

She stirred suddenly and her leg dragged off of him. "Wouldn't be a good idea," she said.

She'd misunderstood. He hadn't been suggesting marriage, thinking about them. But he found himself probing, defending the idea. "Why wouldn't it?"

"Didn't work out so well for either of us last time."

"You were married to a drug lord," he reminded her. She didn't like to talk, or even think about, her years with the late Roberto

Gomez, who'd blamed her for the death of their stillborn child and tried to kill her in retaliation.

"But *you* weren't married to someone who was in that kind of life, Fred. And your marriage still failed."

She could play mean, all right. Carver had struck a nerve and should have backed off. But he didn't. Carver the moth.

"Marriage might be convenient, if nothing else," he said. "We're going to have a child, you and I, and the legalities ought to be clear."

She raised her head and stared over at him, the moonlight highlighting her beautiful dark features, prominent cheekbones. She had the haughty air of an African princess, out of time and place, but royalty nonetheless. "This is going to be a racially mixed child, Fred. What problems there'll be will have nothing to do with legal formalities. You want to get all legal, we can have an attorney draw up a prenuptial agreement."

"You only have a prenuptial agreement if you're planning on getting married," he pointed out.

She let her head drop back on the pillow and laughed. "A few weeks ago you were willing to agree to my having an abortion," she said. "Now you're talking marriage. What's next, a barbecue pit and a minivan with a flip-out infant seat?"

Carver didn't think those infant seats were a bad idea. "I always wanted this baby," he said. "You were the one considering an abortion. I would have gone along with it, not held it against you. It was your decision to make. That's how I felt and still feel. There was never any doubt about that."

She rolled over to face him, propped up on one elbow. She was smiling. "We arguing, Fred?"

He was quiet for a moment. "It does sound that way."

"You gonna press me to get married?"

"No." He hadn't really thought hard about it, somehow knowing she wouldn't consider it.

"I decided not to have an abortion," she said. Her long forefinger with its bright red nail touched his lower lip. "Isn't that what you wanted?" The nail was sharp and might have cut his lip if she hadn't quickly withdrawn it.

"Is it what *you* wanted?"

"Yes," she said. "That's why I made the decision. I want this baby, Fred. Want it in the worst way, when I'm not sick in the morning or I don't wake up with second thoughts."

I never have any second thoughts.

But he didn't say what he was thinking. He figured he'd better lay off talking about marriage. At least until he'd considered it some more. Maybe it wasn't such an unacceptable idea. They weren't a couple of kids shacking up in the seventies. He was in his mid-forties. She was thirty-six. Sometimes he was bothered by the idea of growing older. She never seemed to think about it. She was a survivor; maybe she assumed she could somehow survive old age, somehow manage to skip over the unpleasant and inconvenient business of death.

"You thirsty?" he asked.

"No. What I am is tired, and I'd better get some sleep. I've got an appointment tomorrow morning to interview John York."

"Isn't he the guy who wants to make handguns and automatic weapons illegal in Florida for anyone but police?"

"Yeah. *Burrow* wants to do a feature on him." *Burrow* was the small and aggressive newspaper Beth wrote for. It specialized in going after stories that for one reason or another the mainstream press shied away from covering. Being a giveaway paper, it couldn't afford to pay its journalists much, so for Beth her job was mostly a labor of love, an outlet for her own outrage and resentment at the abuses of power.

John York had built a surprisingly large organization that was becoming a pest in the state legislature, lobbying for a change in Florida's lenient gun control laws. Carver wondered where Beth stood on the issue. She was familiar with guns and he'd seen her use one without hesitation. Even with enthusiasm.

He decided to avoid the subject. Why start another argument? And as a private investigator with a class G license, he'd continue to be able to carry a gun if he needed one. Any change in the law wouldn't affect him, except perhaps to make his world a little safer and more predictable.

He sat up, swiveled around, and sat on the edge of the mattress. "I'm going to get something to drink," he said.

She didn't answer as he reached for his cane, levered himself to his feet, and limped barefoot into the cottage's kitchen area. He opened the refrigerator, found a can of Budweiser hiding behind a plastic container of lettuce, and opened it. Some of the foam fizzed coolly over his hand, and a little of it dripped onto his bare right foot.

He stood for a minute or two leaning on the sink, taking pulls on the beer can and looking out at the immense blackness of the moonlit ocean beyond the wide window with its hanging potted plants. In the quiet night, the surf sounded closer than it was, rushing and slapping against the beach.

Carver returned to stand next to the bed, holding the Budweiser can out for Beth. "Sure you don't want a drink?"

"I'm sure."

He leaned his cane against the wall and lay down beside her. Stretched out on his back, his head propped on his wadded pillow still damp with sweat, he sipped the cold beer and listened to the ocean.

"We happy, Fred?" Beth asked drowsily beside him.

"We're happy."

2

IN THE MORNING, Carver went for his daily therapeutic swim in the ocean. It always made him feel better to swim far out from shore, kicking from the hip with both legs and stroking with his lean but powerful upper body. He was at no disadvantage in the sea, and not at as much of a disadvantage on land as some people might think. Using a cane, along with regular exercise, forged a strong torso and arms and a conditioned quickness. His grip was iron, and his walnut cane could become a lethal weapon in an instant.

He floated on his back for a while, looking in at the few early swimmers and sunbathers on the public beach beyond the crescent of land where the cottage sat. Near a corner of the cottage his ancient Olds convertible was parked beside Beth's newer, white LeBaron convertible. The canvas top on his car was up, the LeBaron's top was lowered. The grouping of three palm trees that had shaded her car when she parked it there yesterday afternoon were now casting their shadows in another direction. The LeBaron's interior would already be hot to the touch.

He saw Beth walk out onto the cottage's plank porch, raising her hand to her forehead to shield her eyes from the morning sun as she gazed in his direction. He lifted an arm and waved to her.

As he rolled over and began swimming toward shore, he caught a glimpse of her turning and going back inside. Then he scanned the beach, found his cane jutting from the sand as a marker, and stroked toward it. He swam hard in an Australian crawl, breathing rhythmically as he swiveled his head, keeping up a steady kick with his legs and reaching far out with his cupped hands with each powerful stroke. He'd taken it easy this morning, with too much floating on the gentle swells and luxuriating in the sun, and he wanted to extend himself, so he was breathing hard when he reached shore.

CARVER ENTERED the cabin still dripping with water, his towel slung over his shoulders like a cape. His breath was still a little ragged from his sprint to shore. He tracked sand on the plank floor as he made his way into the bathroom, removed his trunks, and showered.

After drying himself with a clean, rough terry cloth towel, he wiped the fog from the center of the medicine cabinet mirror and regarded his tanned features—catlike blue eyes tilted slightly upward at the corners, a bald pate, and a thick fringe of curly gray hair around his ears and growing too far down on the back of his neck. He ran his fingertips over his chin. Paperwork awaited him in his office on Magellan Avenue in nearby Del Moray. Only paperwork, no clients. Nobody to impress. Why not take advantage of the silver lining? He decided to skip shaving this morning.

Five minutes later, wearing gray slacks, black loafers he didn't have to lace, and a white polo shirt, he poured himself a cup of coffee from the Braun brewer and sat on a stool across the breakfast counter from Beth.

She was almost finished with a plate of eggs, dry toast, and some asparagus spears left over from dinner last night.

Pregnancy.

"I left the eggs out for you," she said. "If you don't use them, put them back in the fridge."

He sipped some of the strong black coffee, figuring he'd catch the news on TV before having breakfast. "I thought you had an interview to do this morning."

"I do," Beth said around a bite of egg. "At nine-thirty. I've gotta get out of here within a few minutes."

"Better take a towel to sit on," he told her. "You left your car's top down."

She smiled at him in a way he recognized. Oh-oh.

"It isn't running right," she said, "and I didn't want to waste battery power raising or lowering the top. The engine's missing like I might have bought some cut-rate gas that has water in it. Mind if I borrow your car for the interview?"

"I need to get into the office," he said, "catch up on paperwork, pay some bills, see if the electric company's turned off the power."

She thought for a moment, chewing toast. "How about if you follow me into Del Moray, make sure I make it to the interview? Then if the LeBaron quits running I can call you on the cellular and you can pick me up." She used the edge of her fork to cut an asparagus spear in half. "That is, if it starts in the first place."

"I'll follow you," Carver said, "and after the interview phone me and we'll take your car to a repair shop where they can drain the tank, if water in the gas is the problem." He didn't want her stranded somewhere in the summer heat. After all, she was pregnant. "If you got a bad tank of gas, you shouldn't be driving around much anyway. Rough on the engine."

She agreed to that plan, then sprinkled pepper on and consumed the asparagus spear. She glanced at her watch and frowned. Maybe she was going to eat it next.

Carver looked wistfully at the carton of eggs on the counter. Now that he knew breakfast would have to be delayed, he was hungry.

He took a throat-scalding gulp of coffee, then got down off his stool and put the eggs in the refrigerator. The second part of his plan would be to stop at Poco's taco stand on Magellan for a take-out Mexican breakfast after making sure Beth got safely to her interview.

The day could be starting better.

3

CARVER FOLLOWED the LeBaron down A1A, which jogged east just outside of Del Moray and for a few miles became Magellan Avenue. It was easy to keep the LeBaron, which had started easily and seemed to be running okay, in sight. Despite its advanced age, the Olds, with its powerful V-8 engine, was faster than the newer convertible, and Beth was wearing a very visible bright yellow headband to keep her hair neat in the swirl of wind.

They passed the strip mall on Magellan where Carver's office was located next to Golden World Insurance, drove south for a while, then turned west on Flamingo. South again on de Leon Boulevard.

De Leon was a wide street with a grassy median lined with palm trees whose trunks were painted white to a height of about five feet. There were mostly office buildings and shops on both sides of the street, then farther west de Leon narrowed and the neighborhood became residential. In the extreme west end of Del Moray, it ran through a poor, mostly Hispanic neighborhood, then continued west through orange grove country and ended near Interstate 101. John York, the subject of Beth's interview, lived outside Del Moray, so they still had a long drive ahead of them. Carver didn't mind. He had the top up on the Olds, but all of the windows were cranked down and the morning breeze bounced and buffeted through the car's interior. The vibration of the rumbling, prehistoric engine ran from the accelerator pedal and steering wheel through his entire body. Shadows were still soft and the digital sign on the bank they were passing indicated that the temperature hadn't yet touched eighty. He felt good, following Beth's jaunty little convertible and watching errant strands of dark hair escape from beneath her headband and whip in the wind, loving her and contemplating their future with more pleasure than uncertainty. He didn't mind the drive at all.

Brake lights flared on the LeBaron, and it slowed and veered toward the curb.

At first Carver assumed Beth was having trouble with the car. Then, ahead of them, just before the street began to narrow, he saw a crowd of people on the wide median directly across from a low brick building.

Beth let the LeBaron coast forward and parked half a block from the building. Carver saw now that the crowd was made up of demonstrators, many of them carrying placards. He couldn't make out what the crudely printed signs said as he braked the Olds to a halt behind Beth's car. The building they were picketing was, as far as he could determine, without lettering or a sign to indicate what went on inside.

Beth climbed out of her car and walked back toward Carver. He saw that she was wearing her sunglasses with the large round lenses. She was such a tall and graceful woman that her pregnancy, in its tenth week, was barely noticeable beneath the green blouse she wore loosely over tan slacks.

The sun was reflected in both lenses of her glasses as she approached the car, then leaned over to speak to Carver through his rolled down window.

"I've been meaning to phone this place and cancel my appointment," she said. "Since we're here, I think I'll go in and cancel it in person."

"This place is what?" Carver asked. But he had a pretty good idea. And he knew why Beth had stopped even though she was pressed for time.

"It's Women's Light," she said. "An abortion clinic."

Which explained the lack of a highly visible sign, Carver thought. "It would be easier to phone later from the cottage," he said.

She shook her head. "No. I'm here, and it will only take a few minutes to cancel personally."

"You were going to drive past it, then you saw the pro-life demonstrators."

"I think of them as anti-choice."

"Beth—"

"I don't want them to scare me away. I've got a right to go in that building if I want to without being hassled."

"Sure, but you don't have to go in there at all. Not now or ever."

She lowered her glasses on her nose and gazed over their rims at him with serious dark eyes. "You were me, Fred, would you go in there?"

"No."

"Ha! You'd go. You're the most stubborn, obsessive bastard I know. I don't like you lying to me, Fred."

"I wouldn't go in there if I was pregnant. That's God's honest truth."

She stared at him with disdain. "Well now, Fred, I think you're pretty safe in saying that. Otherwise you wouldn't say it."

He knew she was right. Knew she was going.

"I've got business in there," she said. "I'm just gonna walk in, cancel my appointment, then walk back out. No trouble. I'll simply make my point, then leave."

There was shouting coming from down the street, in front of Women's Light. Beth straightened up and turned, and Carver watched through the windshield as a young woman with blond hair got out of a red Jeep with a canvas top and ran the gauntlet of demonstrators. The law prevented them from crossing the street to be close enough to the building to physically block access, but several of them were waving signs angrily and screaming at the woman. A man and a woman in jeans and red T-shirts with black lettering on them ran across the street and tried to stuff some literature into the blond woman's hand. She tried to avoid them, batting the literature away, then hurried inside through the clinic's glass double doors. Carver got a glimpse of someone just inside the clinic greeting her. The two demonstrators who'd flaunted the law hurried back to the median. The man was waving his brightly colored, glossy pamphlets in the air as he ran, as if they were the scalps of enemies.

Beth leaned down again so she was looking at Carver, her dark glasses back in place on the bridge of her nose. "I won't be long, Fred."

"Don't rise to their bait," he cautioned.

"I be cool," she said jokingly.

He didn't like that. A bright and educated woman who'd fought her way out of a Chicago ghetto, she slipped into street jargon only when she was angry and determined.

He watched her stride past her parked car, then along the sidewalk in the direction of Women's Light. A few of the demonstrators had noticed the tall, regal figure heading toward the clinic and were either staring at her or telling others of her approach.

Carver waited a moment, then put the Olds in drive and glided it around the parked LeBaron and back in close to the curb, rolling forward slowly but staying twenty feet behind Beth. He could make out the demonstrators' signs now, mostly red-lettered anti-abortion slogans on plain white backgrounds. A few of them featured reproductions of color photos of aborted fetuses. Some of the demonstrators were carrying long, white wooden crosses, thin and light enough to march with and wave without getting tired. The red T-shirts were lettered OPERATION ALIVE across their chests.

Carver stopped the car at the curb, turned off the engine, and continued watching Beth and the demonstrators. Several people were jabbing the air with their signs and crosses, their faces masks of rage as they screamed at Beth that babies were being killed inside the building and she shouldn't be one of the murderers. Several of them shouted verses from scripture, and a tall man with white hair was waving a Bible frantically in his right hand and pointing to it with his left. Two large women wearing shorts and carrying aborted fetus signs screamed insults at Beth in perfect unison, as if they'd practiced in the manner of a singing duet. Unruffled, Beth removed her sunglasses, glanced over at them, and smiled.

When she was ten feet from the building, the man and woman with pamphlets darted across the street toward her. Several other people crossed the street west of the building, staying just outside the legal limit.

Instead of ignoring the pamphleteers or swatting their thrusting hands away, Beth clutched the man's wrist and squeezed it hard, dragging him for a moment toward the building. He fought to pull back, dropping his pamphlets in the struggle, and she grinned and released him, then pushed inside through the glass doors. As soon as the man scooped up the dropped literature, he and his partner ran back across the street. Carver was aware of several other figures racing back across the street to the legal sanctuary of the median. At the same moment, a Del Moray police car approached from the other direction and parked about a hundred feet west of the demonstrators. Carver was relieved to see it.

Then the blast roared through the hot air and seemed to rock the heavy Olds. Stunned, Carver saw Beth come flying back out through the shower of sun-touched glass that had been the building's doors and land hard on the sidewalk. She stayed propped up in a sitting position for a few seconds, then fell back. Even from where he sat, he could see her head bounce off the concrete. Black smoke began to roll above the building against the backdrop of bright blue sky.

Carver couldn't move. *Jesus! Is this real? Is this* real?

Figures casting stark shadows were running in every direction. As he recovered from his shock and climbed out of the Olds, Carver saw two Del Moray cops pile out of the cruiser and race toward the building, leaving the police car's doors hanging wide open. Placards and glossy pamphlets littered the street and median.

The stench of ruin was in the air. The feel of death.

Already sirens were screaming as Carver set the tip of his cane on the baked concrete and hobbled as fast as he could toward Beth.

4

CARVER FOLLOWED the ambulance back into the center of Del Moray, his heart pounding as the air was split by emergency sirens and flashing red-and-blue lights that fought the sun.

Beth had been bleeding and unconscious when they laid her on a gurney and got her into the ambulance. Carver told himself the bleeding was only from minor cuts made by flying glass, but he knew he was only hoping.

The ambulance veered to the right lane, then turned into the circular driveway of the emergency entrance to A. A. Aal Memorial Hospital. By the time Carver found a parking slot in the adjacent lot, Beth had already been removed from the ambulance and taken inside.

As he entered through the double-wide pneumatic doors, he found himself in an area of green walls, carpeted cubicles, and beige-curtained partitions. A medicinal scent mingled with the acrid smell of Pine-sol, so cloying that Carver wondered if the air itself could heal minor illnesses, hung in a coolness that chilled like icy water after the warmth of outside. Green-gowned doctors and white-uniformed nurses were roaming the wide corridors, but there was no sign of Beth. Carver's heart plunged to depths out of proportion to the simple fact of losing sight of her.

She isn't dead, he reassured himself; she's only in one of the diagnosis and treatment rooms. *But I don't know that for sure.*

A heavyset nurse with pale lips and wild red hair sat behind a long counter with a gray computer on it. When Carver approached her, she looked up from writing on a yellow form and smiled. For some reason the perfunctory smile angered him. He wasn't here to make small talk or return a toaster; someone he loved might be dying, and this woman was smiling!

She seemed to read and understand his anger, and the smile faded. "Yes, sir?" she said. She had round, flesh-padded cheeks that made her eyes seems small, but there was a pleasant quality to her features that would exaggerate expressions of cheer. He realized that she hadn't really given him the kind of smile he'd assumed.

"Beth Jackson," Carver said. "She was just brought in here from the explosion on de Leon."

"Explosion?"

"Where is she? Can I see her?"

"You a relative?" the nurse asked.

"Closer than that."

"You're assuming responsibility for payment?"

"Of course!"

She turned away from him and picked up a phone with a curved shoulder rest on its receiver, then talked for a minute in tones too low for him to overhear.

The wide doors to outside hissed open and a blond woman on a gurney was wheeled in by two somber attendants. Beyond them Carver could see the back end of the ambulance with its doors open. The woman was covered to her chin with a white sheet and had an oxygen mask over her face. Her entire body seemed to be trembling beneath the sheet. As the gurney was wheeled past, Carver saw that most of the hair on the left side of her head was singed black. He remembered the young blond woman who had walked into the clinic ahead of Beth.

Standing and watching the attendants wheel the woman down the hall and into one of the curtained cubicles, he hadn't heard the nurse behind the counter.

". . . will come out and talk to you in a little while."

He turned. "What?"

She was sitting on a stool and working at the computer now. "Beth Jackson's being examined in room seven. A doctor will come out and tell you her status as soon as possible."

"Where's room seven?"

"It's not a regular hospital room." She motioned toward the wide hall. "One of those curtained diagnostic rooms." She played the keyboard, smiled, and said, "Ah, there we go. I have a few forms for you to fill out, Mr . . .?"

"Carver. Fred Carver."

She stretched far to the side and lifted some pink and yellow forms from a nearby metal tray, then set them on the counter. "It will probably be a little while before the doctor talks to you. Do you want to take care of these now?"

Carver stared at the forms. *In the midst of life, in the midst of death, there are forms.* "Sure," he said. Maybe it would occupy his mind, hold at bay the dread that would double him over if he gave it a chance.

"I need you to answer a few questions first," the nurse said. "Is Ms. Jackson covered by insurance?"

He patiently fielded her questions while she fed his answers into the computer.

Ten minutes later, when he was finished with the questions and the forms, the nurse directed him to the emergency waiting room.

It was a square room divided from the corridor by a low bank of potted ferns. The walls were green, like the rest of the walls in emergency, and the carpet was dark brown. An even darker brown vinyl sofa sat with its back to the ferns, and along two of the walls were alternatingly red and gray molded plastic chairs, somehow fastened together so they stayed neatly aligned. In a corner sat a table holding a Mr. Coffee and stacks of foam cups. Some of the cups were sitting upright and held packets of sugar and artificial sweetener and powdered cream. There was also an opened box of tea bags, though Carver didn't see any hot water. Directly above the coffee brewer was a TV mounted on a steel arm that elbowed out from the wall. The TV was tilted down slightly and aimed so that its screen was visible from most of the chairs in the room. A talk show was on without sound. A grim-looking woman wearing dark glasses and an obvious black wig was seated in a chair directly facing the camera. Beneath her a caption read "Slept with her mother's boyfriend." Carver poured coffee into one of the foam cups, then sat down in one of the plastic chairs facing the corridor. On the wall adjacent to the TV was a square clock that read 9:45. The coffee was bitter. He was alone in the room except for the woman who'd slept with her mother's boyfriend.

At a few minutes before ten, a woman even more grim than the one on TV walked into the waiting room and slumped on the vinyl sofa. She didn't look at the TV or at Carver. He thought she was about forty. She had dark hair that was mussed and hanging over one eye, and she would have been attractive if it weren't for the fact that she'd obviously been crying and was under a strain that seemed to clutch at her face from the inside. She folded her hands in her lap, bowed her head, and stared at them, moving one finger then the other, as if testing to make sure they still worked. Her jaw was set. He could see the play of muscles in front of her ears as she rhythmically clenched and unclenched her teeth.

Ten minutes later a tall man in his early twenties, still with the gangly build of his teen years, shuffled into the waiting room. He was wearing Levi's and a gray T-shirt and seemed upset. As he sat down in one of the plastic chairs, he glanced at the TV, then promptly stood up. He paced, sat down again in another chair. He bent forward, elbows on his knees, and stared at the floor, digging the toes of his dirty white jogging shoes into the carpet and jiggling his legs. He acted as if he were the only one in the room. Carver realized that everyone was acting that way, himself included. Waiting room etiquette. This kind of trouble didn't like company.

The wall clock acted as if time didn't exist and it was pretending to be a painting. Carver tried not to look at it.

Only a few minutes had passed after the gangly man's arrival when a doctor in a wrinkled and stained green gown appeared and rested a hand on the woman's shoulder. Without a word, she stood up slowly and followed him into the corridor and out of sight, like a sleepwalker half awake with dread.

The young man in the chair stared briefly at Carver, then let out a long, loud breath and stood up. He turned up the volume on the TV and sat back down. "I don't care about other people's morality," shouted a gray-haired man sitting next to the woman who'd slept with her mother's boyfriend. He was wearing a suit and tie and had on dark glasses like the woman. He smiled as the audience applauded. A black woman in the audience stood up, leaned close to the microphone extended to her by the bald black man who apparently was the show's host, and shook her finger at one of the guests on stage as she said, "You're hurting other people besides your own self!" The gangly young guy got back up and turned the volume down too low to hear again. Carver was glad.

Another doctor in a green gown appeared, this one a slight young woman who appeared to be of Indian descent. Carver tensed his body and gripped the crook of his cane to stand up, but the woman crossed the room and said something to the gangly man. He looked stricken as he rose from his chair and followed her from the waiting room and down the corridor in the direction the woman and the other doctor had gone.

Carver didn't at all like the way this was going.

A long time passed, even according to the clock on the wall. Two nurses entered the waiting room, sat side by side in plastic chairs, and exchanged copies of papers from folders they were carrying, then left. Later an elderly man wearing work clothes came into the room, glanced at the TV, then at Carver, and sat down on the sofa. He leaned sideways as if reaching for his wallet but instead pulled a paperback book from his hip pocket, crossed his legs, and began reading intently. Carver got only a glimpse of the title: something about angels.

"Mr. Carver?"

Carver looked up to see the surgeon, the one with the badly wrinkled green gown who'd left earlier with the woman, standing near him. He was a weary-looking, fiftyish man who would soon be as bald on top as Carver but for now combed his hair sideways in a pathetic attempt to camouflage his gleaming scalp.

As he parted his lips to ask Carver's identity again, Carver nodded. There was a lump in his throat that made him afraid to try his voice.

The doctor, whose name was Galt, according to the plastic tag pinned to his gown, understood and smiled.

"Beth's going to be okay," he said.

Something heavy and dark seemed to shift from Carver. He leaned back in the chair with relief and wiped at his eyes with his knuckles.

Dr. Galt looked around, then at the cane leaning against Carver's chair. "Want to come with me?"

Carver nodded and stood up.

He followed the doctor down the corridor to a small, neat office with a desk, an extra chair, and a small, round table with a vase with artificial flowers in it sitting precisely in its center. There was no sign of the woman or the young man from the waiting room. Carver sat down in the chair in front of the desk. Dr. Galt sat on the edge of the desk and crossed his arms. There was a window behind the desk. Carver could see numerous birds fluttering in a tree on a patch of grassy ground near the parking lot. It was a happy scene, another world.

"How seriously is she hurt?" Carver asked.

"Concussion, and we picked some broken glass out of her." Dr. Galt paused. "And a badly bruised hip and abdomen." He stared at Carver uneasily, with a tired compassion.

It took a second for what he'd heard to hit Carver full force. *Hip and abdomen!* "The baby?"

"I'm sorry, Mr. Carver. She lost the baby."

"You're sure?" He knew it was a stupid question even as he spoke; the words had simply slid out from between his lips.

Dr. Galt treated it like any other question. "Yes. We've already done a D and C. We had no choice."

Carver listened to his own breathing for a while. "Does she know?"

"Not yet. She won't be conscious for at least another few hours."

"Because of the anesthetic?"

"No, we used locals on her. She hasn't yet regained consciousness from the blow on the back of her head and the trauma from whatever struck her pelvic area. We surmise a heavy object or piece of debris propelled by the force of the explosion hit her there. That might have been the impact that sent her out through the glass doors, where the paramedics said they found her. All her cuts are superficial, needing only a few stitches to close some of them." Dr. Galt studied Carver for a moment, then forced a smile. "The thing is, Mr. Carver, she's alive. You might have lost them both."

Carver swallowed. Beth was alive. But the baby . . . again, like her first pregnancy.

"I'm sorry, Mr. Carver. I *can* tell you it's still possible for her to bear children. That's something."

"Something," Carver agreed. He was sweating. The room was cool but he could feel his clothes sticking to his flesh.

The doctor straightened up from where he was perched on the edge of the desk. "I'd better get back to my patients. You going to be okay?"

Carver nodded and stood up, leaning on his cane.

"I'll have the duty nurse tell you what room Beth's going to be in. Check back in a few hours and you can go up and see her."

"Have they found out anything about the explosion at the clinic?" Carver asked.

Dr. Galt shrugged. "I don't know anything about it other than that it was lethal. Two dead, two injured. We're going to have to amputate the other injured woman's lower right leg. She'll lose her foot and most of her ankle."

"We should count our blessings, is that the message?"

"We really should do that, Mr. Carver. Every day."

"Beth didn't even have to be in that clinic."

Dr. Galt held the door open for him. "Usually none of us really has to be anywhere." He shook his head sadly. "Still, things happen to us."

5

THE ONLY thing in the hospital cafeteria that looked remotely edible was the salad. Carver used tongs to place some in his plastic bowl, got a cup of coffee from a nearby self-service urn, then paid the cashier. He found a table off by itself near the single row of windows that ran the length of the cafeteria.

He wasn't really hungry, but he knew he had to eat, both to keep up his strength in case there wouldn't be a chance later today, and to pass the time. So he dutifully chewed forkfuls of lettuce and sipped coffee between bites. A group of women were clustered around the table closest to him, apparently employees chatting about hospital gossip on their lunch hour. Beyond them sat two men in white uniforms—nurses, Carver assumed. They were eating quietly. One of them was studiously reading a folded newspaper. Most of the other tables were occupied by one or two people, friends or relatives of patients, reading paperback books or staring pensively at nothing while they ate, wondering and worrying. At the far end of the cafeteria, on the other side of a low railing, sat several doctors in suits and ties. Carver recognized one of them from earlier that day when the man was wearing a surgeon's green gown.

As Carver returned his attention to his food, he noticed the gangly young man from the Emergency Department waiting room. He was seated at a table near the wall opposite from where Carver sat. There was no food on the table, only two cans of soda and two white foam cups. Sitting across from the gangly youth was a slim woman with short, curly black hair, a ballerina's long neck, and dark eyes. She was wearing white shorts and a white blouse, what in other surroundings might have passed for a tennis outfit. She probably hadn't seen thirty and had a very sweet, oval face of the sort seen in cheap religious paintings. Her expression was one of compassion, and she seemed to be trying to console the young man, leaning toward him and talking earnestly, once even patting his hand.

The man suddenly seemed to sense Carver staring at him and glared over at him. Carver quickly looked away and concentrated on his salad. It embarrassed him to intrude on someone else's grief, to the point where it was sometimes even awkward for him to express sympathy. He was a private person and didn't like his own emotions trespassed upon. "Out of touch with his feelings," a female friend had once said of him. But he knew it wasn't that at all; he simply assimilated grief and other powerful emotions gradually as he adjusted to them—perhaps because he was *more* sensitive than his friend the amateur analyst.

When he chanced another look at the table where the man and woman had been talking, they were gone.

After lunch he sat for a while trying to kill time by reading a Del Moray *Gazette-Dispatch*. But it was too early for any news of the Women's Light Clinic explosion, and he couldn't concentrate or remember what he'd read ten seconds after his eyes had passed over it. He gave up on the news, set the paper aside, then went back to emergency and asked the nurse at the desk if Beth had been transferred yet to a regular room. The nurse checked on her computer, then shook her head no and told him it would be a little while yet.

He wandered outside and went for a walk, but the afternoon was heating up and within a few blocks he became uncomfortably warm. He wasn't wearing a hat, and though his bald pate was tanned and fairly impervious to being burned, he could feel the sun blazing down on it and figured maybe it had reached its limit. Sweat was streaming down his face, and his legs were weak. There were days when he'd felt better.

After standing for a while in the shade of a building canopy, leaning against the wall, he felt stronger and realized he was near the entrance to a large discount store. He entered and wrestled a can of Coca-Cola from a vending machine. Enjoying the coolness and quiet, he roamed the aisles, gazing at lotions, loud silk shirts, and a 50-percent-off sale on swimming suits, suntan oil, and beach towels with sunsets and flamingos on them. He thought he might have one of those flamingo towels at home.

He finished his Coke and he dropped the can into a metal trash receptacle on the way out of the store. Then he walked back to the hospital and entered through the Emergency Department door.

This time the nurse at the desk didn't disappoint him as she smiled and checked her computer. "She's in four-fifteen, Mr. Carver."

He thanked her and rode the elevator up.

AFTER KNOCKING SOFTLY, he cautiously pushed the wide door of 415 half open and peered inside.

Beth seemed to be sleeping soundly. There was an IV packet of clear liquid dangling from a vertical metal rod attached to the bed, and a clear tube coiled down from it to the back of her right hand. Carver eased inside and let the door swing shut behind him. The room was cool. It had beige walls that were almost white, beige drapes that stopped at the marble windowsills, beige metal furniture except for the green padded chair at the foot of the bed. Vertical white metal blinds were angled so that the room was softly lighted. There was a medicinal scent in the room, but no smell of Pine-sol like in the Emergency Department.

Carver went directly to the bed. Though Beth was resting supine, he could see that the back of her head was bandaged. A cut about an inch long on the side of her neck was stitched and smeared with pink antiseptic. Half a dozen fine cuts were peppered over her face, two of them on her right eyelid, but the doctor had said nothing about her eye being injured. Her lips were dry and her features drawn.

She opened her eyes to swollen slits and saw him, then gave the faintest of smiles. Her dry lips parted. "Shoulda driven on past that place," she said in a grating whisper.

He couldn't speak, so he nodded and rested a hand lightly on her shoulder. She slipped her hands beneath the white sheet, IV tube and all, and he could see them stirring beneath the thin material. They moved tentatively to the area of her stomach, where new life had existed this morning. He watched her face for a change of expression, but there was none.

"What happened?" she asked.

"Almost certainly a bomb." Evasive Carver, not ready yet to tell her. But he'd never be ready.

"A nurse told me I could have been killed. Doctor said I'd be okay, though, after a few days in here. Told me I had a concussion. Am I talking sense, Fred?"

"Perfect sense."

"I don't have a headache. Aren't you supposed to have a headache with a concussion?"

"Been my experience. I guess you're on medication for the pain."

He'd talked enough that she'd picked up something in his voice. She stared up at him. She didn't blink.

"There's something I don't know," she said.

He swallowed loud enough to hear his throat crack. "The baby."

"What?" It was as if she'd forgotten she was pregnant and he'd reminded her. But he knew she hadn't forgotten. Some part of her knew what must have happened and didn't want to hear it or believe it. Everything would be different once he uttered the words and it had been confirmed, made real.

"The baby." He found that he was squeezing her shoulder and loosened his grip. "We lost it."

She closed her eyes but still didn't change expression. Her hands stirred again like frightened thoughts beneath the thin white sheet. She moaned softly.

He leaned over and kissed her cool forehead. He didn't know what else to do. Didn't know what he could do for himself. He felt like sobbing.

"It isn't fucking fair!" she said in a flat voice.

"No," he agreed, "it isn't."

She opened her eyes again and gazed up at him. Her eyes were moist but she smiled thinly. "You gonna cry, Fred?"

"No."

"Me either. This is rough, though."

He said nothing.

"I'm bad luck for babies, I guess."

"Don't say that. None of it was a matter of chance, any more than the rest of life is chance."

"But that's what it all is, don't you see, Fred? Nothing means anything . . . it's all chance, no matter what we do."

It was a notion that scared him because it might be true and no one could afford to believe it. "You can't think that. Think about yourself instead. Please!"

She sniffled. "I guess I have to."

"Yes. No choice."

"It isn't gonna break me," she said.

"I didn't think it would."

A rhythmic squeaking out in the hall grew louder, stopped, then the door swung open and a plump blond nurse with kind brown eyes and a serious expression walked in on soft-soled shoes that squeaked with each step. She nodded to Carver and smiled at Beth. The serious expression disappeared entirely and her eyes lit up with her smile, as if she really felt the good cheer she projected. "We doing okay?"

"More or less," Beth said flatly.

The nurse bent over her and examined her pupils, then took her temperature and blood pressure. After marking something on the clipboard she was carrying, she went to where the plastic IV packet was slung on the metal rod. She got a hypodermic needle from the drawer of a nearby beige metal cabinet, filled it with clear liquid from a vial she was carrying, then injected the liquid through a plastic connection in the IV tube. "To help you rest," she said to Beth.

"Should she sleep with a concussion?" Carver asked.

"At this point it's okay. She has other trauma." Again the smile. "Don't worry, we're keeping a close watch on her."

But Carver was worried.

"You don't have to stay, Fred," Beth told him.

"I want to stay," he said.

"It isn't necessary," the nurse assured him.

"I'm not going to let this fuck me up," Beth said softly, and closed her eyes.

Carver and the nurse watched her as her breathing deepened and evened out.

"She'll sleep for several hours," the nurse said. "Maybe longer. You're welcome to stay here if you want, but you don't have to.

Why don't you leave a message at the nurses' station where you can be reached if she wakes up and wants you or needs something?"

Carver didn't like the idea of leaving Beth, even though she obviously didn't need him for anything at the moment. He hesitated, then nodded and left the room with the nurse.

He dropped off both his office number and the beach cottage's phone number at the nurses' station down the hall from Beth's room, then limped to the nearby elevators and pressed the down button.

It took awhile for the elevator to arrive. Carver's mind kept circling what had happened, playing on the screen of his memory the images of Beth flying backward out of the clinic in a shower of fragmented glass, falling back, her head bouncing off the concrete walk. People throwing aside placards and diving for cover. Figures running in the edges of his vision. Something there he couldn't quite grasp. Maybe something important. Now Beth was in a hospital room, and the baby . . . their baby . . .

He felt shaky as he entered the elevator, and tears brimmed in his eyes. He drew a deep breath and held it.

As the elevator dropped toward the lobby, he fumbled in his shirt pocket for his sunglasses and put them on, then leaned against the hip-high metal rail along the back wall. Casual Carver.

The elevator lurched to a stop at the second floor, and a large man with a stomach paunch and a loud tropical print shirt stepped in and unnecessarily punched the glowing button for the lobby. Carver allowed himself to breathe.

When they reached lobby level, Carver and the paunchy man waited patiently for the elevator doors to slide open. Through his dark glasses, Carver saw that the tropical shirt was festooned with a pattern of brightly colored parrots flitting among brilliant flowers. The man stared directly at him, even raising himself slightly on his toes as if he could peer over the rims of the sunglasses and see what Carver might be concealing.

"You okay, buddy?" he asked.

"I'm fine!" Carver snarled at him as the doors slid open on the lobby.

The paunchy man stood and stared at him as he hurried past him out of the elevator.

"Hey, buddy," the man said behind him in a loud, annoyed voice, "don't take it personal."

But Carver didn't answer or look back. He tightened his grip on the crook of his cane and limped quickly toward the exit and the cauterizing sun.

6

BETH SLEPT most of that day. At six that evening she was examined and was awake for another hour, during which she and Carver were never alone. Within minutes after the doctors and nurses had left, she was asleep again. Carver stayed with her in the room until eleven o'clock, then left and drove back to the beach cottage.

He lay awake in the dark for a long time, listening to the ocean and wondering. The evening news had revealed that the explosion at the clinic definitely had been caused by a bomb. The somber and handsome newscaster quoted police as saying they had leads and expected an arrest to be made soon. Then there was an interview with Operation Alive members who'd been picketing at the clinic that day. All of them denounced violence and professed to know nothing about the bombing. Carver stared into the shadows and thought about the irony of the bomb injuring a woman who had gone to the clinic to cancel her appointment for an abortion. What would Operation Alive think about that?

Probably that it was too late for her to be exculpated after the sin of making the appointment in the first place.

From up on the highway came the sound of a truck accelerating along the curve that paralleled the coast, a faraway whine of tires on still-warm concrete, then gradations of engine noise as the driver shifted through the gears.

It was the last thing Carver heard in the sultry night before falling asleep.

IN THE MORNING, when he returned to the hospital to visit Beth, he was pleased to see that she was sitting up in bed. She had her head wrapped in a pale yellow scarf wound like a turban. The IV needle had been removed from the back of her hand, leaving a black-and-purple bruise tinged yellow with antiseptic. She looked much better, more clear-eyed and alert.

Carver walked to her and kissed her on the lips, then placed the valise with the clothes and cosmetics she'd requested on the chair next to the bed.

He was suddenly aware of an odor in the room that didn't belong. It had about it the cloying sweetness of something rotting in the sun.

"Just who I wanna fucking see," said a voice he recognized.

He turned around to see Del Moray police lieutenant William McGregor, and he realized the familiar odor was the cheap deodorant McGregor used as a substitute for bathing. The lieutenant was nobody's favorite cop. He was corrupt and ambitious and blatantly reveled in his evil. He hated Carver. Carver hated him.

"I've been talking to your dusky friend here," McGregor said. He was a skinny but strong man, six and a half feet tall, wearing his usual rumpled brown suit and stained shirt, his boat-size brown wing-tip shoes. He had a lean face, lank blond hair that flopped down over his forehead like Hitler's, and a wide space between his front teeth through which the pink tip of his tongue habitually peeked like a serpent. He didn't approve of interracial love affairs, said his mean little blue eyes, and he didn't feel at all sorry for Beth. If Carver had asked him, he probably would have said as much.

Carver looked at Beth. "Do you feel well enough to talk to the police?"

She nodded. "Might as well get it over with. It can't take long, because I don't have much to tell. All I know is that I walked inside the clinic, then got blown back out through the door."

"Wages of sin," McGregor said with a wicked grin, pulling a small, leather-covered note pad and a pencil from his pocket. The movement made his suit coat open wider and revealed the checked butt of his shoulder-holstered nine millimeter. Also fanned the stench and failure of his deodorant across the room.

"What sin?" Carver asked.

"Yours and hers, dumbfuck. You knocked her up and she let you do it, or she wouldn't have been anywhere near that explosion."

Beth knew how McGregor fed on other people's misery and tried not to show she was upset. "I thought you were going to tell us you were pro-life or pro-choice, but that would mean you believed in something other than yourself."

McGregor looked over at Carver and grinned, poking his tongue through the space between his teeth at the same time. It made him look incredibly lewd. "Hey, she's still feisty, even after getting her ass blown through some glass doors."

"Still thinking clearly, too," Carver said. "She's got you figured out."

McGregor shrugged. "Pro-life, pro-choice, who gives a flying fuck? I'm pro-me and I'm not ashamed to admit it." He poked at his concave chest with a long forefinger. "Pro-me, just like everybody else is, when push comes to shove."

"You sound proud of it, though," Beth said. Despite Carver's warnings, she was always surprised anew by the totality of McGregor's evil. He wished she'd be quiet; inspiring others' loathing was

McGregor's crude way of communicating with people. It would have been pathetic if it weren't so . . . well, loathsome.

"Damned right I'm proud," McGregor boasted. "Charles Darwin would be proud of me, too. He and I both understand nature, including human. I accept my nature, which is just like yours. Only you don't accept what you are. Don't even admit it to yourselves. Hell, I admit it and like it. Tell you, Carver, I feel good about myself, just like all the psychology assholes advise."

Carver tried to imagine McGregor reading psychological self-help books but couldn't. Maybe *I'm Despicable, You're Despicable.*

"You're as repugnant as anyone I've ever met," Beth told McGregor.

He smiled at her, happy to have roused her ire. "Thanks. And you should be a good judge, considering you've slept with repugnant characters. Even married one. Way it goes, you lie down with shit, and you can't help but get up with it all over you."

Carver felt his anger surge and took a step toward McGregor. He wanted to grab him by his wrinkled brown lapels and knock out some of his oversize yellow teeth.

He almost raised his cane to swing it at McGregor's head. Then he stopped. McGregor was staring at him, still smiling. This was what he wanted. Anything he'd said that was out of line could be denied, and McGregor could lie like a corrupt choirboy. And a scuffle would bring people, leave evidence. The kind McGregor wanted in order to nail Carver with the law he sometimes wielded like a hammer.

"Keep right on coming, dickface," McGregor said, obviously disappointed that Carver had stopped. "This is exactly the kind of thing I'd expect from a dumb gimp like you." He moved his hand slightly so it was resting on the butt of his holstered gun.

Carver didn't move. "Find out what you need to know, then get out," he said tersely.

"Humph!" McGregor said, opening his notebook. "You'd think

you gave the orders around here. Dr. Carver, pilfering drugs from the supplies between fucking the nurses. You should be so lucky." He turned his attention to Beth. "What did you see when you entered the clinic?"

Beth thought for a moment. "A reception desk with nobody sitting behind it. A hall leading to some doors. A woman in the hall, well ahead of me. Then I saw . . . I don't know, the explosion, pieces of wall and wreckage flying upward, outward, toward me. The force of the blast lifted me up, and I found myself sitting outside on the sidewalk. That's all I can remember about it. The next thing I knew I was here, at the hospital."

McGregor kept writing for several seconds after she'd finished talking, his tongue protruding from a corner of his thin-lipped mouth. Then he lifted the pencil and said, "Notice what was going on outside the clinic as you were walking in?"

"You mean the demonstrators?" Carver asked.

"I'm not questioning you, Carver," McGregor said "I wanna do that when your lies won't help you. That day's coming."

"Most of the demonstrators were across the street," Beth said. "They were waving their signs around and yelling at me."

"Yelling what?"

"Insults. A few of them called me a murderer. One said I was a nigger bitch and was going to hell."

"Some of those people must know you," McGregor said.

Carver stirred.

McGregor grinned.

"Notice a blond man carrying a sign come out from around the building at about the time you entered?"

"I don't think so," Beth said.

"Think before you answer," McGregor told her.

She closed her eyes, then opened them. "I can't remember much in the way of details from that time, but I don't think I saw anyone run out from behind the building."

"Run?" McGregor thrust out his long scoop of a chin. "I didn't say anybody was running. You probably saw this man running and forgot till now." He began scribbling in his note pad.

"I saw people running," Beth said. "I remember that now. They were down the street, though. I think they were, anyway."

"What about a blond man? Dark pants, white shirt, carrying a sign?"

"No," Beth said, "I don't remember anyone in particular."

"Then you *might* have seen him."

"Well, yeah, I suppose he could have been there."

"Good. You might have to testify to that."

"The news said it was definitely a bomb," Carver said. "And that you've got a line on the bomber."

"Of course it was a bomb, Mister Fucking Curious. And we've not only got a line on a suspect, we got the suspect himself in custody. Brought him in about an hour ago. Mechanic named Adam Norton, got himself an arrest record for assault, and he's a member of Operation Alive. That's the bunch of religious nutcakes that were picketing the clinic yesterday morning. Beth's not the only one who saw Norton run out from behind the clinic just before the explosion."

"What's Norton say?"

"Nothing, to you."

Carver leaned on his cane and stared at McGregor.

"Okay," McGregor said. "You read the papers anyway, and I want it made clear there's no reason for you to go sniffing around this case, maybe fuck up some evidence we need. Norton claims he's innocent and only went behind the clinic so he could wave his sign where it would be seen through an operating room window."

"Not much of an alibi," Carver said.

"Hardly one at all. Why would he wave a sign in a back window, so some pregnant bitch would look over and read his message while the doctor was taking a half-baked roll outa her oven? It'd be too late by that time."

"If Norton—"

But Carver stopped talking as he heard Beth sob. McGregor had become too much for her. Carver understood.

"Time for you to leave," he said to McGregor.

"Oh, we on a schedule here?" Then he too noticed Beth had her head lowered and was sobbing. Tears were tracking down her cheeks, spotting her gray hospital gown. He smiled and shook his head. "Well, it appears our patient's having a relapse."

Carver tightened his grip on his cane. McGregor took a step toward him, suitcoat held open to reveal his gun.

"Please give it a try," McGregor said. "Go ahead and swing that cane."

"Ring for the nurse," Carver told Beth, without looking away from McGregor.

She pressed the button pinned to her sheet. Neither Carver nor McGregor moved.

Beth stopped sobbing.

When the nurse entered, she stopped and stood still also. She was the same serious nurse with the shockingly mirthful smile who'd been in the room yesterday. She looked at Beth, then at Carver and McGregor.

"We think it's time for Lieutenant McGregor to leave," Carver said.

There was no hint of the smile on the nurse's face. "Time for both of you to go," she said.

"No," Beth said. She pointed at Carver. "Not him. Please."

The nurse glared at McGregor. "That leaves you odd man out," she said in a voice that would have made Dirty Harry proud.

McGregor grinned, snapped his note pad closed, and slid it and the pencil into his shirt pocket.

"I was leaving anyway, sweet cakes," he said to the nurse. "I've had my health fix for the day."

He strode over and pushed out through the swinging door, leaving behind only the lingering scent of his cheap deodorant.

"That is a man," the nurse said, wrinkling her nose, "who is not very nice."

"Like cancer isn't a cold," Carver said.

7

CARVER DIDN'T like the feel of McGregor's dead certainty that Norton was the bomber. This was a high-profile case, and a successful rush to judgment would be beneficial to McGregor's career. It wouldn't concern him at all if an innocent man was imprisoned for murder. Why should it? He figured there were no innocent men.

Not that Carver was feeling any particular sympathy himself right now for Adam Norton. Especially if he really was the bomber. Carver's concern was in seeing that whoever was responsible for what happened to Beth and their unborn child would be caught and punished. He wanted revenge. Not so much justice as revenge. His pursuit of his unborn child's killer wasn't simply a job, like McGregor's. It was a mission.

He parked the Olds outside Vinny's on Egret Road. Vinny's was a lounge where off-duty Del Moray police hung out. It had in a previous incarnation been a hardware supply warehouse and was a narrow but long building of cinderblock needlessly painted a dirty gray, about the color of cinderblock. Its garish red-and-green

neon sign featured tilted champagne glasses with bubbles rising
from them to spell VINNY'S, but Carver was sure champagne was
never served there. Vinny himself was Vincent Carbello, a retired
Del Moray vice detective. He ran an impeccably clean and honest
operation, or at least was experienced and clever enough in his
corruption that he wasn't suspected of misdeeds.

One of the regulars at Vinny's was Paul Geary, a cop promoted
to detective first grade after a recent shoot-out with drug traffick-
ers in which he'd apprehended two suspects while bleeding from a
bullet wound in his arm. A couple of years ago Carver had helped
Geary's daughter out of a problem concerning a manslaughter
charge. Geary owed him, and Geary hated McGregor. When
Carver phoned and asked for a meeting, Geary suggested Vinny's.
Carver liked that. It was very possible that if the two men met and
talked at Vinny's, someone would carry news of their meeting to
McGregor, Geary's superior. Geary obviously didn't give a damn.

Vinny's was cool after the noon heat outside. It was filled with
a soft buzz of voices against the background noise of a country-
western song coming from the speakers mounted behind the long
bar. Randy Travis was crooning in his deep voice about something
profound that had happened in a pickup truck somewhere in Ten-
nessee. Carver paused inside the door, waited a few seconds for
his eyes to adjust to the dimness and acrid tobacco smoke, then
looked around for Geary.

Most of Vinny's business was in the evening, but even now, a
little before noon, most of the stools at the bar were occupied.
There were booths on the wall opposite the bar, and farther back
toward the rear of the place were more booths along the walls and
tables set out in the middle. The walls were paneled in light knotty
pine and were decorated with clusters of sports memorabilia and
photographs. About half of the tables and booths were occupied.
There were only a few uniforms in the place, but Carver recognized some of the other faces and knew many of the customers

were cops. Some of them surely recognized him, but gave no indication. Discretion was the better part of complication.

He noticed Geary seated in a booth toward the back, his bulky body hunched over a mug of beer. Geary had seen him enter and was watching patiently without expression as Carver made his way toward him. He was a medium-height but very broad man with a face that was ugly in an amiable way, like that of a veteran boxer who'd started his career handsome and whose features had been coarsened by years of battle. He always looked as if he needed a shave, perhaps all over his body. Hair sprouted thick and dark on his forearms and the backs of his hands. The hair on his head was worn in a dark buzz cut, short and bristly. Carver had never seen him with any other hair style and could easily imagine him having been born with such a haircut, as well as the rest of his body hair, the offspring of half-human, half-bear creatures.

When Carver approached, he didn't stand up, but he extended his hand and smiled. He had long, yellow bicuspids that made him look even more like a bear when he smiled, but a sly bear.

Carver shook hands and slid into the seat opposite Geary in the booth. On the wall over the table were two crossed bats, and a Marlins baseball cap hung on a peg between their barrels. A tall, thin barmaid with long brown-gray hair, whose name Carver remembered was Tammy, came over and Carver ordered a Budweiser and a replacement for Geary's half-empty beer mug.

"How's Beth?" Geary asked.

"She's going to be okay," Carver said. He didn't mention the baby. Geary didn't know about that and didn't have to.

Neither man spoke as Tammy returned to the booth and placed their drinks on the table. When she'd gone back behind the bar, Carver said, "How are you getting along with McGregor?"

Geary showed his yellow canine teeth again. "Nobody gets along with McGregor, he can only be endured."

Carver slowly poured some of his beer from its bottle into a frosted mug, creating a small head of foam. "He got a statement from Beth this morning at the hospital."

Geary grunted. "He should have sent somebody else."

"He came himself because he enjoys the fact that she's hurt, and that—it's because she and I are together. You know, the racial thing."

"McGregor!" Geary said with disgust, making a face as if he might spit. His wife was Cuban, as was their beautiful daughter Rachel, whom Carver had helped two years ago. "Was he rough on Beth?"

Carver poked at the head of his beer with his finger, as if that might deflate it and he could sip sooner without acquiring a foam mustache. "He would have been rougher if I hadn't shown up. He tells me there's a suspect in custody in the clinic bombing."

"Yeah, a guy named Norton. It'll be on tonight's TV news, along with McGregor bragging and hogging time in front of the cameras."

"You think Norton's good for it?"

"Might be."

"McGregor seems positive about him."

Geary took a sip of beer. "Norton was in the wrong place at the wrong time—from McGregor's point of view, anyway. He's an auto mechanic lives over in Orlando, got a wife and kid. Religious fanatic. We got a warrant, searched his house and garage, and found detonators and books on bomb making. That's when McGregor decided the charge would stick."

"Heavy evidence," Carver said.

"Sure is. And witnesses place him at the scene, inside the legal limit for demonstrators and running out from behind the building a short time before the blast."

"He sounds good for it," Carver said.

"He will be, if McGregor has his way."

Carver watched Tammy serve a scotch to a compact black

woman in a white dress, seated in the next booth. He thought she might be a police officer, Frances something . . . but he might have been thinking of someone else. "You don't sound as sure as Mc-Gregor about Norton," he said to Geary.

Geary rotated his beer mug on its cork coaster, leaving a dark, damp ring. "You gotta wonder if Norton acted alone or somebody put him up to it. McGregor doesn't wonder. He figures if he wraps up this case all neat and tidy, he's a cinch for a promotion. The slimy bastard wants to be chief someday."

"But you don't want him to be."

"No cop working under him wants it. He only kisses ass and bullshits his superiors. Other people, he cuts their throats then steps over them on his way up, careful not to get blood on his shoes." Geary raised one of his meaty hands, palm out. "But don't get me wrong, Carver. If this Norton guy actually did the deed, I want him to go down for it. Every other cop on the force does, too."

Carver wondered if by "every other cop" Geary meant one out of two.

"My brain tells me he's guilty but my gut says he might be innocent," Geary said. "Or that he was acting as part of somebody else's plan."

"What about Norton's membership in Operation Alive?" Carver asked.

"They're a religious group from Orlando, been demonstrating around the South against abortion. Some of them are extreme. There's been violence at their demonstrations before. Nothing like what happened here, though."

"Was Norton involved in any of the violence?"

"Not as a matter of record." Geary took half a dozen swallows of beer, tilting his head way back. The tendons on each side of his thick neck stuck out like cords. When he set the half-empty mug back down, he said, "The thing about Norton is he says he's innocent, but he also says he would have done it if he'd had the chance. He's glad the clinic was bombed. He thinks abortion doctors are fair game." Geary played with his beer mug and coaster again. "Guilty men don't usually talk that way."

"So there are reasons to doubt his guilt," Carver said.

"Not many, but some. You have to look hard."

Carver leaned back and gazed toward the front of the lounge, at the drinkers at the tables, some of them munching snacks or hamburgers. The drinkers slouched at the bar were more serious about their booze; no food visible there. That said something about them. Maybe. Psychology. It was easy to read so much into things, and so much of what you read could be wrong. The collar seemed to him to fit Norton almost perfectly.

Randy Travis was singing now about something profound that had happened in the backseat of a Buick convertible in Kentucky. Tammy started toward their table, but Geary waved her away.

"I don't know," Carver said. "Norton seems like the ideal suspect."

"Ideal patsy, too. Guy's a true believer."

"You think the real bomber might have set him up?"

"Anything's possible," Geary said. "People like him are suggestible."

"Does Norton claim somebody set him up?"

"No, just that he's not guilty."

Carver looked at Geary. The man was a war-weary cop, and an honest one. Not the smartest, maybe, but a plodder who never gave up. One who took great pride in his work. But no superior officer could inspire disloyalty in his men more effectively than McGregor. Sometimes that disloyalty was conscious and flagrant, sometimes unconscious and subtle. But it was there nonetheless, like an infection that waxed and waned.

"Maybe it's not all that complicated," Carver suggested. "Maybe you're not so sure about Norton's guilt simply because McGregor is."

Geary didn't argue. He nodded. "And because he's McGregor."

Both men understood the odious lieutenant whose very thoughts were corrupt enough to draw flies, and who had the minds of his own officers muddled out of sheer hatred for him.

Carver sat back and worked on his beer. The woman who might be a policewoman named Frances glanced at him and smiled. But he wasn't thinking about her, he was thinking about McGregor.

McGregor, who was completely cynical about humanity, and who was often in the way of justice because he didn't believe it existed.

Carver sometimes hated himself for weakening and thinking McGregor might be right.

8

GEARY LEFT Vinny's after finishing his beer, and Carver asked Tammy to bring him a hamburger and a morning *Gazette-Dispatch*, if there happened to be one lying about.

Five minutes later Tammy returned with a delicious-looking hamburger heaped with tomato, lettuce, and onion on a sesame seed bun, and a badly wrinkled but readable newspaper that had been left by a previous customer. Most of the sports section was missing, but the front section was intact even if the pages had been shuffled. Someone had torn out a ten-minute oil change coupon, but there had been nothing printed on the back of it about the clinic bombing. Instead the interrupted news item had to do with a hostage situation in the Middle East. *Trouble all over the map*, Carver thought. He smoothed out the front page and read as he ate.

The dead in the clinic bombing were Dr. Harold Grimm— ostensibly the target, if there was one besides the clinic itself—and a patient named Wanda Creighton, the woman who'd walked into the clinic ahead of Beth. She had come to the clinic, which concerned itself not only with abortion but with many phases of women's health, to talk to Dr. Grimm about amniocentesis to determine the sex of the child she had decided to bear. The injured were Beth and volunteer nurse and receptionist Delores Bravo. Only slightly injured, and not requiring hospitalization, was a nurse named Janet Havens who had been preparing an operating room for an abortion scheduled for later that morning.

The paper was an early edition and made no mention of Adam Norton. It did mention Operation Alive, describing it as an extremist anti-abortion organization based in Orlando and headed by a Reverend Martin Freel. The Reverend Mr. Freel was quoted as denying that Operation Alive had any connection to the bombing, and that any such allegation was absurd and part of a plot instigated by pro-choice fanatics to undermine the operation's effectiveness. The Bible was quoted by Mr. Freel, the commandment about bearing false witness. Then he refused to say anything more about the bombing and referred any further questions to his attorney, Jefferson Brama.

Carver set the paper aside and finished his hamburger, thinking the law and the Bible sure made life confusing.

The news item had mentioned Dr. Grimm's widow, Adelle. Carver paid Tammy, then went to the phone booth against the back wall and tried to look up the Grimms' number and address in the directory.

But there was no Dr. Grimm listed in Del Moray or environs. Obviously the Grimms had an unlisted phone number, which made sense, considering they were the target of people who were violent.

Figuring Geary was either back at his desk by now or in the field where he could be reached by phone, Carver dropped his change in the slot and pecked out the number of police headquarters. Geary would probably tell him the Grimms' address and phone number. When Geary had walked out of Vinny's, he was in the mood to help Carver do anything that might cause McGregor trouble. And if it happened to cause Carver trouble too, that was acceptable. Life in law enforcement was rife with politics and political victims.

THE GRIMM HOME was on Phosphorus Lane in west Del Moray, in a palm-lined section of modest stucco houses with tile roofs and attached garages at the end of long gravel driveways. Most of the garages were made of brick and looked more substantial than the houses. Practicing in an abortion clinic was apparently less profitable than other places where a physician might ply his trade. Harold Grimm probably hadn't been the sort of doctor who spent much of his time on a golf course.

The new widow Adelle Grimm's house was yellow stucco with a green tile roof, green awnings, and a small front porch with a wooden glider at one end. The front door was painted dark green and had a small, triangular window in it.

Carver thought there was something mournful in the drooping canvas awnings, the sagging gutter over the porch, the shaded windows like the eyes of the dead, as if the house somehow knew and shared the grief of its inhabitant.

He climbed out of the parked Olds and walked toward the house. The small front lawn was green and closely cut so that parallel stripes of varicolored grass from recent mowings showed in it, and the flower bed around the porch was tended and colorful. Birds chirped, bees hummed. The yard wasn't mourning along with the house. There was no sign out here that one of its owners had died unexpectedly and violently.

Carver took the two low steps up onto the porch and stood in the shade. There was no sound from inside the house. He pressed the brass doorbell button with the tip of his cane.

Still no sound.

A jet airliner roared overhead, rolling constant thunder through a cloudless blue sky, and he didn't hear anyone approaching on the other side of the door, inside the house.

But suddenly the door was open and the dark-haired woman he'd seen in the emergency waiting room yesterday morning was staring out at him.

She wasn't a tall woman, but she seemed tall because she stood very erect and her features had a narrow, rectangular line about them. Her hair was mussed and brushed back off a high forehead. The swelling around her red-rimmed eyes narrowed them and added to the straight-lined symmetry of her face. Too old to bounce back after the death of a spouse, too young to bear the burden of sudden widowhood with philosophical acceptance, she gazed out at Carver from her new situation and did not smile or say hello.

Carver tried a smile. A fierce-looking man in repose, he knew that his smile was surprisingly beatific and reassuring, transforming his face and putting people at ease in his presence. One false impression replaced by another. Was that how it was with Beth's nurse? The somber one with the mirthful smile?

Carver suspected she might be somber all the time, considering what she saw almost every day.

"I saw you yesterday at the hospital," Adelle Grimm said, not returning his smile. There was a delicacy about her, not of physique but of attitude, that suggested she wasn't strong enough to survive emotional storms. And right now she was in a hurricane.

"We have something in common," Carver said. "You lost your husband in the clinic explosion, and I lost a child."

"A child?" She appeared puzzled. Then she said, "Oh," and the lines of her face softened. Her eyes, which were a dark violet, became moist. Carver hoped she wouldn't cry. "You mean the pregnant woman who died?"

"No. The mother lived. She's still in the hospital."

Adelle nodded, understanding. "The African-American. How is she?"

"She's going to be okay."

"I'm glad." She said it with such sincerity that, looking into her sad, violet eyes, Carver felt an interior tug and was afraid his own eyes would brim with tears.

"My name's Fred Carver. Would you mind if we had a talk?"

"About what?"

"I'm a private investigator, Mrs. Grimm."

"Are you working for someone?"

"No, I consider this a personal affair. I'm my own client. I want to know what happened. I *need* to know. Do you understand that?"

She seemed to give it some thought. She was a woman who thought a lot about things, Carver figured. More a deliberator than a creature of impulse.

"Come in out of the heat," she said, opening the door wider and stepping back to allow him room to enter.

The house was furnished in a clean but cluttered way that must make people feel at home. The carpet was gray with a red border. There were two matching gray-and-red chairs, and before a wide window with white curtains was a cream-colored sofa with a bright floral design. A long coffee table sat in front of the sofa and had a vase of plastic daffodils and some dog-eared *Home Companion* magazines on it.

"This is nice," Carver said, leaning on his cane and glancing around. "You have the homemaker's touch."

Adelle Grimm managed a smile. "I suppose that's a compliment, even if it isn't politically correct."

Carver didn't see why it was politically *in*correct. "I mean, you make a home look comfortable and attractive."

She motioned for him to sit on the sofa, then sat down in one of the gray-and-red chairs and crossed her legs, lacing her fingers over the top knee.

"I'm, uh, sorry about your husband, Mrs. Grimm."

She nodded and looked around her, as if suddenly finding herself in strange surroundings. "Harold never really spent a lot of time here. He was so . . . dedicated."

"He did useful work," Carver said.

She stared at him with her red-rimmed eyes. "Do you really think so?"

"Yes. Did he spend a lot of time at the clinic?"

"Every other day. He alternated with Louis—Dr. Benedict. But on off days he was usually on call at Kennedy Hospital." Again she glanced around, as if appraising her life from this new and terrible perspective and wondering if her husband's effort and dedication had been worthwhile. So many missed dinners and parties, so many nights home alone. "Harold did sincerely believe in his work. It consumed his thoughts and his time and eventually it got him killed. Murdered." For a second it appeared that she might begin to cry, but she took a deep breath again, even managed a smile that came and went in an instant. It was a smile that pierced Carver's heart like a beak.

"It's . . ."

"What, Mr. Carver?"

He didn't want to put it into words. Why should he, when she had to know how he felt? "Life can be surprising and unfair at times," he said inadequately.

"Yes," was all she said.

"They caught the man, at least."

"I hope they execute him," she said dispassionately. "Harold wouldn't approve, but I hope they convict Adam Norton and then kill him. He's the kind of zealot who's ruining this country." She sniffed and bowed her head, placing the heel of her hand against her forehead. "Not that he isn't entitled to his point of view, if all he wanted to do was argue it and demonstrate."

Carver thought that was an odd thing to add to what she'd just said.

"Then you're convinced of Norton's guilt?" he said.

"Of course. Witnesses place him at the scene, and the police found explosives and instructions on how to make bombs when they searched his home. But if you ask me, he's not the only guilty one."

Another surprise for Carver. "He's not?"

"I don't mean anyone else is legally responsible," Adelle Grimm said, "but that bastard Reverend Martin Freel should pay some kind of penalty for killing my husband. He's one of the people who feed religious zealotry and murderous delusions to maniacs like Norton, feed it to them by the bucketful knowing the more they eat, the hungrier they get. Then when someone is injured or killed at a women's clinic, people like Freel step back and cluck their tongues and profess to have no connection to the violence." She gazed at Carver with her sad, swollen eyes. "When is this country going to have enough of this kind of thing?"

"I don't know," Carver said. It was a good question, all right. "In the months before his—before the bombing, did your husband receive any threats on his life?"

She laughed hopelessly. "Are you joking? He was a physician at an abortion clinic. He received threats almost every day. Vicious phone calls in the middle of the night, threatening letters, graffiti on the side of our house or on the sidewalk out front . . . it's all been an intimate part of our lives. A few months ago someone even sent us an aborted fetus in the mail." She swallowed and wiped at her eyes. "It was gift wrapped so it looked like a box of candy."

Death is like a box of chocolates, thought Carver with revulsion. He could better understand why she thought Norton should be executed.

Adelle stood up and walked to a small cherry wood secretary and opened one of the desk's wide drawers beneath the fold-down writing surface. She withdrew a bundle of envelopes bound with a large rubber band.

"Here," she told him, handing him the bundle. "You can take them with you. The police have already seen them, and I'd just as soon have them out of the house."

Carver accepted the envelopes, then planted the tip of his cane in the soft gray carpet and stood up. He handed Adelle Grimm one of his cards.

"If you think of anything that might help," he said, "or if you need help, call me."

She nodded, then preceded him to the door. Her step was heavy and deliberate, as if she were weighed down by her loss. He felt that he should say something more to console her, but he couldn't find words that wouldn't seem contrived and hollow.

"I wish you well with your grief, Mr. Carver," she said from behind the closed screen door, as he limped from the porch and along the bright sidewalk toward his car.

So she had found the words for him. Women were so strong and savvy about such things. In the depths of her own grief, she'd been aware of his and known what to say to him. It was a demonstration of empathy and strength worth admiring.

He noticed now that the lawn, though it appeared well tended and neat from a distance, was beginning to fall victim to weeds.

9

IN HIS OFFICE on Magellan, Carver examined the letters given to him by Adelle Grimm. For the most part they were the usual nutcase notes, written or typed with misspellings, deliberate or otherwise, and for some reason with very narrow margins. They conveyed the sense that while they were threatening and irrational, the writers were unlikely to pose an actual danger.

Two of the letters, however, interested Carver. They were signed, and they seemed to amount to more than the venting of paranoia and frustration.

One, from a man named Xaviar Demorose, with a Del Moray address, went into detail as to how he was going to abduct, torture, then murder Dr. Grimm. The other letter was more temperate but quoted scripture fluently and was signed by a Mildred Otten, who identified herself as a member of Operation Alive.

Carver folded both letters and slid them into his shirt pocket. Then he dragged the desk phone over to him and pecked out the number of A. A. Aal Memorial Hospital and Beth's room extension.

Her voice sounded throaty and weary when she answered the phone by her bed. Maybe she'd been asleep, or she was groggy from her medication.

"You feeling better today?" he asked.

"Fred?"

"Yes."

"Just a moment." There was a pause. Then, "I had to switch the receiver to my left ear. I keep forgetting I still can't hear well out of my right."

"The doctor didn't tell me you suffered a hearing loss."

"Told me," Beth said. "Whispered it in my left ear."

Carver almost smiled. It was good to hear her usual acerbic tongue. "Has the hearing in your right improved any?"

"Yeah. They tell me it should return to eighty or ninety percent normal eventually."

"We can settle for that," Carver said. "If you'd walked into the clinic a few seconds sooner you might have been killed."

"Timing and luck, maybe they're the same thing." There were faint sounds in the background, as if someone had entered the room, and Beth said something he couldn't understand, muffled, as if she had her hand over the mouthpiece. "The nurse was here looking in on me," she explained a few seconds later. "And McGregor was here about an hour ago, Fred. He was looking for you."

Carver glanced again at his answering machine; the digital counter registered no messages. McGregor hadn't called. "Did he say why?"

"No. He was only here a few minutes. He urged me to leave you and sleep with men of my own race, then he left."

"Did he upset you?"

"No. I wouldn't let him. I know how he is, how he tries to draw out people's rage or humiliation so he can feel superior."

"If he comes back, don't tell him I called. I'll avoid him."

"That would be my advice, Fred. To anyone."

"Can you get through the afternoon without me? I've got to talk to some people."

"Concerning the bombing?"

"Yes."

"About Adam Norton?"

"More or less."

"You don't think he's the bomber?"

"I want to make sure. And if he did the actual deed, I want to know who if anyone put him up to it."

"What about tonight?"

He smiled. "You're full of questions."

"That's my job, just like it's yours."

"I'll be there tonight to see you."

"Good. But don't worry so much about me, Fred. I'm on the mend."

"I know you are."

"It's just that . . ."

"What?"

"The baby." There was a catch in her voice.

Something bent and broke inside him with an abruptness that surprised him. Was he *that* vulnerable?

"I'll drive over there now," he said. "I should have come earlier today."

"Don't you dare." She sounded angry with herself. Determined.

He listened to his own breathing for a moment. "You sure you'll be okay alone?"

"I'm not alone, Fred. Including staff, there are about a thousand people in this building. Half of them come and go in this room, checking on me, giving me medication."

"So you don't need me."

"I didn't say that. Bring my Toshiba when you come tonight."

"Why would you want a notebook computer?"

"I'm going to write a piece on the clinic bombing for *Burrow*. I talked on the phone with Jeff Smith about it this morning."

"You shouldn't be thinking about work."

"I'm thinking about my work and yours, Fred. I'll need you to keep me up to speed on the investigation."

He almost cautioned her again, but in truth he was glad to find her well enough to be interested in her work. He knew how work could displace pain.

"Okay," he said, "I'll brief you when I get there this evening."

"The nurse just walked in again, Fred, this time with something that looks like a turkey baster. I've got to hang up."

"Beth—"

"Don't forget the computer."

The line went dead.

Carver, whose cooking skills and experience were limited, sat thinking that it had been years since he'd seen a turkey baster.

XAVIAR DEMOROSE'S address turned out to be the Golden Time retirement home in West Del Moray, not far from Women's Light. Carver had to drive past the clinic on his way there. The low brick clinic looked normal except for the boarded-up front doors and windows, and the wreathes and bouquets of colorful flowers laid out on the step that led to the entrance. Across the street, two dour looking men were walking back and forth with signs. One sign appeared to show a blown-up photograph of a fetus with a red *X* slashed through it. The other said simply HIS TERRIBLE SWIFT SWORD beneath a crude drawing of an explosion. Carver pushed down his anger and drove on.

Beneath whatever they used to scent the air, the lobby of the retirement home still smelled like medicine, stale sweat, and desperation. Three very old women sat side by side in wheelchairs, staring at a television set showing a soap opera. On the other side of the lobby, where sunlight fell through a high window to the tile floor, an old man with long white hair sat in a rocking chair, a knotted sheet wrapped around his midsection holding him in place. His head was bowed and he was staring vacantly at his lap. A thread of saliva caught in the sunlight stretched from his slack lips down to his chest.

From behind a reception desk, a young woman with brown hair and bangs smiled at Carver inquisitively. Her right hand was poised with a pencil, but there was nothing she might have been writing on beneath or anywhere near the hand. She had a round face that swelled when she smiled and made her look overweight even though her body was quite thin. She seemed incredibly young in contrast to the residents in the lobby. The brass plaque on the desk said her name was Claire. Lucky Claire, Carver thought, with all that life ahead of you.

"I'd like to talk to one of your residents," he said, returning Claire's smile. "A man named Xaviar Demorose."

"Oh. I'm sorry," she said in a despondent tone that made both smiles disappear. "Are you a relative?"

"No. I'm acquainted with the family."

"Mr. Demorose passed over this morning."

"Passed over?"

"Died."

That was better, Carver thought. Dying wasn't like flying over the roof. Or maybe it was.

Claire was absently pressing the sharp pencil point into her left palm, as if she'd somehow been responsible for Demorose's death and was punishing herself. "He suffered a heart attack two days ago, and he pass—he died early this morning."

"He had a heart attack the day of the Women's Light Clinic bombing?"

"I'm afraid that's so. The news excited him to the point where his heart couldn't take it." She realized what she was doing and put down the pencil. "He'd had three bypass operations, you know."

"No," Carver said, "I didn't. Can you tell me, was Mr. Demorose in the habit of writing letters?"

"Oh, sure. He wrote to everyone in the news. And when he wasn't writing to them, he was sending letters to newspaper editors and politicians, just about anyone he could think of. People in here get awful lonely sometimes. Their families forget them after awhile, and they need outside contact. Mr. Demorose, he had an opinion about almost everything, and he needed to share his opinions."

"Were they, uh . . . rational opinions?"

"Sometimes," Claire said, not willing to speak ill of the passed over.

"How old was Mr. Demorose?"

"His ninetieth birthday would have been next Tuesday." She seemed especially moved by the fact that Mr. Demorose had come so near and then missed making yet another round number. "It's all so sad, isn't it?"

"It's sad," Carver agreed, and told Claire good-bye.

MILDRED OTTEN, the second letter writer, was a different story.

She lived in an apartment on Evers Avenue a mile from the ocean, where the neighborhood began to decline. Her building was a four-story white stucco structure with green iron balconies and a front walkway that passed beneath a rotted wooden trellis rich with flaming red roses. Her unit was on the fourth floor, rear, and when she opened the door to Carver's knock, heat rolled out at him.

Mildred Otten didn't seem to notice the heat, though her thin yellow-and-white cotton dress was plastered with perspiration to her gaunt body. Her face, narrow as a board and with a mottled red birthmark covering most of its left cheek, was gleaming with sweat and she was blinking her tiny green eyes as if they stung. A lock of damp hair dangled down over one ear in a spiritless little curl. It was a strange color between blond and gray, as if she'd begun to dye it and then changed her mind.

Carver identified himself and showed her his license with its color photo that looked a little like him. She seemed satisfied, as if she didn't distinguish between private and public cops, and stepped back and invited him in. He was careful not to step on her toes; she was wearing sandals made out of tire tread with rubber loops over the big toe of each foot. On several of her toes were the kind of flesh-colored, circular bandages used to treat corns.

The apartment was steaming hot. The furniture was cheap and stained, and there was a woven oval rug on the scarred hardwood floor. On gray walls that needed paint were hung various unframed religious prints that appeared to have been clipped from books and magazines. One print was of Prometheus chained to a mountain while his liver was being devoured by a vulture. Carver wondered if Mildred realized she was mixing Greek mythology with scripture. Maybe it didn't matter. The theme seemed to be suffering. There was no sign of an air conditioner, and only one window was open—about two inches. There was no screen.

Mildred saw him looking at the window. "I don't open it wider because of the gulls," she explained in a firm, positive voice. "They're the devil's agents and they might fly in and pluck my eyes out if I allow it." She glared at him. "It happened to a woman down in Boca Raton."

"I think I read about that," Carver said.

"Two summers ago, it was."

"Yes." Carver pulled out the letter she'd sent to Dr. Grimm. The paper was damp now, and some of the printing was blurred. "Did you mail this, Ms. Otten?"

She studied it. "Of course. Isn't that my signature?"

"The letter's a death threat," Carver pointed out.

"The other police have talked to me already about that. Didn't they tell you? I explained to them it wasn't a death threat, it was a vision from the Lord. The sower hath reaped the whirlwind."

"Dr. Grimm, you mean?"

"Of course. He took lives, and someone took his own. Wasn't that just?"

"It depends on your point of view."

"Just is just," she said, shaking her head.

"Were you at the clinic the day it was bombed, Mildred? May I call you Mildred?"

"Yes and yes. I saw the wrath and lightning of the Lord loosed on the house of death."

"Innocent people were killed," Carver pointed out.

"Innocent people are killed there every day, day after day."

"Again a matter of opinion, Mildred." Carver was trying not to get angry, remembering Beth flying backward out of the clinic in a sunlit shower of glass fragments.

Mildred shook her head again, this time violently, as if flinging away his words before they might stick in her mind. "'As you know not how the wind blows, nor how a babe within the womb grows.'"

"The Bible?"

"Ecclesiastes. We haven't the wisdom to judge living tissue other than alive. It is the Lord's work. That is plain in the Word."

"I understand you're a member of Operation Alive."

"I am that, and proud of it. 'Look at my agony; my maidens and my youth are in captivity.'"

It took Carver a few seconds to realize that she was quoting again.

"Ecclesiastes?"

"Lamentations," she said. "'He slaughters and kills the children, the delight of our eyes.' That verse refers to Dr. Grimm and his kind. So I do what I can, Mr. Carver. I make picket signs, I stand before passersby whose eyes are blind and try to make them see. Ever since they released me from that place of doctors and sins, I've worked for the force of life and the reward of life ever-lasting."

"What place was that?" Carver asked. But he knew.

Mildred suddenly appeared sly. She grinned like a mischievous schoolgirl. "Ask your friends among the Romans."

"Romans?"

"The police. The ones who are crucifying Adam Norton."

"Do you know Norton?"

"He is me and I am he."

Carver stared at her. She smiled broadly. He decided she'd had nothing to do with bomb making or conspiracies; they were beyond her. Whatever anger he'd felt toward her dissipated, leaving only pity. She was probably certifiably insane.

"The police know that when the lightning struck, I was on the other side of the street picketing," she said, "toiling in the service of the Lord. He is my salvation and my alibi."

Maybe not so insane, he decided, thanking her for her time and easing his way out the door.

Maybe it was the heat.

10

AFTER LEAVING Mildred Otten, Carver drove to Poco's Tacos on Magellan near the public marina, where he sat outside at one of the small, round metal tables and had two burritos and a Diet Coke for supper. He watched the white-hulled pleasure boats bobbing gently at their moorings. They appeared impossibly clean and pure in the slanted bright sun of early evening; emblematic of money and position. Florida was different if you possessed wealth. It could be a vast playground then, Disneyworld bounded by Georgia, Alabama, and the sea.

When he was finished eating, he disposed of his paper plates and cup in an orange-and-white trash receptacle around which bees buzzed, then walked over to a bench where he wouldn't bother any of Poco's other customers and fired up a Swisher Sweet cigar. He put on his tinted glasses so the sun's reflection off the water and the white hulls wouldn't hurt his eyes. Then he sat back and smoked and looked out at the sea and the pelicans, so awkward on land and so graceful in the air, passing low over the water.

Beth hated Poco's and had refused to eat there with Carver. She'd warned him that the food tasted tainted beneath the hot spices and he was going to contract some sort of illness from it. It had all started, he was sure, when she became sick here during the early days of her pregnancy, though she didn't see it that way. He decided not to tell her he'd been here when he saw her that evening. Why upset her? He'd mention having eaten supper in the hospital cafeteria. A lie to facilitate healing.

More pelicans arrived. They put on a show, skimming low, sometimes splashing down to dive for a fish, always coming up empty. Beyond them at sea, boats with brightly colored sails tacked and canted to the wind. And beyond the boats, white clouds lay low and immense on the horizon. It was such a beautiful world, Carver thought; why did people have to plant bombs in it? But he knew the sick and the pained and possessed were out there, the ones who were sure they were striking back at something. They always had been, but now there seemed to be more of them, and coming from both ends of the spectrum. He'd always tried to practice and endorse the politics of reasonableness. He hadn't moved much in his basic beliefs. But the rest of the world had moved. People he had admired and with whom he had agreed had made a journey from dedication to zealotry to fanaticism. He couldn't go with them. He tried now to be apolitical, but people were dying.

The light had dimmed and he no longer needed the sunglasses, and there were no more pelicans. He tossed the dead stump of his cigar into a trash container next to the bench. Then he stood up and limped to his car to drive to the cottage for the Toshiba to take to Beth at the hospital.

It was official visiting hours, so the hospital parking lot was almost full. He had to park the Olds in a slot at the far end, near a low stone wall and a row of palm trees that marked the property line. It was a long walk to the entrance. The day's heat lingered and with each step the tip of his cane sank slightly into the warm, graveled blacktop.

A nurse he hadn't seen before was leaving Beth's room as he entered. Beth was sitting up in bed, leaning back on her pillow and reading a *Gazette-Dispatch*. Her hair was pulled back and tied with a red ribbon, and the front of her gown sagged to reveal the cleavage of her large breasts. Carver knew it wasn't the time to be thinking what he was thinking. She smiled at him, as if maybe she knew what he was thinking, and he went over and kissed her.

"How are you?" he asked when he straightened up, leaning on his cane. He saw now that her eyes looked weary and her features were strained.

"Better. Mad."

"Better, all right."

She straightened her gown, then touched his hand where it gripped the crook of his cane. "Just set it on the table where I can reach it."

"What? Oh." He'd forgotten he was holding the notebook computer in its black carrying case. He moved a plastic water pitcher and placed the case on the table.

"The battery charger in there?"

"Everything," he said.

She folded the newspaper, which she'd laid aside, and tossed it onto a nearby chair. "They've indicted Adam Norton."

"No surprise," Carver said. "He's probably guilty. Question is, was he put up to it?"

"I think he was. By Operation Alive."

"He might have been simply a fanatic acting on his own. There are plenty of them these days. We tend to look for reason and conspiracy sometimes when they don't exist. It's not always a rational universe."

"Hardly ever. Did McGregor find you?"

"No. Lucky me."

He thought she was reaching for her computer, but instead she picked up the plastic water pitcher. She poured water with a few chunks of ice into the plastic cup that served as the pitcher's lid, then leaned back into her pillow and sipped. When her thirst was assuaged, she held the cup in her lap with both hands and said, "Tell me about the outside world, Fred."

He filled her in on his visits with Dr. Grimm's widow and with Mildred Otten.

"There's a lot of rage out there," she said.

"There is around abortion clinics."

"The paper said the police found blasting caps in Norton's car, and traces of dynamite in his garage workshop. Not to mention several books on how to make bombs."

"He'll need a good lawyer," Carver said.

"He's got one. Name of Jefferson Brama. *Burrow* did a piece on him last year, when he was defending a pro-life demonstrator in a property damage case. He won, despite a ton of evidence against his client. He's aggressive and smooth and a winner."

"He's also the attorney for Operation Alive," Carver said, remembering reading about the Reverend Martin Freel referring media questions about the bombing to his attorney and naming Brama. "You'd think Operation Alive would be trying to distance itself from Norton."

"Oh, no. He's one of theirs. You know how those kinds of organizations play it. They goad their members into doing something drastic, then step back and deny culpability. But while they emphatically don't condone what was done, they don't actually condemn it. So they're acting as if Norton is merely a sheep strayed from the flock, instead of a calculating killer on a mission. That's how Operation Alive is playing it. Tongue clucking, but with a 'well, that's what you can expect when you murder babies' tone."

"How do you know all this?" Carver asked, glad to see her angry, taking an interest as a victim. Righteous rage was preferable to depression.

"I've been reading the papers, watching TV. That Reverend Freel is like all the rest of the smug bastards who're causing the trouble, putting themselves above the law, frightening pregnant teenage girls and calling them murderers on the way into clinics."

"And you think he's behind the Women's Light bombing? That he hired or instructed Norton?"

Her jaw set. "I think he motivated him. The Freels of this world, they yammer about saving lives, but they killed my—" She stopped talking suddenly and looked as if she might break into sobs.

"I know," Carver said softly to her, thinking she was more delicate right now than she appeared. Balanced on a fine edge. "I know what you mean and I feel the same way." He sat down on the bed and held her, waiting for her to cry, but she didn't.

She sucked in a deep breath and lay back. He noticed that she cocked her head slightly to the right on the pillow so she could hear him better with her left ear. Her face was dark stone. "Keep me informed on what's going on, Fred. When I get out of here, I want to help you pin this on whoever's responsible."

"Maybe Norton really did act on his own."

"I don't think so."

Neither did Carver, but he didn't say it. He angled his cane and stood up from the bed.

"Do you know a tall, broad-shouldered man with black horn-rimmed glasses and a blond crew cut?" Beth asked.

"No."

"He was wearing a dark blue suit, white shirt, and red tie. I thought he might be police."

"Maybe he was. Or FBI. Where'd you see him?"

"He stepped into the room earlier today, while a nurse was in here. Then he only smiled, nodded, and turned around and left. I thought he might be one of McGregor's men, looking for you."

"Could be he was. Or just some guy who wandered into the wrong room."

"He was kind of creepy. That's why I thought he might be connected to McGregor."

"Logical," Carver agreed. "Creepy how?"

"I'm not sure. I guess because he was so perfectly groomed and conservatively and neatly dressed that it almost had to be a front. He was like an automaton who'd been to Brooks Brothers."

"Ask a nurse who he is," Carver suggested.

"I did. The nurses don't know him. And he was such a straight-arrow, all-American WASP, I'm sure they'd know who I was describing if he worked here at the hospital."

"A visitor, then. Here to see one of the patients."

"Maybe."

"You're worried about him."

"Yes. I'm not sure why, but I am. He seemed surprised to find a nurse with me. Or more like disappointed. I got the feeling that he had the right room and he'd come in for a reason, then changed his mind."

Carver didn't see much basis for her fear, but he'd come to trust her instincts. "I'll find McGregor," he said, "and see if there can be some protection assigned here for you."

"I don't think there's much chance of that," Beth said.

Carver didn't either, actually. "I can spend the night here."

She shook her head and smiled, then winced at some sudden pain in her damaged body. "That's not necessary, Fred. I'm probably just more suspicious than usual."

"No one could blame you." He leaned forward and kissed her cheek. "You're a woman who was blown up."

"Fred, if you learn anything pertinent you think might upset me, I want you to tell me anyway. I need to know the truth about this."

"So do I. That's why I've been looking into it."

"And you think it might be as simple as a deranged man planting a bomb all on his own during a pro-life demonstration?"

"Might be."

"You wouldn't lie to me, Fred?"

"Of course not."

She grinned and glanced at her wristwatch propped on the table so she could see the dial. "You had supper yet?"

"Sure. Down in the cafeteria."

11

DUSK HAD closed in while Carver was in the hospital. He walked across the lot to where the Olds was parked, all by itself now near the stone wall and the line of palm trees swaying in the breeze as if they were doing a lazy hula.

As he neared the car, he reached into his pocket for his car keys. The keys jingled softly as he pulled them out and reached for the door handle. The wind kicked up harder, making the hula more hectic, and rattled the palm fronds above his head.

"Fred Carver, isn't it?"

A man's voice, neutral.

Carver turned around expecting to see a tall, crew cut WASP wearing a business suit and dark-rimmed glasses. Instead he was looking at a dumpy little man wearing a rumpled gray suit with a tie that was too long for him and whose pointed end dangled almost at crotch level. If he wore glasses they were contacts. He had the kind of curly brown hair that would always look mussed, and for that matter a face whose features would always look mussed. He smiled, looking even more rumpled, but friendly. Everybody's best friend who always dies in the movies so the audience hates the villain.

"I'm Special Agent Sam Wicker, FBI," he said. He flashed ID that appeared genuine enough to Carver even in the dim light.

"You don't look FBI," Carver said.

"I know. People tell me that all the time. They expect a guy who looks and dresses like a Sears suit model with a law degree. Pretty often that's what they get."

Carver understood then that the man who'd looked in on Beth probably had been a federal agent.

Wicker had been standing near the stone wall. Now he shambled around the back of the car to stand near Carver. He was taller than he'd first appeared, maybe five feet ten. It occurred to Carver that Wicker dressed a lot like McGregor, only he was cleaner. The breeze blew again, cool and fresh, rattling the palm fronds harder. "It's nice down here," Wicker said. "I spend too much time up north." He spoke as if he'd come to Florida for a vacation rather than a social hot button murder investigation.

"You in charge of the Women's Light bombing investigation?" Carver asked. He still couldn't quite believe it.

"Sure am. I've got my agents looking at all the leads, investigating the hell out of everything. Seems I've got you investigating, too."

"I've got a personal interest."

"Uh-huh, I understand. Something you need to understand is that you best stay out of the bureau's way. As much as you can, that is. And when and if you find out anything pertinent, you get the information to us pronto. To me personally if at all possible." He handed Carver a card. It was embossed in gold. Very official and meant to be impressive, very like the bureau Carver knew.

"What about doing this in both directions?" Carver asked. "Will you share information with me?"

"Hell, you're a private citizen. I can't confide in you about bureau business." Wicker's face broke down into its creased smile again. "Except maybe in a very general way, if conditions warrant it, if the planets are in proper alignment."

"Just your occasional opinion, maybe?" Carver said.

Wicker peered up at the darkening sky, possibly at the planets, then back down. "Maybe. Now and again."

"Do you think Norton did the bombing on his own?"

"That I honest to God don't know. In that respect, you and I are sniffing along the same trail. That's why you need to tread careful and make sure everything's above board. I wouldn't want to see you get in trouble. Even more so, I wouldn't want to see you cause trouble."

"When are you going to question Beth Jackson?"

"Oh, real soon. It's not for you or her to worry about though. She's a victim, not a suspect."

"She can't tell you much," Carver said. "She walked inside and got blown back outside."

"We'll let her tell it, make it official." Wicker grinned and turned slightly to face in the direction of the sea, as if to luxuriate in the cool ocean breeze that came with the evening. When he looked at Carver, it was with a slight sideways tilt of his head. "We know about you, how you were an Orlando cop, got the bad luck and the bad leg and a pension. Went private, stayed honest. Making out okay most of the time."

"That's me on a postcard," Carver said.

"You witnessed the clinic explosion."

"From some distance. I was sitting in my parked car half a block away."

"What did you see?"

"Not much. Beth walked in, right behind another woman, then the bomb went off."

"Were the demonstrators a proper distance away from the clinic?"

"Yeah. Maybe because they knew the bomb was going to blow."

"Did you see anyone run out from behind the building?"

"I think I glimpsed someone, carrying a sign. But there was so much confusion and running around after the bomb went off, I can't be sure, much less if whoever I might have seen was Norton. I was concentrating on Beth, trying to put together in my mind what had just happened, figure it out."

"Maybe there is no way to figure it out," Wicker said. "At least figure it all the way so everything makes sense. Crazy bastards might not really know themselves why they do things like that."

"I don't think anyone really knows why they do anything. They only think they know, if they think about it at all."

Wicker ran his tongue around the inside of his cheek for a few seconds, considering that somewhat nihilistic philosophy. "That's a fact. But it's up to people like us to tell them why, when what they do is a crime. What's your take on the locals?"

Carver knew he meant the police, not the average Del Moray citizen. "They're mostly okay. Some rotten wood here and there."

"Like Lieutenant McGregor?"

"Just like."

"Local law resents the bureau moving in on them, usually. They got a nickname for us they use behind our backs: feebs, they call us. You know that?"

"I've heard," Carver said.

"Abortion clinic bombing's a federal offense, though, so they got to learn to get along with us. Even your Lieutenant McGregor."

"Not *my* lieutenant. If he were mine I'd have a vet put him down."

"He didn't have many kind words for you, either," Wicker said. "Doesn't matter. We got a line on both of you real fast. It's true McGregor's no good."

"Worse than no good."

"Still, nothing can be pinned on him. He's a real artist at covering his ass. And this is your town and he's the local law, so you've gotta stay legal with him, play along and follow the script. Just like we do."

"He knows that, takes advantage of it."

"Oh, I'm sure he does. And he sort of sees himself in competition with us to solve this case, either prove it was Norton or prove it wasn't and catch whoever did it."

"Or whoever hired Norton or gave him orders."

"Exactly," Wicker said. "Anyway, in a sense McGregor's right about competition. It's not a bad thing through and through. It tends to keep people concentrating on the job, gets it all done faster and closes the book on a case."

"Competition's a good thing," Carver agreed. "I'm thinking of baseball, football, basketball players, how it makes them and the team better."

"Not thinking of FBI agents and local police lieutenants?"

"Yeah, as long as the competition doesn't get in the way of cooperation."

"Uh-huh. Like you cooperate with Lieutenant McGregor?"

Carver had gleaned Wicker's angle. "Don't you *want* me to keep cooperating with him, Special Agent Wicker?"

"Oh, I sure do. The question is, how fast? I mean, you got this piece of maybe important information, say. You're gonna give it to both of us, but how soon and in what order? You understand?"

"I think so. You want to win this competition."

"I want the bureau to know all about whatever and whoever was behind this bombing, and I want the bureau to make the arrests."

"If there are going to be more arrests," Carver said.

"I think there will be. I've heard tapes of Norton's interrogation. He's not what you'd describe as the mastermind type. He's hung up on God, pickup truck, family, flag, in whatever order. That kind of guy."

"God way out in front, I imagine," Carver said.

"His idea of God, anyway. Angry old man with a white beard, hurling lightning bolts down at folks who don't share Norton's views."

"Has he got a lot of views?"

"Uh-huh. And about a lot of things. Government conspiracies, the United Nations, bar codes, secret world governments, gun control, the Trilateral Commission, bankers of a certain ethnicity plotting to control the world's economy, the Internal Revenue Service's secret agenda, covert NATO operations meant to destabilize Europe so arms manufacturers can make a fortune, the murders of Marilyn Monroe, Vincent Foster, Elvis . . . the usual list. He's a fool for talk radio."

"Think he might be right about just a few of those things?" Carver asked.

Wicker stuffed his hands in his pockets and shrugged. "Elvis, maybe."

Carver slid Wicker's card into his shirt pocket. "Okay, you feebs are first on my list. Mostly because I hate McGregor."

"Fine," Wicker said. "I like the folks I'm involved with to know exactly where they stand. That was the real purpose of this conversation—so you'd know."

"I've known from the beginning where I stand," Carver said. "I'm in the middle."

|12|

THERE WAS MCGREGOR.

His feet, anyway.

As Carver got out of the Olds and limped toward the cottage, he saw what had to be the soles of McGregor's huge wing-tip shoes propped up on the porch rail. They weren't simply long shoes, they were wide. Size fourteen double-E, McGregor had once bragged to Carver. Good for kicking ass, he'd pointed out.

When he got closer, Carver saw McGregor's long form in the shadow of the porch roof. He was leaning back in one of the webbed aluminum lawn chairs with his legs propped at an extreme upward angle.

Carver stopped at the base of the three wooden steps that led up to the porch. He stood for a while looking at McGregor, listening to the surf whisper and slap on the beach, feeling the pressure of the ocean breeze against his back.

"You should have let yourself in," Carver said, "helped yourself to a mint julep before you got all comfortable on my porch."

McGregor held up a can. "Did go in and help myself to a beer."

Carver was sure he had locked the door. "Through an unlocked window?"

McGregor grinned, yellow as mustard in the moonlight. "Nope. You didn't answer my knock, door was unlocked, so I went inside to make sure you were okay. My professional duty, to serve and protect." He took a long sip of beer, then lowered the drained can, squeezed it until it made a loud metallic pop as it buckled, then tossed it aside on the porch floor with a clatter.

"Where's your car parked?" Carver asked.

"Outa sight, dickhead. I thought I'd just sit here in the dark and wait for you without you knowing anyone was around. No telling what I mighta seen, observing an odd mutt like you. Maybe you were gonna bring home a stray bitch to bed down with, what with your regular bang laid up in the hospital. You do fuck white women once in a while, don't you?"

Carver felt his blood race hot, but he refused to let McGregor get him to show anger. He set the tip of his cane and thumped up the steps onto the porch. "What do you want?"

McGregor shifted his long body and let his feet clunk down on the plank floor, making the porch vibrate with the impact. Then he stood up, towering over Carver's average height. "The feebs have come to town."

"What'd you expect? You've got an abortion clinic bombing, a murder here that's a federal case. That means FBI every time."

"Oh, I expected them." McGregor threw open his wrinkled suit coat and scratched an armpit. Body odor wafted to Carver. McGregor let the coat flop down to hang naturally, but he didn't button it. He wanted his holstered nine millimeter to show. "Agent in charge is a guy named Wicker, little jerk-off dresses so sloppy you wouldn't believe."

What Carver couldn't believe was what he'd just heard. He wanted to point out that Wicker was half as wrinkled and didn't smell bad like McGregor, but that would mean he had to have met Wicker.

"Wicker's gonna talk to you," McGregor said, "if he hasn't already. He's gonna want you to pass on information to him immediately—which means seconds after you obtain it. I want it within nanoseconds."

"And I know why. You don't want the FBI exposing the clockwork behind the bombing before you do, don't want them soaking up your limelight."

"Nothing wrong with ambition. Even a slug like you must have some spark of it, so try to understand. I expect to be front and center throughout this case, Carver. Someday you'll be able to tell your fellow losers you know Del Moray's chief of police personally. Maybe even its mayor. This is a great country and an enterprising fella with balls can go far."

"What if the FBI's smarter than both of us and puzzles it all out first?"

"Smarter than one of us, is what they are. I want the dumber of the two of us to let me know if Wicker talks to him."

"You mean starting right now, Mr. Mayor?"

"You got it, fuckhead. Soon as I leave here. Or sooner, if your phone rings. Also, I want to know whatever information you tell him, which better not be anything you haven't already told me."

"If you want me to let you in on anything new," Carver said, "you should tell me what you already know."

"Can do. It's all in the papers anyway. Eyewitnesses sharper than you saw Norton run out from behind the clinic just before it blew up. He says he went back there to wave his sign at a window, never was inside or threw anything inside. We got a search warrant and found bomb-making literature inside his house. Later we found wires and blasting caps in his car, pushed back under the seat in a locked metal box. He claimed he was making bombs and planned to blow up a clinic, but hadn't yet. His wife backs him up. When we brought him in he was spouting a lot of religious dribble, calling himself the swift sword and arm of the Lord. Now he's not saying anything 'cause his attorney's in on the game. Which is okay by me, since he was just transferred today to federal custody."

"They going to leave him in Del Moray so the field agents can interrogate him from time to time?"

"That's what they tell me, but you never know when to believe those ass wipes. Half of them are lawyers, the other half are accountants keeping track of how much the lawyers steal from the taxpayers."

Carver had heard McGregor rant about suffering the disdain of federal agencies before and didn't want to hear it again.

"How does Norton strike you?" he asked before McGregor could go off on a riff about the incompetence and audacity of the FBI.

"That wasn't in the newspaper, Carver."

"Is one of your FBI antagonists a tall blond guy, well groomed, with a crew cut and black horn-rimmed glasses?"

"I haven't seen one fitting that description."

"Any of your men look like that?"

"Not unless he's working undercover at a CPA convention."

"You want my cooperation, you've got to give me something," Carver said.

"Okay, Norton's an obvious nut case, one of those true-believer dingbats out to save the world from itself. His method is explosives. There, you have something."

"That's not what I meant."

McGregor looked sly. He grinned and probed the space between his teeth with the tip of his tongue. "Oh? What is it you want from me in return for your cooperation, which you better give me anyway or I'll see you *under* the jail and the key'll be in the pocket of some pants I never wear and have forgot all about?"

"I want you to provide some protection for Beth at the hospital."

"Huh? You know I couldn't do that even if I wanted. Anyway, who'd want to hurt her now? Norton's in jail. And she's only a witness anyway, and not a damaging one. You think that clinic was blown up in an attempt on *her* life?"

"No. But I think somebody might want to scare me off the case through her, which means there's something to be scared away from. And if I spend my time protecting Beth instead of investigating, there might be facts you and I never learn." Actually Carver wasn't sure Beth was in any danger, but *she* suspected she was. Possibly her instincts were affected by her grief and injuries, yet they were usually accurate. Then there was the WASP with the horn-rimmed glasses; maybe there was nothing to him as a threat, but only maybe. Beth would feel better, and Carver would, if she had protection until she was well enough to be released from hospital care.

"There you go, overestimating your own importance, dickhead," McGregor snarled.

"You know better. I'm private and can do what you can't, maybe follow a hunch that leads to the right place. If you didn't think that was true and you didn't think I was good at my work, you wouldn't be here talking to me."

"If you're talking about breaking the law, using any means to gain an end, hell, I do that already."

"But you've got superior officers watching you, and subordinates who hate your guts and'll toss you to the wolves if they see the chance."

"Well, that's a fact . . ." McGregor rubbed his long chin with a long forefinger, then brushed back the lock of straight blond hair that was hanging over his forehead. "You know I've got a manpower shortage."

"Always. That's why you want me out there like another cop working for you. You need people who know which rocks to turn over, what to look for when they flip, and how to deal with whatever crawls out."

"Stop trying to bullshit me. It can't be done unless you're more corrupt and devious than I am, and you're not. You're too naive and weighted down with scruples that are gonna take you to the bottom and drown you someday. Dumb fucking gimp."

Carver knew McGregor was weakening. "I told you the deal, that's all. There's no bullshit involved."

"You're lucky," McGregor said. "Timing and luck, that's what's kept you alive and outside the walls. It so happens I got a policewoman's not worth spit. I can assign her to the hospital to watch over Beth. One useless cunt to guard another so your time's freed up, that's not a bad trade."

"And politically correct of you," Carver said.

"Well, we have to watch that stuff these days," McGregor said earnestly, apparently missing Carver's irony.

Carver would see to it that he missed more than that.

13

CARVER WENT for his usual therapeutic swim in the sea the next morning, stroking far out from shore. He rolled over and floated on his back, feeling the heat of the morning sun soak into him as he rode the swells, still gentle this far from shore before they met the resistance of land and began their rise. He liked to gaze in at his cottage perched on the crescent of beach that lent it some privacy, at his life. It gave him the perspective of distance, providing a core of peace if not understanding. It was the need to understand that kept him alive in a business where knowing too much could prove fatal.

On the public beach to the left of where his cottage sat, beyond the curve of sandy shore, a few sunbathers and swimmers were already appearing, spreading out towels or venturing down into the cool surf. A woman carrying a child on her hip was walking gingerly parallel to the surf, now and then allowing the white foam to reach and engulf her bare feet and ankles, while behind her a man was carefully setting up some sort of portable lounger. A young man and woman walked past the man with the lounger, their steps kicking up rooster tails of sand at their heels, each of them gripping a handle of a large white plastic cooler with a blue lid. A woman's happy shouts and high laughter drifted out to Carver from shore. He turned his head in the water and saw a young woman with long blond hair running and splashing in the surf, while a man with his pants legs rolled to the knees stood with his arms crossed and observed her as if he were going to grade her.

Carver watched them for a moment, then rolled over onto his stomach and began to swim for shore, feeling the coolness of his wet back warming quickly in the sun. He glanced toward the beach where his white towel lay folded and his cane jutted like a beacon from the sand, then changed the angle of his direction slightly and lengthened his strokes. He cut through the water swiftly, swiveling his head to breathe regularly and deeply as he kicked gracefully from the hip. By now he was so at home in the ocean that he almost felt he was experiencing evolution in reverse. He told himself that, rather than suppose his occasional thoughts of succumbing to the pull of distance and swimming straight out toward the misty horizon line of sea and sky were suicidal musings.

After returning to the cottage, showering, and getting dressed, he prepared a breakfast of Cheerios, toast, and coffee. He ate seated at the breakfast bar while he watched CNN on the TV that was angled so that it could be seen from the kitchen area.

It wasn't long before the Women's Light Clinic bombing was covered. Bobbi Batista, an anchorwoman with luminous blue eyes, was seated between a woman in a severe pinstriped business suit who was an abortion rights activist, and a man wearing army camouflage fatigues who was referred to as Major. Both guests were talking at once, gesticulating animatedly and arguing about the difference between murder and political terrorism. None of this was comprehensible. Carver used the remote to mute the TV as Bobbi went to a string of commercials about hidden germs in the mouth, a phone company's offer of long-distance discounts for far-flung family members, and the ergonomics of a Japanese car. Carver took a last bite of toast and washed it down with coffee.

When the news came back on, a correspondent was interviewing a man standing in front of a colorful stained glass window. The man was about fifty, stockily built beneath a tailored gray suit that had a lot of silk in the material. He had wavy gray hair parted as neatly as if he'd used a ruler and combed sharply to the side, and strong features frozen into a perpetual smile that was more a chance arrangement of muscle and bone structure than an expression of good humor. He would be smiling even as he slept. The caption at the bottom of the screen identified him as the Reverend Martin Freel of Operation Alive.

". . . might indeed be God's way," he was saying as Carver used the remote to bring the sound back up, "but he certainly wasn't acting at the direction of Operation Alive."

"And was Adam Norton?" asked the correspondent, a somber-looking black man in a white shirt and wild tie, but without a coat.

"Of course not. We don't even know if Mr. Norton is guilty."

"But he was a member of your congregation here in Orlando, and of Operation Alive."

Freel widened his frozen smile. "Many people are, but they don't resort to violence, and neither did Mr. Norton on behalf of Operation Alive." The smile turned wise and tolerant. "I certainly don't think the media should convict him even before he's tried. And I might add that if any one person or thing influenced whoever committed this sad, sick act, it could easily have been the media with its lurid coverage and inflammatory rhetoric concerning other such acts."

"Wasn't it Operation Alive and not the media who instigated the violence at the abortion clinic in Houston last year, Reverend Freel?"

"That was certainly the media's spin on what happened. Our

view and the view of true Christians everywhere is that those who instigated the violence were the people inside the clinic who were slaughtering unborn innocents."

"But one of your own demonstrators was badly injured when a car drove over her legs."

"The young woman was and still is a soldier in the army of the Lord and told me personally she doesn't regret what happened. And of course we know her accident was the result of overzealous and overreactive police."

"Thanks for taking the time to talk to us, Reverend Freel," the correspondent said. Then, in another tone of voice, he said, "Bobbi," and stared into the camera until Bobbi Batista appeared on the screen again.

"We'll be right back," Bobbi said only to Carver. The same commercial about ergonomics came on again, a sleek black sedan cruising along a wickedly curving road while its unconcerned driver, a blissfully smiling woman, switched on the windshield wipers and adjusted the stereo's volume as she chatted on a car phone while driving through a virtual hurricane. Carver used the remote to switch off the TV.

Maybe it had been the car phone. He pulled the phone on the breakfast bar over to him, then got out Special Agent Sam Wicker's card and pecked out his number.

He was surprised when Wicker himself answered. That kind of directness and efficiency didn't suit the bureau's hierarchical image.

"Ah, you have information for me," Wicker said when Carver identified himself.

"Actually I want information from you," Carver said.

"You're turning out to be a disappointment."

"Give me time. Do you have an agent who's tall, broad shouldered, sharply dressed, maybe in a blue suit, has a crew cut, and looks like a typical WASP, wears black horn-rimmed glasses?"

"Other than the glasses, that could be me."

"Let's include the glasses."

"None of my people fits that description. Why do you ask?"

"A man like that wandered into Beth's room at the hospital yesterday. There was a nurse with her, and when he saw she wasn't alone, he smiled and ducked right back out."

"Maybe he was there to visit somebody and entered the wrong room."

"Probably something like that," Carver said. "But he spooked Beth, and normally that's not easy to do, so I thought I'd ask you about him."

"Uh-huh."

Carver waited. Apparently Wicker was thinking on the other end of the line, deciding how much importance to place on an injured woman's concern.

"Well, I'm sure he's not ours," Wicker finally said. "My guess is he was one of McGregor's men."

"McGregor says no."

"Okay, I'll pass the description around and we'll see if anything comes of it."

So Wicker wasn't brushing Beth off as an alarmist amateur. Carver was impressed. "McGregor's going to assign somebody to keep an eye on Beth."

"That doesn't fit with what I know of him."

"Every ten, twenty years, he's struck with understanding and a compulsion to do his job. It'll quickly pass."

"Uh-huh."

"You say that a lot—'uh-huh.'"

"Seems to cover a lot. Remember to let me know about anything even remotely pertaining to the bombing."

"Of course. What have you—"

But Wicker had hung up. Acting very FBI now.

"Feeb," Carver said into the phone, then replaced the receiver.

. . .

AFTER WASHING and putting away the breakfast dishes, Carver drove in to the hospital to look in on Beth before going about the business of the day. The first item of that business would be to talk to Dr. Louis Benedict, Women's Light's surviving abortion doctor.

When Carver knocked lightly and pushed open the door to Beth's room, he found himself facing a short, dark-haired woman with a heart-shaped face and intense brown eyes. She was wearing a police uniform and the flap was unsnapped on the belt holster of her .38 Police Special. Behind her, Beth was sleeping on her side in the bed.

"Help you?" asked McGregor's policewoman who wasn't worth spit.

"I'm Fred Carver. I, uh, sort of requested you."

"Oh, you a friend of Lieutenant McGregor?"

"Christ, no!"

The policewoman smiled with very small, very even teeth. "Let's step outside into the hall, Mr. Carver."

She didn't move, letting him lead the way.

In the hall, she stood watching as he softly closed Beth's door. Without being asked, he pulled out some identification and showed it to her. She looked at it, then her eyes took a walk up and down him.

Carver flashed her his most winning smile. "How many men with bad legs and canes are likely to come calling on Beth?" he asked.

She handed back the ID. "You don't have to have a bad leg to walk with a cane. And you hardly hear that expression anymore, 'come calling.'"

She had a point. Two points.

"I'm Officer Linda Lapella," she said. "Beth told me about you, but I needed to be sure. She had a bad night. The doctor gave her something, and she's been asleep for about an hour."

"What did McGregor tell you about this duty?"

"Nothing other than to come here and guard the—the woman in this room until I'm relieved."

"He tell you to watch out for anyone in particular?"

"No. He doesn't tell me much going into things. Usually I get a certain kind of make-work assignment, then I'm left alone so I'm out of the way. He tells me later where I fouled up."

"This isn't that kind of assignment," Carver said in a voice harder than he'd intended. His tone made Officer Lapella stare at him.

"Okay," she said.

Carver described the crew-cut WASP type who had entered Beth's room.

"Beth mentioned him before she fell asleep," she said. "She didn't know anything about him. Can you tell me anything?"

"Only that he's not FBI, and the nurses didn't know him as an employee or visitor. So maybe he's something else."

"Big hospital," Lapella said skeptically.

"Big world of possibilities."

She smiled with her tiny, perfect teeth. There was a lipstick stain on one of the front ones. "Yeah, you're right. Sorry, Mr. Carver."

"Fred."

"Then it's Linda. And don't worry about Beth. I'm not the screw-up Lieutenant McGregor might have described."

"I didn't think so. He's not lavish with his praise. Now that we've met, though, I feel better."

"Me too," Linda said. "McGregor wasn't very complimentary when he told me about you."

Carver told Linda to let Beth know when she woke up that he'd been by while she was sleeping, then he rode the elevator down and used a pay phone in the lobby to call Women's Light.

A recording informed him that the clinic on de Leon Boulevard was temporarily closed and gave him another number to call. When the phone was answered by a woman, Carver asked to speak to Dr. Benedict, then realized he was speaking to another recording. This one told him that Women's Light patients were being referred to A. A. Aal Memorial Hospital. As Carver was standing in the lobby of said hospital, he phoned the information desk and asked for Dr. Benedict. He was transferred to surgery and told by a nurse that Dr. Benedict wasn't on duty today. He asked for the doctor's home number but was politely refused. After hanging up, he looked up Dr. Benedict's home number and address in the phone directory and was surprised to find them listed.

Detective work.

14

DR. LOUIS BENEDICT'S address belonged to a low, modern ranch house on Macon Avenue in what Carver thought of as an upper-middle-class neighborhood. The grassy area between curb and sidewalk was lined with palm trees, front yards were large, and the homes were set well back from the street and often secluded behind trees and shrubbery.

The Benedict house, however, was plainly visible at the end of its long, straight driveway. The carpet of lush green lawn sloping uphill toward it was unbroken except for a circular flower bed vivid with the bright colors of geraniums and yellow and red roses. The house itself was mostly brick, vast planes of tinted glass, and angled exposed beams. There was a two-car garage attached to it by what looked like a breezeway that had been converted to an additional room. Money here, Carver thought, but nothing grand.

He parked the Olds in the street so it wouldn't drip oil on the pristine concrete driveway, then used a stepping-stone walk parallel to the driveway to go up to the long front porch. There was so little overhang on the roof that there was no shade on the porch, and the late morning sun bore down on Carver's bald pate and the exposed back of his neck as he waited for an answer to his ring.

There was a faint sound behind the door, then it was opened by an attractive woman in her late thirties with tousled blond hair, a square jaw, and inquisitive blue eyes. She possessed an elegant figure beneath a loose-fitting blue dress and had on white toeless shoes with built-up heels. The arch of her eyebrows was accentuated by eyebrow pencil darker than her hair, making her appear mildly surprised.

Carver introduced himself and asked to see Dr. Benedict.

"I'm Leona Benedict, the doctor's wife," the woman said in a voice that sounded more Boston than Del Moray. "Could you tell me what this is about?"

"It's about what happened at the clinic."

She looked wary as well as surprised. "The bombing, you mean?"

"Yes. A woman who was injured in the explosion was carrying our child."

A fleeting expression of pity crossed Leona Benedict's handsome face. A doctor's good wife, she wanted to deflect Carver so he wouldn't disturb her husband's time away from the operating room, but there was no denying that Carver had a claim on that time.

She smiled, not totally erasing the pity, and invited him inside.

He was in a cool living room that seemed dim after outside. The view through the wide window was of the vast stretch of lawn and the street, his rust-spotted Olds convertible squatting at the curb like a last weary warrior from Detroit in the land of BMWs, Lexuses, and Volvos. Leona Benedict left him alone and disappeared down a wide hall in search of her husband.

Carver turned his attention from outside to inside, appreciating the white leather sofa, soft beige carpeting and drapes, original oil paintings, and glass-shelved bookcases that contained an extensive collection of small pewter figurines. Expensive and tasteful. This was probably one of the better-furnished homes on Macon Avenue.

A medium-height, dark-complexioned man with a barrel chest and thinning black hair entered the room. He was wearing a gray-and-white striped short-sleeved shirt open at the collar and navy blue pleated pants. His feet were almost bare in skimpy leather sandals. He said he was Dr. Benedict as he shook Carver's hand. His soft, commiserating tone suggested that his wife had already explained Carver's connection with Beth. He had bushy black eyebrows above dark eyes whose pupils moved quickly and seemed to see a lot. He wasn't a handsome man but there was a heartiness and energy about him that women might find attractive. The doctor appeared to be about ten years older than his wife. Carver wondered if the expensive furnishings were for Leona Benedict, who might well object to the long and unpredictable hours of her physician husband.

"I'm sorry about Miss Jackson," Benedict said. "How is she?"

Not "your wife." The doctor was up on things.

Carver told him Beth was doing very well but was still depressed over the loss of their child.

"It will take time for her to assimilate that," Benedict said in his soft, soothing voice. "If you help her, she'll heal from the loss." He smiled in a way that made Carver like him. "Perhaps someday there'll be another pregnancy."

"The last one wasn't deliberate," Carver said.

"I see. Most pregnancy's aren't, you know." Again the smile. "That's what keeps me in business."

"I understand you and Dr. Grimm alternated days at the clinic."

Benedict frowned at the mention of his dead partner's name and nodded. "Yes, with only Sundays off. Of course, both of us were always on call." He shrugged. "That's the life of a doctor.

Complications and special circumstances don't follow the calendar."

"So it's possible that Dr. Grimm was the bomber's target."

"If either of us was," Dr. Benedict said, "I suppose it was Harold. More likely it was a symbolic act and the bomber didn't have a specific victim in mind." He took a deep breath. There was a change of light in his eyes, and Carver was surprised to glimpse the depth of anger in this amiable-looking man. "The religious right hates us. The bombing was simply an act of hate and desperation."

"Desperation?"

"Yes, because we've won the war and they don't want to surrender. The law is on our side and will continue to be, and they can't face that. They simply won't accept or can't grasp the fact that the courts and public opinion aren't in line with their own extreme beliefs. There isn't much left for them other than to wave signs and shout and throw bombs. You wouldn't believe the things they put us—and the women who come to us—through. Often the women they scream at and frighten aren't even coming to the clinic for an abortion. We do other medical procedures there. But that doesn't matter to the maniacs in the street. They act out of ignorance."

"You sound more angry than frightened."

"Well, I suppose I am. I happen to believe in women's reproductive rights as strongly as the shouters and haters believe in their own warped concept of religious responsibilities. Maybe even more strongly."

"I was surprised," Carver said, "that you had a listed phone number. You aren't difficult to find, Doctor."

"I don't want to be. Once you give in to the kind of terrorism our opponents practice, you've lost. I receive threats regularly, as does my wife. We're used to it. I'll continue my work regardless of what the anti-choicers do, because my work is important—essential."

"Does your wife feel the same way?"

Leona, who had returned to the room and was seated at the far end of the low white sofa, said simply, "Most days."

It was obvious to Carver that the Reverend Martin Freel had run into an opponent whose zealotry might match his own. A great deal of animosity had to exist here. He wondered if it was possible that Benedict had been the target of the bombing.

"Was Dr. Grimm as . . . enthusiastic about his work as you are?" Carver asked.

"He was dedicated enough," Benedict said. He paced a few steps this way and that, frowning. Then he stopped pacing and punched a fist into his palm. "Damn it! The clinic was doing good work, helping people. Then this madman's act of violence. It's a tragedy for so many people, Mr. Carver."

"But it won't stop us," Leona Benedict said in a flat voice from the end of the sofa. She didn't sound nearly as enthusiastic as her husband.

Carver turned toward her. "After what happened at the clinic, are you afraid?"

"Sometimes," she admitted.

"This place isn't as vulnerable as it appears," Benedict said. "There's an excellent alarm system, and the glass is double-thick and shatterproof." He sounded more like a general, boasting about the strength of his position, than a doctor describing his suburban home.

"Bulletproof too?"

"No."

"At night we draw the drapes," Leona said.

"The danger's lessened for the time being," Benedict said. "The bomber's in custody, and Operation Alive is under scrutiny and pulling in its horns, on the defensive for a change."

"They wouldn't appreciate you describing them with horns," Leona said.

"Then you're sure Norton's guilty," Carver said.

Dr. Benedict stared at him. "Of course he's guilty. He was spurred on by that maniac Freel and his Operation Alive's outright lies and statistical distortions. The anonymous threats have increased since the bombing, but right now I think that's all they are—threats."

"Then you assume the source of these threats is Operation Alive?"

"That's where most of them come from, I'm sure. Of course there are plenty of stray extremists, but generally the ones who give us trouble are members of organizations."

"I understand you're keeping patients' appointments and performing abortions at A. A. Aal Memorial."

"Yes, though I don't advertise it, for the hospital's sake. I'm sure Operation Alive knows about it, though. I don't care. In fact, I want them to know about it. I want them to know that no matter what they do, I'll continue my work."

A phone began to chirp well back in the bowels of the house. Leona stood up and excused herself, then hurried away to answer it. The chirping stopped.

She returned a minute later carrying a white cordless phone with a stubby flexible antenna.

Dr. Benedict knew it was for him. He shrugged and accepted the phone from her, then said hello into it and wandered off down the hall and out of earshot.

"Your husband's a dedicated man," Carver said to Leona.

"He's an idealist," she said. "He believes in what he's doing, and so do I."

"But you're not an idealist, are you?"

"Not like my husband is. Few people are."

"Martin Freel, maybe."

"Martin Freel definitely," she said. "In a way, Freel is very much the personification of what Louis hates: smug self-righteousness, intolerance, a willingness to sacrifice other people for your cause and personal aggrandizement."

"Do you think Freel sacrificed Adam Norton for his cause?"

"Probably. My guess is that Operation Alive is behind the clinic bombing, but it will be almost impossible to prove. Norton will be tried and convicted unless that sleazeball lawyer Jefferson Brama can get him off on some sort of technicality. But I'm not sure it really matters in the long run. Some other certain and wrong true believer will make another bomb and set it off where it will kill someone. This thing seems never to end."

"It will someday."

"How?"

"A pill, maybe. A morning-after pill that makes whether a woman chooses abortion her personal and private decision."

"The French RU-486 pill?"

"Or something like it."

"God, how I look forward to that day!" Leona said. She glanced around as if to make sure Benedict wouldn't overhear. "I do understand the other side's point of view. I mean, how some people, because of honest religious convictions, can't condone abortions. But that's quite different from the kind of things Freel believes and says and does."

Carver knew what she meant, even agreed with her, but he said, "How so?"

Her arched eyebrows rose higher and she looked particularly surprised that he would have to ask. "Why, taking a life is just that—taking a life. If you don't believe in it, you don't do it. Freel says he believes in love and tolerance and life, but he preaches the opposite and urges his followers to commit acts of violence that can result in people's deaths."

"Do you consider him a phony out for fame and fortune? A con man?"

"No. He's a madman. And a dangerous one."

Benedict had disappeared and might be involved in his phone conversation for quite a while, so Carver told her to thank the doctor for his time, then said good-bye and left.

Leona Benedict stood in the doorway with her arms hanging limply at her sides and watched him drive away.

Despite the fact that the low brick house was exposed on the wide lawn and had a great deal of glass area, it reminded Carver of a military bunker.

HE STOPPED by his office to check his mail and phone messages. The mail contained no checks, and not much of interest except for an advertisement for a sport jacket with a dozen hidden pickpocket-proof pockets. Carver had once owned a jacket with a lot of hidden pockets, though not a dozen, and found it a damned inconvenience. He never could remember which one held whatever it was he needed. Still, he'd never fallen victim to a pickpocket.

He put the mail aside and pressed the play button on his answering machine to check the two messages that had been left for him.

Beep: "This is McGregor, fuckface, call me and report whatever it is you've been doing."

Carver decided to ignore that one.

Beep: "'Never imagine I have come to bring peace on earth; I have not come to bring peace but a sword.'" A man's voice, so it couldn't have been Mildred Otten quoting scripture at him again. "You are tolerating that Jezebel of a woman," the voice went on. "I have given her time to repent, but she refuses to repent of her sexual vice. 'Lo, I will lay her on a sickbed and bring her paramours into sore distress if they do not repent of her practices.'"

Carver waited. Whoever had left the message didn't hang up

right away. He could hear deep, even breathing until the tape reached its limit and the machine clicked and rewound.

He erased the message, then sat back and thought about the last one. The Jezebel who lay on her sickbed would be Beth. He supposed that if Beth were a Jezebel—and he sometimes thought she was, and enjoyed it—then he, Carver, would qualify as her paramour. Was in fact glad to be her paramour. Though he didn't like the prospect of "sore distress" for either of them.

He locked the office behind him, then limped out to the parking lot and lowered himself into the Olds. After propping his cane in its usual position against the front seat, he started the engine and drove toward A. A. Aal Memorial Hospital. Paramour or not, he'd had enough sore distress in his life.

And so had Jezebel.

15

BETH WAS sitting up in bed with a green hospital tray across her lap. On the tray were rust-colored Jell-O, brown bread, and a substance resembling beef stew. The pungent scent of the stew chased away the usual medicinal scent in the room. There was also a small container of frozen yogurt on the tray, alongside a glass of ice water. Cooking for the sick was an art no one seemed to have mastered.

"Where's Officer Lapella?" Carver asked as he entered the room.

She fixed him with a stare that made him think she was indeed improving. "I told her to go eat lunch in the cafeteria. I appreciate her company, but I don't want the woman living with me."

"She can't guard you from the cafeteria."

"Can't do me much good if she's starved to death, either. Besides, I can take care of myself for half an hour, don't you think?"

"No." He'd spoken more sharply than he'd intended.

"Ease up, Fred." She studied him. "Has something happened?"

He told her about his conversation with Dr. Benedict and Leona and about the biblical message waiting for him on his office answering machine.

"Revelation," she said, and forked some beef stew into her mouth. She chewed and swallowed. "And I think the first part, about the sword, was from Matthew."

Carver was astounded. "How can you know this?"

She took a sip of water and placed the glass back on the tray. "I grew up on the Bible. Had an aunt who'd been married to a preacher man. She could almost recite the entire book of Esther. That's the one where Queen Vashti gets replaced for refusing to obey the king, who then takes up with the more beautiful Esther. Preacher man left my aunt for a younger woman, and she never forgot."

"The point is," Carver said, "this is a threat directed toward you."

She paused with another bite of stew halfway to her mouth. "You saying I'm the Jezebel in the phone message, Fred?"

"Er, yeah. I mean, it isn't me saying it, it's the caller. And my guess is he's the straight-arrow overgrown WASP who walked into your room and then left when he saw a nurse was with you. Who knows what he might have done if that nurse hadn't been here?"

"Jezebel, huh." She seemed less angry now, maybe even oddly flattered.

"We're living in sin in the eyes of this nut case, and he probably thinks you were entering Women's Light to have an abortion or to make arrangements for one—another sin. In fact, it's the sin du jour. Then of course there's the fact that I'm white and you're black. That causes problems among some of the folks who perceive only one path to heaven."

She grinned at him. "Never thought of myself as so bad. Hmmm, Jezebel."

"What it all means," Carver said, "is that for whatever reason, the oversized, overdressed WASP is out to make you pay what he calls the wages of sin."

"That's death, Fred. 'The wages of sin is death.' That's Romans." She didn't seem so amused now.

Carver felt as if he should be struck dead himself. "I'm sorry . . . I forgot that. I got carried away. I'm not a Bible scholar."

"You really think that big creep is out to do something to me?"

"Haven't you suspected he was going to try something?"

"Yes, but only suspected."

"I don't know it for sure," Carver said, "but if he is, I think his object is to place you in danger in order to keep me from investigating the Women's Light bombing. It only makes sense that way."

"A certain kind of sense," she admitted. Fear moved in her dark eyes and she looked away quickly, aware that he'd noticed it.

He didn't like to see her frightened, even a little bit. But at least she wasn't brooding about the baby if she was afraid, on her guard.

"Lapella can't stay with me every minute," she said.

"When she's not here, I'll stay."

"Not a chance, Fred. Have you considered that might be exactly what the caller wants? You stuck in a hospital room reading old magazines instead of out doing what you set out to do?"

It was possible. He didn't answer.

"I think I should go home," she said.

He shook his head. "You need to be in here. There's no way you could have recovered yet from what happened. Have you forgotten you were hurt in an explosion?"

"Hardly. What you need to remember is I survived. Now I want to be back in the outside world. I want to know what's going on, and to be a part of it."

"I come here," Carver said, not liking at all where the conversation was going. "I tell you what's going on, just as I promised. You're a part of everything I do, every minute of every day."

"Not the same thing, Fred," she told him, unimpressed by his calculated romantic drivel.

She was determined. He was sorry to see it, but he was buoyed by the fact that her spirit had returned full force even if her body was still ailing.

"I'll talk to Dr. Galt," he said. "We'll see what he thinks of the idea."

She nodded. "Fair enough." She pried the lid off the little paper container and began to eat yogurt with a white plastic spoon. "You want some of this stuff?" She motioned toward what was left on the tray: part of the ersatz stew, most of the rust-colored Jell-O, and the brown bread, which she hadn't touched.

"I'll get something in the cafeteria," he said, "after I tell the nurses to watch for our WASP friend, then make sure Lapella is on her way back up to your room."

"She's been here since seven-thirty this morning, Fred. She needs a break."

"She's getting paid to do a job," Carver said, a little angry that Lapella, after all her big talk about being more effective and responsible than McGregor gave her credit for, was sitting down in the cafeteria while anyone could walk into Beth's room.

"Go easy on her, Fred. She's all right. Her only flaws are she needs to eat and sleep. I haven't even noticed her leaving to go to the bathroom."

"Two F's and an A," Carver said, irritated.

He could read the look in Beth's eye. She saw how he was and had given up on trying to calm him. He was on his own and could live with the consequences. Sometimes she was too much like a mother to him.

Only sometimes.

He went to the bed and leaned over and kissed her lips, still cold from the last bite of frozen yogurt.

"You're right," he said. "I'll make sure she comes back up to your room, though, so one of us is here. And I'll try to find Dr. Galt and talk to him about you leaving. You might be safer back at the cottage anyway."

"I can work there better, that's for sure."

"Don't do anything without me," he said, moving toward the door.

"Never, Xerxes."

"Who's that?"

"Damned fool that got rid of Queen Vashti, book of Esther."

He nodded and left the room.

At the nurses' station down the hall, he described the WASP to the head nurse and asked her to call security immediately if the man appeared on this floor. Then he walked toward the elevators at the other end of the hall.

"Mr. Carver."

He stopped and turned. Officer Lapella was seated on an orange vinyl chair in a tiny alcove that served as a waiting area for radiology. She had half a sandwich in her hand and a crumpled potato chip bag in her lap.

"I thought you were down in the cafeteria," Carver said.

"That's where I told Beth I was going, but I bought some stuff from the vending machine and ate here, where I could see anyone coming or going into her room. I saw you enter about fifteen minutes ago, so I relaxed a little and enjoyed my sandwich."

Carver smiled. His world made sense again; McGregor, as usual, had misjudged someone under his command.

"No one's been by except the doctor," Lapella said. "Nothing unusual's happened."

"How does Beth seem to you?"

"She's a willful woman, Mr. Carver. That's why I gave up and agreed with her that I had to have something to eat and was going to the cafeteria."

"She's a Jezebel," Carver said.

"I hope not, Mr. Carver. Jezebel was willful, too, but cruel. She was eventually killed and her body was thrown to the dogs."

Carver was astonished. "What is this? Is everyone but me an expert on the Bible?"

"That's just Sunday school stuff," Lapella said. "I used to teach it in my church over in Sarasota." She raised her eyebrows. "But what did you mean about Beth being a Jezebel?"

He told her about the message on his answering machine.

"I'd say that sounds serious," Lapella said when he'd finished. She automatically glanced toward the door to Beth's room, halfway down the hall. "I'll be here at the hospital the rest of the day."

"What if McGregor orders otherwise?"

"Hell, Mr. Carver, McGregor's probably forgotten I exist. I'm just another dumb broad-assed cop, not important to him. That's why he gave me to you in the first place. It gets me out of the way."

"He did me a favor."

"And me," she said with a slight smile. "I'm finished eating, so I'm going back to Beth's room. You had lunch?"

"No."

"So go on down to the cafeteria and eat, then maybe you should come back up and drop in on room three-eleven, talk to Delores Bravo."

"The nurse who was hurt in the clinic explosion?"

"Right. The one who lost a foot and part of her leg. I talked to a nurse who spent some time with her. She told me about some things she said about the bombing. You go see Delores Bravo, she might be able to shed a little light."

"You've shed more than a little light," Carver told her, patting her shoulder.

And he did go down to the cafeteria and ate a salad and a roast beef sandwich. But he was preoccupied and ate in a hurry, hardly tasting his food.

Then he took an elevator to the third floor, wanting but not wanting to see what the bomb had left of Delores Bravo.

16

DELORES BRAVO was sitting up in bed the way Beth had been, only the hospital tray had been removed and there was a *People* magazine folded in her lap. She was a beautiful Latin woman in her twenties, though right now she looked old and drawn and had deep, shadowed circles beneath her eyes. Someone had combed her long, lush hair, and it lay in graceful dark waves over the white surface of her angled pillow. A thin white sheet covered her slender body; there was a tentlike contraption beneath the material where her foot had been amputated.

"Miss Bravo?"

She looked over at Carver with pained dark eyes. Don't hurt me, they screamed. I've had all I can take.

Gently he told her who he was, and that he wanted to talk with her.

"The police have already asked me questions," she said with a trace of accent, perhaps Cuban. "Lots of them."

"Mine might be different," Carver told her. "Besides, the police don't always share their information with me."

"The FBI was here, that man Wicker."

"We know each other," Carver said.

"But you don't share confidences?"

He smiled and shook his head no.

She glanced down at his cane. "You get around okay with that?"

"Not bad. My knee's locked so my leg's bent at a thirty-degree angle. It'll be that way for life."

"You have an accident?"

"Shot. When I was a cop in Orlando."

"That's a shame."

"What happened to you is a shame, too, Delores."

"You gonna tell me there are worse things than losing your foot and part of your leg?"

"No. You know there are worse things. You'll develop a new way of looking at yourself and other people. One day you won't think about your artificial leg and your limp until somebody reminds you of them by glancing at you oddly as you walk past, but the look they give you won't bother you much anymore. By then you'll know who and what you are."

"What if who I become isn't okay with me?"

"It will be."

She sighed and scrunched her head back into the pillow. Her black hair caught and held the light. "How's your friend Beth Jackson?"

"She's better."

"The nurses told me about her. She lost her baby."

"We both did."

"Dr. Grimm was a fine doctor, a good man. The man who killed him and did this to me, I've been reading about him. He's a religious person, yet he could do something like this and not think it wrong."

"You believe Norton did it?"

She looked at him, surprised that he had any doubt. "Of course I believe he did."

"I mean, on his own?" Carver amended.

She waited awhile before answering that one, obviously thinking it over. "The papers say it might have been Operation Alive, and that makes sense. Of course, my whole world made sense a few days ago, and now it doesn't. At least not in any way I can figure out. So I guess the truth is I really don't know who might have put him up to it, or if anyone did. But the actual planting and blowing up of the bomb—I think Norton did that on his own. Don't know it, but I think it."

Carver limped over and lowered himself into the chair next to the bed. It was identical to the chair in Beth's room. "What did you see the morning of the explosion?"

"I was walking down the hall to see how soon Dr. Grimm would be finished in the operating room, hurrying because I saw your friend Beth entering and had another woman waiting, a patient named Wanda Creighton. There's a storage room to the right of the hall. Its door was standing open, I remember. Outside the window at the end of the hall, I saw that Norton man running. He glanced in at me and had a horrible grin that I won't forget. A few seconds later the bomb went off, and I don't remember anything afterward until I regained consciousness here. The blast came from the storage room, right next to the operating room. It's a wonder the woman on the operating table wasn't injured. They say she was protected by the fact that she was prone, and by Dr. Grimm's body. The storage room has—had a window that might have been open or was broken and provided access for Norton to have planted the bomb." Tears glistened in her large brown eyes. "He did it, Mr. Carver. I saw him running away. I remember that grin, like it didn't matter that I saw into his ugly soul because soon I'd be dead."

"Would he have had to enter the clinic to plant the bomb? Might he have tossed it inside and then run?"

"I think it's possible that he threw it into the storage room through the window. An organization like Operation Alive, I'm sure they have floor plans of most of the women's clinics that perform abortions."

"Were there more than the usual threats to the clinic in the weeks leading up to the bombing?" Carver asked.

"Yes. We always got threats. It was part of what we did. In the last few weeks, they'd become more extreme because most of them came from Operation Alive, even though they deny it. Then there was the bullet hole."

Carver sat straighter. "Bullet hole?"

"A week before the bombing, someone fired a bullet into Women's Light during the night, when the building was unoccupied. The next morning, when I arrived early and opened the clinic, I saw that the front door glass was shattered. The police said it was a drive-by shooting. They figured out the angle of the shot, then they found the bullet buried in the wall opposite the door."

"Did you mention this to the FBI?"

"No, I don't think so. I just told them about the threats, the letters and phone calls. I'd just finished talking to the police and didn't tell them about it because they already knew. So I told the FBI pretty much what I'd said to the police but forgot to mention the gunshot last week. I was still shook up from what happened, so maybe I wasn't thinking clearly. Do you think it's important?"

Carver wondered how she could doubt its importance. But she'd been in an explosion and lost part of herself. That sort of thing tended to change your priorities in an instant.

There was no point in burdening her with a sin of omission. "It could be important," Carver said, "but probably isn't."

The gunshot was almost surely a piece of information McGregor had kept from Wicker in their competition to discover who if anyone other than Norton was behind the bombing. More specifically, to gain proof that it was Operation Alive. Norton might know about the drive-by shooting, but he wasn't talking to the authorities at all now on advice of counsel. If it weren't for Jefferson Brama, the FBI would be wringing facts out of Norton like water from a wash rag.

But now Brama would be doing the talking, either himself or through Norton, and it would be artful talk that revealed nothing.

"Do you know who Jefferson Brama is?" Carver asked.

"Sure. The lawyer for Operation Alive. He's been to the clinic to threaten us with murder charges and lawsuits." Delores twisted up her mouth as if she might spit. "Him I don't like."

"Had you seen or met Adam Norton before catching sight of him outside the window?"

"No. The only time I saw him was that day, just before the explosion. I know I shouldn't, but I want him to die now for what he did."

"He might," Carver assured her.

"Probably not, with Brama as his lawyer."

Carver didn't argue with her. She might be right.

He gripped his cane and stood up. "Is there anything you need?"

"No," she said, "my father visits me regularly, brings me things every day. My boyfriend, I don't know . . . He was here once, said he'd be back, but he hasn't."

"Serious boyfriend?"

She smiled sadly. "Maybe not."

"Don't give up on life, Delores."

She sniffled and wiped her nose with the back of her hand. "Well, doesn't that sound simple?"

"It is simple, and it's good advice, considering the alternative."

"Why don't you tell me I'm young and beautiful and have my whole life ahead of me?"

"Is that what you want to hear?"

"No."

"You know all those things are true, when you're not feeling sorry for yourself. Not that you don't have the right, but sometime it's got to end."

"I know." She clutched her hands tightly, forming fists with the thumbs tucked inside her fingers, the way women do. "I'm furious, Mr. Carver, and I'm terrified of the future."

"You'll get over both, the fury and the terror. It might be hard at first, but the future can be good for you."

She looked again unabashedly at his cane and his ruined leg, then up at his face. "I know you're right."

She tried a smile, but when he left the room she was crying.

Carver's own eyes were stinging with tears. Like Delores Bravo, he found himself furious, and afraid of the future.

Not without reason.

Sitting in his office late that afternoon, he got a call from the head nurse on the fourth floor at the hospital. There had been trouble in Beth's room.

|17|

WHEN CARVER left the elevator on the fourth floor and hurried
down the hall, the first person he saw was McGregor standing
outside the door to Beth's room. The lieutenant's wrinkled brown
suit coat was open and hitched back on one side, as if to allow him
to reach his gun, whose checked butt was visible in its leather holster. It was a pose Carver had seen McGregor affect before when
he wanted to be especially authoritarian.

McGregor reached out a long arm toward Carver as he approached the door. "Not so fast, asshole."

Carver avoided the arm, shoved him aside, and continued on
his way, expecting McGregor to follow him into the room. His
knuckles whitened on the crook of his cane. He was ready to deal
with McGregor if he came in.

But McGregor, an expert on the remaining length of burning
fuses, stayed outside.

Wicker was in the room, standing at the foot of the bed. So was
a uniform from the Del Moray Police Department and a stocky
plainclothes cop with acne Carver assumed was FBI.

Beth was standing near the bed, alongside Wicker, tall and elegant in her hospital gown. She was barefoot and looked perfectly all right except for the stitches still in place on the side of her neck.

The woman lying across the foot of the bed was battered and bleeding, and one of her hands was wrapped in a white towel. Someone had done a thorough and skillful job of administering a brutal beating to Officer Lapella.

Everyone other than Lapella stared at Carver. Lapella continued to face the ceiling. Wicker nodded to him. Beth walked over to him and leaned against him, placing a hand on his shoulder near his neck. He felt her fingers squeeze, loosen, squeeze, loosen.

"Beth saw the guy, and a nurse saw him leave," Wicker said. "He was tall, broad shouldered, well-tailored blue suit, red tie, blond crew cut, black horn-rimmed glasses. Looked like a government official or an accountant, the nurse said."

"The WASP," Beth said to Carver.

"Why Lapella?" Carver asked. In the corner of his vision he saw McGregor enter the room and slouch against the wall with his arms crossed.

"It seems he was using her as an example," Wicker said, looking particularly dumpy and disheveled next to Beth. "It was a way to demonstrate what he could just as easily have done to Miss Jackson."

The door opened and a spoke-wheeled gurney thumped and nosed into the room, followed by a nurse and a male attendant. They worked a backboard beneath Lapella. No one spoke as she was transferred from Beth's bed onto the gurney. Lapella glanced over at Carver and smiled weakly with split and puffy lips. It looked as if her nose was broken, and both her eyes were almost swollen shut. Carver reached over and gently touched her elbow.

The nurse affixed an IV needle in the back of Lapella's left hand and hung the clear plastic pouch on a metal stand attached to the gurney, draping the tube so it wasn't bent or kinked before adjusting the valve for the proper drip rate. She nodded to the attendant, then held the door open while he wheeled the gurney out. McGregor waved a hand at the plainclothes cop with bad skin, who followed the gurney. Apparently he wasn't FBI after all, but was one of McGregor's men.

"What do the doctors say?" Carver asked.

"Aside from cuts and contusions," Wicker said, "all of the fingers on her right hand are broken."

"They sounded like twigs snapping," Beth said. She didn't change expression or sound horrified when she said this, it was simply a statement of fact. McGregor and Wicker looked at her. Only Carver knew how tough she could be.

"Lapella was in the room here when the guy came in," McGregor said, pushing away from the wall with a lanky, whiplike motion of his long body. "Didn't have time to get to her gun, she said. I don't know about that. Gun or not, you'd think she'd have taken him on. Hell, she's had training."

"She really didn't have time," Beth said. "Not to get her gun out or do anything else. He was smiling and didn't say anything, and within two seconds after he'd walked in, he slapped her so hard she almost lost consciousness, then he just kept beating on her. When I started to get up, he drew her gun from its holster and pointed it at me, ordered me to lie back down."

McGregor looked pained. "He took Lapella's own gun? Where was she and what was she doing when this was happening?"

"She was on the floor then, and he started kicking her. He kept kicking her, all the time looking at me over the barrel of the gun and talking about wanton women and being burned with fire and lightning. I remember one phrase: 'For fear of her torture, shall they stand crying.' He repeated it several times all the while he was kicking. He . . . he seemed to relish what he was doing."

She sat down on the bed.

"Why don't you lie down," Wicker suggested.

"No, I'll just sit."

"Did he hurt you at all?" Carver asked, controlling his anger with difficulty, He yearned to do something about this, to do something *back*!

"No, he didn't even touch me. And while he was . . . doing things to Linda, he was careful to stand so I'd see what was happening. He wanted me to watch. More than that, he wanted to watch me."

"Why the hell didn't you ring for the nurse?" McGregor asked. His tone suggested that what had happened was partly Beth's fault. The fire in Carver's stomach threatened to spread.

"I started to," Beth said, "but he reached over and ripped the call button from the wall. He picked up Linda and threw her across the foot of the bed." Her voice quavered with emotion. "Then he bent back and broke her fingers over the top of the footboard."

"Did he say why he was doing this?" Wicker asked.

"No. He kept up a stream of casual chatter about God and the Bible and the arm and sword and lightning of the Lord. Some of it was scripture, I'm sure. And when he was finished, he left the room fast, moving quickly for a man that large. I climbed out of bed then, yelled down the hall for a nurse, and went to help Linda."

"That's when the nurse saw the man walking toward the stairway," Wicker said. "She gave the same description as Miss Jackson and Officer Lapella. Said he was taking his time and seemed calm."

"He was calm all the time he was in here with us," Beth said. "Calm and in a kind of sadistic daze, but you could tell a part of him was very alert. I've seen men like that before. Women, too."

"I'll bet you have," McGregor said.

"He's the man I asked you about three days ago," Carver said to Wicker. "The one who came into the room and then turned around and left when he saw a nurse was with Beth."

"I know," Wicker said. "We'll learn his identity."

"Ask Norton about him," McGregor said. "Or let *me* ask Norton."

"Norton's under federal jurisdiction," Wicker reminded him.

"Sure he is, which is what's gonna fuck up the case. Whoever beat up Lapella was a Bible-thumping shithead just like Norton, so Norton'll probably know him. These militant religious jerk-offs are a big gang, like the Crips and the Bloods, only they pray."

"Norton's not talking," Wicker said. "He's got an attorney."

McGregor smiled. "I know how to cut attorneys out of the loop long enough to get what's needed here."

Wicker looked at McGregor with distaste, then at Carver.

"He's Del Moray's biggest criminal," Carver said, glancing at McGregor. "The chamber of commerce would make him a tourist attraction, only the tourists would faint."

McGregor started toward him, then stopped abruptly and grinned, probing the space between his yellow front teeth with his tongue. "Have your fun now, Carver, but he who laughs last will laugh standing on your fucking throat."

Wicker stared at McGregor as if he were something that should be stepped on but would make a mess.

"Don't forget it was my man got beat up," McGregor reminded them.

"As if you care about *your man*," Beth said.

"If it'd been an actual man, this probably wouldn't have happened. We'd have the assailant in custody right now," McGregor said disgustedly.

"Or maybe a dead cop," Carver said.

"Let the nurses know when you feel well enough to make a formal statement," Wicker said to Beth.

She nodded.

"Make damned sure my department gets a copy of that statement," McGregor said. "The clinic bombing might be a federal investigation, but there's no guarantee Lapella's beating is connected to that."

"It's guarantee enough for the U.S. government," Wicker told him. "It'll have to be guarantee enough for you."

McGregor glared at him, then at Carver. Then at Beth, the cause of this latest problem that was spoiling his day.

"We'll see how it plays out," he said, then shoved the door open violently and stalked out.

Wicker stared after him and shook his head. "I've dealt with locals all over the country, but that one's as bad as I've seen. He's a cop in name only. How'd he ever get on the Del Moray force in the first place?"

"We think he somehow transferred to the department directly from the Mafia." Carver saw no point in explaining that McGregor had been forced from the Fort Lauderdale Police Department in disgrace and was a Del Moray officer only because he had something on the mayor. Or, more accurately, the mayor's wife.

"We've got agents outside the hospital and on this floor," Wicker said to Beth with a professionally reassuring smile. "Lapella's assailant can't get back in here. No one can without our okay. You'll be safe."

Carver knew better. "I think she should check out and go home with me."

"Why?"

"She'll be safer there. I can make sure of that."

"I don't think so," Wicker said.

"It isn't up to you," Beth told him. "It's up to me."

Wicker stared at her. "I've talked to your doctor, Miss Jackson. He told me you'd asked about leaving the hospital. He recommends at least another day. So do I." He looked at Carver. "Can we compromise on this? One more day?"

"Ask her," Carver said.

Wicker did.

"One more day," Beth agreed, "then I become an outpatient."

Wicker smiled at her and left the room.

Beth lay back on the bed and didn't say anything for a few minutes. Carver sat down in the chair next to the bed and poured some water from the pitcher on the table into a plastic cup and held it out for her. She shook her head, refusing to drink. Carver took a few sips, then put down the cup.

"It was a nightmare, Fred."

"I figured."

"He used poor Linda, tortured her and mutilated her for no reason other than to demonstrate that he could do it to me if that was his choice. So why didn't he simply do it to me?"

"If he'd already done it to you, what he *might* do would be removed as a threat. Whoever's behind the clinic bombing—and it appears that someone other than Norton planned it—sees three threats: the FBI, the local law, and a snooping private investigator with a serious grudge. McGregor and the Del Moray police will be content with the conclusion that Norton acted alone. So might the FBI, after a cursory investigation. Those are the two biggest threats, and they have to be dealt with—and maybe they can be, because they're constricted by the law and are at least somewhat predictable. But I'm a wild card, and they want me out of the deck."

"So beating up Lapella in front of me was simply a precaution, a message to you."

"An obvious warning," Carver said. "They want Norton to go to trial, be convicted, and take the fall. Case closed, news media lose interest."

"Do you think Operation Alive is behind the bombing, and making sure Norton carries the whole blame is his lawyer's real assignment?"

"It's looking more and more likely."

Beth chewed on her lower lip the way she often did when anger smoldered in her. "They're underestimating me, Fred."

"How do you mean?"

"There are *two* wild cards in the deck."

He picked up the plastic cup and took another sip of ice water, worrying, thinking maybe one was wilder than the other.

18

THE HOSPITAL was Carver's second stop the next morning. In Beth's vocabulary, Wicker's "one more day" of hospitalization had meant one more night.

"See that she doesn't exert herself," Dr. Galt told him outside Beth's room. "Her cuts are superficial and the stitches can be removed soon, and there's no lingering complication from the D and C. But her right hip's still badly bruised and will need a cold compress if it begins to swell. I'll prescribe pain pills, and something to help her sleep if she needs it." Galt smiled and touched a hand gingerly to the hair plastered sideways across his gleaming scalp, like a man testing wet paint. "She tends to think she's stronger than she is."

Carver could have told him a few things, but simply nodded. "Is she . . . psychologically okay?" he asked. "I mean, after losing the baby?"

"I wouldn't imagine she's over it yet," Dr. Galt said. "But she *is* very strong in that respect. She's a realist and will accept what's happened and get on with life." He touched his slicked-over hair again. "We all have to do that."

"How's Linda Lapella?" Carver asked.

Dr. Galt looked blank for a moment, then his eyes brightened. "Ah, the police officer who was attacked yesterday. I'm afraid she's unconscious, though she's in stable condition. Blunt-object cerebral trauma, I was told."

Carver remembered Beth mentioning the WASP kicking Lapella while the dazed policewoman lay on the floor. "Does that mean she was kicked in the head?"

"The injury's consistent with that."

"When will she be able to have visitors?"

"I'm not sure. Not today, certainly. You'd have to ask the head nurse on her floor when visitors will be allowed."

Carver shook hands with Dr. Galt and thanked him.

"The nurses should have Beth ready to leave in about fifteen minutes," Dr. Galt said. "Be sure to phone me if there are any complications at all."

Carver said that he would, then decided that while the nurse was preparing Beth to leave the hospital, he'd go to Delores Bravo's room and tell her Beth was leaving. The woman with her foot and part of her leg missing would be interested, and would doubtless need some cheering up.

HE WAS SURPRISED to find Wicker sitting in the chair beside Delores's bed. The rumpled little man stood up when Carver entered. He didn't seem glad to see Carver.

"Is coming here part of your investigation?" Carver asked.

"She's an eyewitness to the bombing," Wicker said. He sounded oddly defensive, as if trying to justify his presence in the room. "She can place Norton at the scene."

"So she told me," Carver said.

Wicker sat back down.

"Anyway, I just wanted to let Delores know that Beth was leaving the hospital this morning," Carver added.

Delores smiled at Carver from the hospital bed. Her long dark hair was neatly combed today, and the shadowed circles beneath her eyes were gone. "I appreciate you coming by," she said.

"Feeling better?" Carver asked.

"Coming along. Our talk yesterday helped."

"I didn't know you were a counselor," Wicker said. Then he remembered and glanced down at Carver's cane. "Then again, maybe you know something Miss Bravo can use."

"I hope so."

"Miss Bravo doesn't recognize the description of the man who beat up Lapella."

"I know. I asked her about him yesterday after Beth saw him enter and leave her room. Same day I asked you about him," Carver added.

Wicker stood again and jammed his hands deep in his pockets, making his belt slip below his stomach paunch and the legs of his pants bag around his shoes. Carver thought he might have insulted Wicker by suggesting that the bureau should have known the WASP was dangerous, but Wicker didn't seem annoyed.

"I think you're doing the right thing," he said, "getting Beth out of here and in different, more familiar surroundings. McGregor can't be counted on to furnish adequate protection here at the hospital. Maybe he couldn't even if he tried. Better to have her away from here and on your own turf."

"How is she?" Delores asked.

"Getting feisty," Carver said.

Delores smiled. "I can imagine that, just from what Agent Wicker has told me."

Wicker shifted his weight from one chunky leg to the other, as if the floor were tilting like a ship's deck and he had to maintain his balance. "I'll have a talk with McGregor, Carver. Use some bureau influence and make sure he knows it would be politically stupid of him to keep leaning on you and antagonizing Beth."

"Thanks," Carver said. "He understands politics."

"Because he's a born asshole," Wicker said, then shot a glance at Delores, as if embarrassed at having used profanity in her presence. Not the FBI way.

Carver thought it was time to share some information with Wicker. He invited him out into the hall. "Did Delores tell you about the shot fired into the clinic the week before the bombing?"

"Just a little while ago. Before you told me," Wicker added in a level voice.

"I've only known about it one day," Carver pointed out, "and I've had a lot to think about."

"Actually," Wicker said, "we've known about it all along. Dr. Benedict told us the day of the bombing."

Carver knew the FBI had exercised a warrant and searched Norton's house as well as his car. "Did Norton possess any firearms?" Silly question in Fort Florida.

"A snub-nosed thirty-eight revolver, a nine-millimeter semiautomatic with a banana clip, and a twelve-gauge Ithaca shotgun. None of Norton's weapons fired the shot. The bullet dug from the clinic wall was a steel-jacketed thirty caliber, probably from a rifle."

"So maybe Norton was careful enough to get rid of the rifle after the shooting."

"Maybe," Wicker said. "But he was careless enough to leave bomb-making manuals lying around his house, and there were blasting caps in his car. I doubt he'd be so cautious as to drown or bury a rifle."

That sounded reasonable to Carver.

They drifted back into the room.

"I'd better get back to Beth," Carver said, looking at his watch.

"Tell her we'll get together after I'm back on my—when I get out of here," Delores said. "We have things to talk about. We both lost something in that explosion."

"I'll tell her," Carver promised.

As he left the room, he saw Wicker sit back down.

BETH WAS being backed from her room in a wheelchair as Carver approached. The elderly volunteer who was maneuvering the chair was also holding the flower-patterned valise that Carver had brought for Beth. The woman appeared to be well into her seventies, a large-framed woman with white hair that had probably once been blond to match her pale eyes and complexion. The breadth of her shoulders and hips suggested she had never been thin. There was a craggy symmetry to her features that lent her stateliness and probably, long ago, beauty of the unconventional sort that haunted.

Carver kissed Beth and took the valise from the woman, then started to take over pushing the wheelchair.

"Sorry," the volunteer said with a smile, "I'll have to take her down to the lobby and see her off. Insurance requires I look after her while she's still on hospital property."

"Insurance rules the day," Carver said, and stepped back.

"I can walk," Beth said.

"Not if you want to leave here," the volunteer said, showing a streak of steel.

Carver grinned at Beth and stood aside to make room for the wheelchair as they started toward the elevator.

"Where were you," Beth asked as they descended, "trying to see Lapella?"

"No, she's still unconscious."

"Dr. Galt told me. That bastard kicked her in the head."

The volunteer studied the numerals on the digital floor indicator. The elevator stopped and the door glided open.

"I was visiting Delores Bravo," Carver said.

The volunteer gripped the wheelchair handles tighter and leaned her weight forward so the chair's wheels would hop over the ridge where the elevator didn't quite line up with the lobby floor.

"How is she?" Beth asked, craning her neck to look behind her and up at him.

"She'll need the wheelchair," Carver said.

Just outside the hospital's side entrance, they waited for him in a patch of sunlight while he went and got the car. As he pulled into the driveway, he saw Beth still sitting motionless in the wheelchair, the white-haired woman standing over her like an aged and wise guardian angel.

The sight scared and saddened him. For the first time he wondered if they were doing the right thing, letting Beth leave the hospital.

Then he remembered Lapella, in the same purgatory between sickness and health, protected by the same corps of angels. They hadn't made much difference the day she was beaten.

He braked the Olds in front of the entrance, then climbed out and helped Beth into the car.

As they were driving away, he glanced in the rearview mirror and saw the angel leaning against the wall by the entrance and lighting a cigarette.

19

HOLDING BETH'S oversize valise and the crook of his cane in his left hand, Carver unlocked the cottage door with his right. Beth stood alongside him, looking tired but obviously glad to be free of the hospital. Behind them on the beach the surf roared and dashed itself on land, while off in the distance gulls screamed.

"What was that?" Beth asked, hearing another, faint sound from inside the cottage over the rush of the surf.

"That's a surprise," Carver said, opening the door.

He went in ahead of Beth, glanced around, then smiled and stepped aside, leaning on his cane and motioning for her to enter.

She took a few steps inside, then stood still, staring at the medium-size black-and-tan dog that was staring at her with its head cocked to the side.

"What is it and why?" Beth asked, never one to be fond of animals.

"German shepherd," Carver said. "I got it from the pound this morning before coming in to the hospital. The woman there recommended it, said they were a very territorial breed and he'd be protective of his house and owner almost immediately. And he's got a good loud bark that'll scare away any intruders."

Beth looked more closely at the dog. "Are German shepherds all swaybacked like that? And aren't both ears supposed to stand up on a German shepherd?"

Carver didn't know the answer to either of those questions. "Maybe its a collie-shepherd."

"What's that?"

"Half German shepherd, half collie."

"But it doesn't have long hair or a pointed snout like a collie."

Carver smiled. "That's because he's a German shepherd." Setting the valise on the sofa, he snapped his fingers and whistled for the dog. The dog ambled over to Beth and stared up at her. She bent down and ruffled its fur between the ears, possibly to get it to quit staring.

"His facial markings are odd," she said. "Makes him look as if he has eyebrows."

Carver had noticed that at the pound, and on reflection realized it was the eyebrowlike markings that gave the dog the quizzical, intelligent expression that had made him feel confident in the animal as a loyal watchdog and companion.

"What's his name?" she asked.

"Al. That's what the woman at the pound said. And he's had some training, she said. He's housebroken and obedient."

"He looks old."

"She told me he was a young dog."

"He's gray around the muzzle," Beth said as Al began to lick her hand.

"So am I," Carver pointed out, "if I neglect to shave for a few days. Al doesn't shave at all."

Beth walked over and sat down on the sofa, next to the valise.

Al followed and sat quietly at her feet. That didn't figure to Carver, since he'd been the one who had fed Al this morning. Maybe his previous owner was a woman.

Al rested his head against Beth's thigh. Carver was getting restless.

Beth ignored Al and unzipped the valise, then withdrew her computer case. She opened the case and removed the computer.

"You should rest," Carver said.

"I've been resting, Fred. I'm going to print out my notes and have you read them, then you can let me know what's missing."

She stood up, causing Al to jerk his head back and stare at her questioningly. He followed her over to where her ink-jet printer was set up on a table, watched as if he understood what was going on as she attached the printer cord to the computer. She hooked up the AC adapter and plugged in the computer and printer.

"I don't think we need to keep Al," she said. Al raised his sort-of eyebrows and stared at her as if shocked.

"He's a great alarm system," Carver said. "He might even fight for you if the WASP breaks in."

"Al is not a fighter."

"You can't tell by looking."

Al barked. It was a deep, dangerous, German shepherd bark.

Beth couldn't help looking impressed. She even smiled.

Carver and Al watched as she switched on the computer and keyed into her word-processing program. In less than a minute, she had the printer grinding out paper.

The phone rang. Carver went over and picked it up before Beth could. She was apparently determined to forget her grief and her injuries by throwing herself back into life. That wasn't what Dr. Galt had in mind when he released her.

"Fred Carver?" a man's voice asked after Carver said hello. "The private investigator?"

"It is."

"I went to your office this morning but you weren't there, so I looked you up in the phone directory. I'm Nate Posey."

Carver couldn't place the name and was about to say so when Posey added, "Wanda Creighton's fiancé. You know, from the Women's Light Clinic."

The gangly young man in the waiting room the day of the bombing. Almost had to be him. "I think we saw each other at the hospital," Carver said. "I'm sorry about what happened."

"So am I. For me, for you, especially for Wanda. I want to talk with you. Can I drive to wherever you are? I'm on Magellan about three blocks from your office."

Carver wanted to talk to Posey, but he didn't want him here. He wanted the cottage to serve as a haven for Beth to fully recover, and he didn't want a visit by Posey to disturb her and spur her on to more activity before she was ready.

"Or we could meet someplace halfway," Posey almost pleaded, reading Carver's silence as indecision about whether to have a meeting at all.

"Drive north on Magellan about four miles," Carver said. "There's a public beach there, some park benches and picnic tables under some palm trees. I'll meet you there in about twenty minutes."

"I know where it is," Posey said. "Thanks, Mr. Carver."

"You'll meet who there?" Beth asked when Carver hung up the phone.

"That was Wanda Creighton's fiancé."

"The woman who was killed in the clinic bombing?"

"Yeah. He wants to talk."

"Maybe I should go with you," Beth said. "I mean, maybe it would be safer for me."

Carver considered that manipulative suggestion. It really didn't make much sense. Posey might not want to talk in her presence, and she'd wind up sitting alone on a bench or in the car while they conversed out of earshot. For that matter, Carver knew nothing about Posey, or even if the man he was going to meet was really who he said he was. Deviousness seemed to be going around like a virus.

"I don't think so," he said. "You'll be safer here. That's why I got Al."

Before she could answer, he went into the sleeping area and pulled the top drawer of his dresser all the way out and laid it on the bed. In a square brown envelope fastened to the back of the drawer with duct tape was his Colt .38 semiautomatic. It was actually an illegal gun for a Florida private detective to carry. The investigator's G license specified .38 revolvers or nine-millimeter semiautomatics. But Carver had never been called on the matter, didn't ordinarily carry the gun, and had seldom used it. Besides, at a glance it looked like a nine-millimeter.

He checked the clip in the handgrip, then racked the mechanism to jack a round into the chamber. Making sure the safety was on, he carried the gun in and laid it next to the printer, which had finished its work and was now switched off along with the computer. He didn't have to instruct Beth in how to use the gun. She was at least as proficient with firearms as he was.

"You'll be safe here," he said, "with this, and with Al."

Beth was frowning at him. "What I might do," she said, "is use the gun on Al." Al arched an eyebrow and seemed to smile, knowing she wasn't serious. He was apparently aware of his charm. Like Carver. Only quite often with Beth, Carver was wrong. He wished he could somehow convey that to Al.

"Lock the door behind me and let no one in," he said to Beth. "I'll come back here immediately after meeting with Posey and let you know what it was all about."

Beth picked up the gun, hefted it expertly in her hand, and stared down at it. "I hope the WASP does come here," she said.

"Don't go to sleep until I come back," Carver said. "Al might go to sleep too."

He kissed her on the lips so she couldn't reply, then limped out of the cottage.

On the porch, he stood still in the shade until he heard the snick of the locks on the other side of the door.

CARVER PARKED the Olds with its front tires up against a weathered telephone pole that had been laid sideways and was half buried to mark the edge of the gravel parking area between the coast highway and the rough, grassy slope of ground that led to the beach. The beach itself was deserted. The only other vehicles were a red Jeep with a canvas top, the one that Wanda Creighton had gotten out of before walking into the clinic just before the explosion—Nate Posey's car—and a silver Honda station wagon with a sun-bleached American flag on its aerial.

Even before Carver climbed out of the car, he saw whom he presumed was Nate Posey sitting on one of the wooden benches beneath some palm trees, facing away from him and staring out at the ocean.

Hearing the car door slam, the man turned slightly, then stood up and watched Carver approach. He was the gangly young man from the hospital waiting room, as Carver had thought. He was wearing a white pullover shirt with a red collar and a wide red horizontal stripe across the midsection, and khaki pants that clung to his legs in the sea breeze and crept up to reveal red socks. The wind molding his clothes to his lean body made him look thin and misshapen. When Carver was close enough, Posey held out his bony hand and smiled.

Carver shook hands with him. "Want to sit back down?" he

asked. Despite the bright late-morning sun, it was almost cool in the brisk wind off the water.

"I'd rather walk." Posey stole a look at Carver's cane. "If you don't mind."

"Let's stay on hard ground," Carver said. "Walking with a cane's kind of tricky on sand."

Posey strolled slowly and deliberately alongside Carver over the sandy but firm soil, about twenty feet away from where the beach began and parallel to the shore. Several minutes passed and he didn't say anything, as if the words would have to be forced out and he didn't yet have the strength. Carver idly studied the ground as he walked, careful not to place the tip of his cane on an uneven or soft spot that might cause him to fall. Like walking through life.

"Wanda's funeral was yesterday morning," Posey said finally in a hoarse voice Carver could barely hear. "I know I'm still in shock . . . or something like shock. But at the same time, something in my heart tells me I'm thinking more clearly now than ever before."

"That's possible," Carver said. He knew shock could work that way when it began to wear off, like an electrical jolt that somehow cleared one's thought processes.

"I've been mulling over what happened, Mr. Carver. How I was ignorant and fooled and the world's never what it seems. One moment everything's normal. All the pieces are in place and all the machinery of your life is humming away. The future seems almost as predictable and unchangeable as the past. The next moment everything changes." He wiped his hand down his face, dragging thumb and forefinger over his eyes to staunch any tears. "Wanda was dead as suddenly and unexpectedly as if she'd been struck by lightning, and everything was different, changed forever."

Carver thought about how close he'd come to losing Beth that morning at the clinic and understood Posey's state of mind. "None of us sees it coming," he said. "That's the nature of lightning—it's sudden, out of nowhere, a blast of change. It happened with my leg."

"Your leg?"

"When I was shot. I was an Orlando police officer, happy with my life, assuming the kind of future you mentioned, useful work rewarded by promotion and eventual retirement. Then one day I was off duty and went into a convenience store to buy groceries, and ran into a boy who was holding up the place. I wasn't playing hero. He was on his way to escaping with the money when he suddenly giggled and lowered the gun and shot me in the leg. I don't think he even knew he was going to do it. And suddenly there was a muzzle flash and his future and mine were radically changed."

"That's why you're a private investigator?"

"I was a pensioned-off, self-pitying beach bum for a long time, then people who cared about me talked sense into me. I needed something to do, so I got into the only thing I knew well. I had the experience, the contacts, and a case came my way. Then I met a woman who changed my life again."

"The black woman? Beth?"

"A different woman. She was there when I needed her. So was Beth, but that was later."

Posey stopped walking and stared down at his dusty loafers. They were the kind with a leather slot on each instep where people used to insert pennies. There was only sand in the slots. "You saying I'll meet another woman?"

"I'm saying the world will keep turning and your life will change. More slowly than it did the morning of the bombing, but it will change."

"Maybe, but right now I'm thinking about Wanda."

"You should be."

"I want to hire you to find out if Norton really is the bomber, Mr. Carver. And if he is, who if anybody was behind him and involved in planting that bomb."

Carver looked over at the youthful face made younger by a sun that revealed no mark of experience or hard-earned wisdom. "You want revenge."

"No. I want to understand what happened, all of it. I need to know why Wanda died; then maybe I can let her go someday."

"She died because she was in the wrong place at the wrong time."

"I can't just accept that. *Why* was it the wrong place and time? The days leading up to the bombing, and earlier that morning, I need to know about them so maybe they can provide an explanation for what happened, how it all fit together and why. I can pay you—I've got money. I can write you a big retainer check right now." He reached toward his back pocket.

Carver gripped his arm at the elbow and held it motionless. Posey winced and stared at him, surprised by his strength. A man and woman, probably from the Honda station wagon, were on the beach, he in baggy red shorts, she in a one-piece black swimming suit. They were strolling along the surf line, staring over at Carver and Posey. The woman said something and they looked away.

"I don't want you to pay me," Carver said. "I'll find the answers to some of your questions because I need to know them myself. Beth was carrying our child. She'd decided not to have an abortion and was at the clinic to cancel her appointment. It was only a matter of chance that she was there, just like with Wanda."

Posey stopped wincing and blinked. "Then maybe you know how I feel. Maybe you feel the same way yourself."

Carver released his arm. "Same bolt of lightning," he said.

20

ON THE drive back to the cottage, Carver thought about his conversation with Nate Posey. Posey was still young and discovering how life could stun him and the future could dart away in unexpected directions.

Carver pitied the grieving youth. Despite the kind words of mourners and assurances of professional counselors, what had happened at the Women's Light Clinic would always be with him, and the pain, even if eased, would remain a part of him. The past was immortal and lived with the present.

Before making a right turn off the coast highway onto the road to the cottage, he pulled the Olds onto the shoulder and braked to a halt.

He'd slowed the car deliberately and studied the area where he knew someone watching or visiting the cottage unobtrusively might park, and he'd caught a glimpse of gleaming blue metal. Almost certainly a car, not quite well enough concealed among tall brush and a copse of sugar oaks. The low rumbling of the Olds's idling V-8 engine was probably carried away by the ocean breeze, but Carver switched off the engine anyway. He reached into the back of the car and got the Gator-lock that in crime-ridden areas he used to lock the steering wheel in place. It was tempered steel and heavier than the cane and would make a more devastating weapon up close—an ideal club. He climbed out of the car, shutting its door quietly. Gripping his cane in one hand and the rubber handle of the Gator-lock firmly in the other, he started walking through the brush toward the parked car below.

Carver was soon out of sight of the highway and whoever might be in the parked blue car. He maintained his sense of direction easily and kept moving toward the sound of the sea. Grit from the sandy soil worked into his moccasins, and once he almost fell when the tip of his cane broke through a crust of sand and plunged about six inches into a sink hole or the burrow of a small animal.

There! He saw blue metal again, slightly off to the left. He veered that way, moving slower and more quietly, and worked his way up to the edge of the stand of trees. Though he was in the shade, sweat streamed down his face and he could feel it trickle stop-and-go down his ribs. Concealed by a wild, thorny bush with tiny red blossoms, he stared at a blue Dodge parked well off the narrow road, in a spot where the driver had a clear view of the cottage and the beach.

But the driver wasn't in the car. He was standing facing away from Carver on the other side of the vehicle, leaning back against its front fender. The first thing Carver noticed was that the man was too small to be the WASP. He was wearing gray slacks and a blue shirt. His suit coat, carefully folded inside-out so that only its gray silk lining was visible, had been laid neatly across the car's waxed and gleaming hood. The man had bright red hair, cut short on the sides and grown bushy on top, combed neatly except for a single lock standing straight up on the left side of his head, displaced by the ocean breeze. A narrow dark strap traversed his back just below the armpit. Another strap lay at an angle across his shoulder. He was wearing a leather shoulder holster. He raised his right hand to his face now and then, as if he were eating something. From his angle, Carver couldn't see what was in the hand.

A sudden soft rustling sound off to Carver's left caused the redheaded man to stand up straight and turn that way. In that instant Carver saw the holstered gun and a pair of binoculars slung around his neck by a black leather strap. Carver turned his head then to see what had caused the rustling sound.

Nothing was visible. The redheaded man walked around to the back of the car, the binoculars bouncing gently against his stomach, and stood by the trunk. Carver saw now that he was carrying a brown paper sack that must have contained whatever he'd been eating.

There was the noise again. The redheaded man stiffened, placed the paper bag on the trunk, and removed the small handgun from its holster.

Carver hunched lower, watching.

Branches moved, the soft rustling resumed, and Al trotted out of the foliage.

The man smiled and tucked his handgun back into its holster.

"Hi there, boy," he said, not loud, but Carver heard him.

Al walked over to the man, who bent down and patted the top of his head. Then the man reached for the paper sack on the trunk and drew out a sandwich. He tore off part of the sandwich and tossed it to Al, who caught it effortlessly in mid-air and scarfed it down.

This wasn't what Carver had had in mind when he got Al. Instead of protecting Beth at the cottage, here Al was accepting food from a man who was obviously spying on Beth.

Carver looked more closely at the man, then at the blue Dodge.

He began to understand. Trying not to make noise, he cautiously began backing away behind the bush, careful to avoid the thorns.

Al suddenly looked in his direction, turned toward him, hunkered down and pointed his nose and cocked a front leg.

"So you're part pointer," the redheaded man with binoculars said, as if delighted. "Well, I'm not hunting quail today, fella."

Al continued to stare and point at Carver.

Carver raised a forefinger to his lips, urging the dog to be quiet, but immediately realized how stupid that was. And the motion caused him to wave the red steel Gator-lock around, which might attract attention.

The man tossed Al another bite of sandwich. As Al broke the classic pointer stance to pick it up from the ground, Carver moved back quickly.

He turned and walked as swiftly as he could toward where the Olds was parked, digging his cane in deep with each step. It wasn't easy, moving uphill toward the highway instead of downhill toward the beach, and he feared that any second Al would begin barking and run to join him.

But apparently Al's stomach took precedence over his pursuit instincts, and Carver made it to the Olds reasonably sure that he hadn't been seen or heard by anyone or anything other than the dog.

Catching his breath as he sat behind the steering wheel, he caught sight of a big semi approaching in the rearview mirror. He timed starting the car with the passage of the roaring and whining truck so that it could not be heard by the redheaded man. Letting the idling engine power the car, he put it into drive and the Olds slowly rolled forward and then back up onto the highway.

Carver drove the quarter mile to the cottage road turnoff and continued on his way to join Beth as if nothing had happened and he was unaware of the man watching from cover.

He saw her right away as he parked beside her recently repaired. LeBaron near the cottage. Beth was sitting in one of the webbed aluminum chairs on the porch, her Toshiba in her lap. She was wearing red shorts and a yellow halter top, slumped over and pecking away at the computer's keyboard. A can of Budweiser sat on the plank floor next to her chair. Her long dark legs glistened with perspiration in the bright sunlight. No wonder the guy parked off the road was using binoculars.

Carver was irritated. He slammed the car door behind him harder than he'd intended. Beth hadn't looked up. "Where's Al?" he asked as he limped toward the porch.

Now she raised her gaze from the computer. "I let him out to do what dogs have to do. He went to the door and stood there. Kept staring at me. You said he was trained, Fred, so I figured he knew what he wanted."

"How do you know he'll come back?"

"You said he was trained," she repeated, and began working again with her computer.

Carver clomped up onto the porch and walked past her, entering the cottage. She had the air conditioner on high and it was cool in there.

He pulled Wicker's card out of his wallet and went to the phone on the breakfast bar.

Wicker answered the phone on the second ring.

"You sound as if you've got a pillow over your face," Carver said.

"Cell phone. I'm in my car. What do you want, Carver?"

"You got an agent about five foot ten, medium build, red hair, drives a late-model cheap blue Dodge, likes animals?"

Silence. Then, "Uh-huh. You spotted him?"

"He's yours, then?"

"Must be, though I didn't know about the animals. That's Anderson. He's assigned to watch Beth."

"Without her knowledge?"

"Better that way, Carver. In case our WASP friend tries to pay her a visit. She won't get careless if she doesn't know she has protection."

Carver didn't know whether to be aggravated with Wicker for posting a watch or to be grateful. What Wicker hadn't mentioned was that if Beth was unaware she was being guarded, she'd act normally and make more effective bait for the man who'd beaten Lapella. On the other hand, Wicker hadn't had to assign anyone at all to protect her. Carver decided on gratitude, but he said nothing. That might only encourage Wicker to make more close-to-home moves in secret.

"Does Anderson know that you know?" Wicker asked in his muffled voice.

"No. We can leave it that way."

"Good. And I assume you won't tell Beth."

"It might be better that way," Carver said, knowing she'd resent being observed. Wicker was right: she might get careless. Might even march down to Anderson, grab him by the shirt, and demand that he leave.

"Fine. Now what's this business about animals?"

"I've got a dog might have torn your man apart," Carver said. "Luckily Anderson had some meat to throw to him."

Wicker said something Carver couldn't understand, fading fast, probably moving between cells or falling victim to some technological glitch beyond Carver's grasp. He said something else, then the line went dead.

Carver hung up the phone, went around the counter to the refrigerator, and got out a cold can of Budweiser. As he popped the tab, the cottage door opened and Al came in, closely followed by Beth.

Al was licking his chops with a tongue that looked as if it belonged on a larger dog. He glanced at Carver as he followed Beth to the refrigerator. He smelled as if he'd rolled in something.

Beth reached in and pulled out a package of all-beef premium frankfurters.

"What are you doing?" Carver asked.

"I'm going to feed Al. He acts hungry, and you neglected to buy him any dog food."

Al raised an eyebrow. Carver thought he might have winked.

"You talk with Posey?" Beth asked, using a knife to slice the plastic wrapper on the frankfurters.

"Yes. He wanted to hire me. He's grieving hard over his fiancée's death, needs to find out what it was all about. He told me he needs a sense of closure so he can get on with his life."

"Sounds as if he's been to a therapist."

"He probably has."

"Did you tell him the only definitive closures in life are orgasms?"

Lord, she was tough! "No. It didn't seem the time or place."

He watched her slice up half a dozen premium franks on the cypress cutting board, then walk over and dump them into Al's dish. She stood holding the cutting board and knife, observing with seeming fascination as the dog greedily and noisily devoured his food with the pure and primal gluttony that only beasts possess.

Carver wondered what she was thinking.

How, in her secret heart, was she dealing with her own grief?

21

"YOU NEED to get this dog's nails clipped, Fred."

He looked down at Al, lying on the cottage floor and recovering from eating six frankfurters. His front nails were plainly visible and looked okay to Carver.

"They wear down naturally," he said.

Beth stared at him dubiously. "Maybe in the city, when a dog's walking on concrete most of the time, but not out here on the beach."

"Sand will wear them down," Carver lied. He actually had never thought about dogs' nails and had assumed that nature took care of such things, the way it did beavers' teeth.

Beth continued staring at him. It struck him that it was good for her to be so nurturing and concerned about Al. It might seem absurd that a dog would in any way take the place of an unborn child, provide an outlet, however misplaced, for a burgeoning maternal care and love, but it was possible. At the very least, Al was a healthy distraction that assuaged grief.

"I'm driving into Orlando to talk to Desoto," Carver said. "I'll buy some nail clippers when I stop to pick up dog food on the way back."

Beth smiled at his sudden change of tack, then bent down and petted the dog. The inert Al made a halfhearted attempt to lick her hand, but it was already gone.

"I phoned the hospital about Linda Lapella while you were gone," Beth said.

"How is she?"

"Better. They wouldn't let me talk to her, but they said she could have visitors. We could drive in and see her tonight. I'd like to thank her for what she went through for me."

"You should stay here and take it easy," Carver said.

"I've taken it easy for too long. I don't like sitting around thinking. It makes me an easy target for painful recollections."

"You up on your medicine?"

"Of course."

"Let's talk when I get back from Orlando."

"Bullshit, Fred!"

"What's that mean?"

"Means you're not playing fair with me. You're patronizing me and dancing around whatever I suggest."

He walked toward her to kiss her cheek, moving suddenly with the cane, and heard a low growl. Al was standing, baring his fangs, his ears back flat against his head and his eyebrows knotted into a tight V of surliness and warning. Carver looked at him in amazement.

Al didn't settle back down until the now-tentative kiss had actually been planted and Carver had withdrawn.

"Dr. Galt made me your nurse, remember?" Carver said. "You're in my care, and I say you need more rest."

She glanced at Al. "Let's take a vote."

"It would be a tie. Al doesn't have a vote."

Al knotted his brow again and growled.

Carver glared at Al.

Al glared at Carver.

"Al gets a vote," Carver said, "if Dr. Galt does." That seemed to give Beth pause. Dr. Galt was at least human and could reason. Even had made it through medical school.

"Get out, Fred."

CARVER TOOK Interstate 95 to save time, then cut west and drove the Bee Line Expressway into Orlando. It was past two o'clock and he hadn't eaten lunch, so he found a restaurant downtown on Jackson Street and ordered a hamburger and a frosty mug of draft beer. From his seat in a booth near the window, he could comfortably watch tourists and office workers walk past on the sun-heated streets.

Two attractive women in light summer dresses molded to their bodies by the breeze walked by on the other side of the street, and he found himself admiring their form and grace more than contemplating their sexual possibilities. Was he growing old? A man and woman with two young boys passed on the sidewalk in the opposite direction of the women. One of the boys, about ten years old, ran out ahead of the rest of what Carver assumed was his family. He was a skinny kid in jeans and a souvenir T-shirt with a porpoise on it. Something about the way he ran, taking long, loping strides while flailing the air with his arms, reminded Carver of his son Chipper, who'd died at the age of eight and would be eight forever in Carver's memory. He wondered if his and Beth's child would have been a boy, and a rage and despair welled up in him that he knew Beth must feel all the time. He took a long pull of beer and looked away from the window.

After lunch, he was glad to find Lieutenant Alfonso Desoto in his office in the police headquarters building on Hughey. Carver had called and Desoto was expecting him, but police work was as unpredictable as crime, and personnel were often unexpectedly on the move, even lieutenants.

Desoto was sitting behind his desk, talking on the phone, when Carver knocked on the open door. With a wave of his arm that flashed a gold cuff link, Desoto motioned for him to enter. Carver closed the door behind him and sat in a chair angled to face the desk. On the windowsill behind Desoto sat a Sony portable stereo that was usually tuned to a Spanish station. This afternoon it was silent.

"We have a match on fingerprints," Desoto was saying into the phone. "When the lab work comes in, we'll have a match on blood." He sat listening for a while, holding the receiver to his ear loosely with a hand bearing two diamond rings in gold settings, looking at Carver. Then: "Yes, DNA, whatever it takes. He's ours. Uh-hmm, uh-hmm, uh-hmm."

Desoto hung up the phone, flashing his matinee-idol white smile. He had a classically Latin handsomeness, moved like a tango dancer, and sometimes dressed like one. But instead of plying the trade of a gigolo, Desoto was a practical and tough cop who had an almost religious respect for women.

"Good to see you, amigo," he said to Carver. "How's Beth?"

"Much better."

Desoto stood up and removed his pale beige suit coat, draped it over a form-fitting hanger, then hung the hanger on a brass hook. He must have been out and just returned to the office when the phone rang. He tucked his white shirt in more neatly, used his hands to smooth the beginning of wrinkles from the elegant material of his pants, then sat back down behind his desk. Automatically he reached behind him with his right hand and pressed a button on the Sony, and soft guitar music wafted from dual speakers into the office.

"I need to know about Martin Freel and Operation Alive,"

Carver said, resting his folded hands over the crook of his cane, finding the rhythms of the guitar restful.

"So you told me," Desoto said. "Here in Orlando, the police know a great deal about Reverend Freel. Few of us are in his flock."

"But maybe one in sheep's clothing?" Carver asked.

Desoto grinned and shook his head. "If there's infiltration in Operation Alive, it's from the FBI, or maybe ATF. We don't have the manpower to send someone to church on a regular basis." He leaned back in his chair and laced his fingers behind his neck. Light from the window glinted off his gold rings, cuff links, and wristwatch and sent reflected light dancing over the walls. He liked gold more every year. "But I can tell you about the good Reverend Freel. He's more of a con man than an idealist. And a wealthy con man. He nurtures his ego and wallet through his congregation. Operation Alive isn't one of the genuine and responsible anti-abortion organizations."

"You think it's completely phony and exists only to make Freel rich?"

Desoto chewed on the inside of his cheek for a moment, causing his lips to pucker. "Completely? I'm not sure. These organizations are almost always part religion, part confidence game. They do from time to time show some obligation toward their members—when they're not tithing them or selling them medallions or plastic figurines. You're asking me if Reverend Freel personally is a true believer, answer's no, I don't think he is."

"He have a police record?"

"Not much of one. He's done some things just this side of the law, but there's wriggle room in the law as well as in the Bible. My feeling is that Freel uses all of that room and then some. Operation Alive's only been in existence three years. Last year they demonstrated at an abortion clinic here in Orlando. Freel stirred up his picketers with a fire-and-brimstone speech and they stormed the place, started breaking things up inside. They did a lot of damage, made a lot of noise. One of the patients undergoing an abortion at the time went into shock and had to be rushed to the hospital. The same night, somebody fired a shotgun blast into the clinic."

Carver remembered the shot fired into Women's Light. A bullet and not shotgun pellets, but still . . . "Were there any arrests?"

"Not on the shooting," Desoto said. "Freel and seven of his Operation Alive demonstrators were arrested for what happened when they rushed the clinic. Freel's attorney got them all out on bond within hours, and now the matter's being ground exceedingly fine in the courts. Demonstrators who did the damage might eventually pay a fine, but none of this will stick to Freel."

"Is the attorney Jefferson Brama?"

"The same. Obnoxious windbag thinks he's Perry Mason."

"He's representing Adam Norton," Carver said.

"So I've heard. He'll probably get him a good plea bargain. Brama knows the law and he knows how to spread money around. A formidable combination."

"Is Brama a member of Freel's congregation?"

"Probably. Lawyers can rationalize anything."

"Know anything about a well-dressed big guy with a blond crew cut, black horn-rimmed glasses, likes to beat up people while he's spouting scripture?"

"Not offhand, and I think I'd remember. Why do you ask?"

Carver told him about the WASP's attack on Officer Lapella, then described him in greater detail.

"Him we'll keep an eye out for," Desoto said grimly.

"I need the address of Freel's church," Carver said. "His home, too, if he doesn't live in some kind of rectory."

"He separates work from his home life. Freel and his wife have a luxury spread about ten miles out of the city."

"He's married?"

"Of course. That's how he can get by ranting and raving about family values. His wife Belinda Lee, a sort of cotton-candy blond, assists him sometimes at the Clear Connection. That's what he calls his church. It's a building with a lot of windows, like a greenhouse only with pews." He picked up a file folder from the desk and slid it over to Carver. "It's all in here, just for you, amigo. Everything's copies, so don't return it. In fact, don't tell anyone where you got it. It's the same information we gave the FBI."

"You've met Special Agent Wicker?"

"Sure. He was in here the day after the clinic bombing, asking the same questions you just asked."

"Has the FBI talked to Freel?"

"Probably."

The guitar music from the radio faded and a soft, syncopated drumbeat began. A woman began singing something mournful in Spanish. Or maybe it sounded mournful because it was in Spanish. Carver picked up the folder and stood up from his chair.

Desoto stood also. "Take good care of Beth."

His concern struck Carver as odd. Desoto had had reservations about Beth because of her marriage to the late Roberto Gomez, one of the bad guys. A cop thing. But he also had sensitive antennae when it came to women; he must know what it meant to her to have lost a child she'd agonized over and decided to bear.

"The FBI's got a watch on her at the cottage," Carver said. "And we've got a guard dog."

"Dog? That doesn't sound like you, owning a dog. *Her* dog?"

"It's working out that way," Carver said.

"What kind of dog?"

"German shepherd, more or less."

"Big dog?"

"Big."

"They're a breed known to turn on their masters," cautioned

Desoto, who knew nothing about dogs and was in fact a little afraid of them.

"Not Al. I don't think."

Desoto looked at him curiously and started chewing the inside of his cheek again.

Carver thanked him for his help and moved toward the door.

"Take care of yourself, too," Desoto said as Carver left.

22

THE CHURCH OF the Clear Connection looked as if it had at one time been a discount store. It was a long, low cinderblock building, painted white, with wide windows that had been installed so close together that steel frames rather than cinderblock separated them. What had probably once been a flat roof was now on a shallow pitch with what appeared to be chains of adjoining skylights. Soaring from the center of the roof was a white metal cross that for some reason reminded Carver of a TV aerial. That might have been the idea. Communication was communication.

The grounds around the Clear Connection, probably once a parking lot, were immaculate—grass as smooth and closely mowed as golf greens, palm trees of uniform size lining the wide stone walk to the building's entrance, colorful flower beds so symmetrically arranged that the blossoms appeared almost artificial. In the center of a round flower bed bordered by low-lying yews was a fountain that made Carver look twice. Looming from the center of a shallow pond was a tall, sculpted crucifix, and from the stone hands of Jesus nailed to the cross flowed water to cause ripples in the pond as it fell and was recirculated by an electric pump to rise in dancing little spurts around the edges of the pond. Colored lights were arranged around the pond to illuminate the spectacle at night. Carver wished he could see that.

He pushed through the tall glass doors into the Clear Connection and was immediately struck by the pure white light that infused the building. What little wall space there was had been painted pristine white, and gray carpeting with a white fleck pattern ran down the two main center aisles toward a bleached-wood pulpit. The pews were also bleached wood, of a lighter shade than the pulpit. Behind the pulpit was a crucifix that at first appeared to have been carved from ice but was actually glass. It picked up the colors of the flowers arranged on either side of the pulpit and seemed to glow with crystalline life. Despite all of the glass and sunlight, the church was cool almost to the point of being cold. The air-conditioning system made a low hum that would be inaudible when there were people here and a sermon was being directed from the pulpit. To the right of the glass crucifix was a wide alcove and a small door that led farther back into the building.

"Hello?" Carver called. His voice seemed to be fragmented and muted by the light, sent in all directions but not very far.

After a few minutes, the door in the alcove opened and a man about sixty with a flowing mane of white hair stepped out and smiled at Carver. He was wearing a cream-colored suit, white shirt, and blue tie and was slightly stooped as he walked up one of the center aisles to where Carver stood at the rear of the church.

As he drew nearer, he got older. Loose flesh hung at the sides of his jaw, and his kindly eyes were faded and surrounded by a web of fine creases in his tanned flesh. Carver changed his estimation of the man's age to at least seventy. "Can I help you?" His voice was soft and sincere, as if Carver had come in for solace and he was eager to comply.

"I'm looking for Reverend Freel."

The man's gaze went to Carver's cane. "Have you been injured?"

"Long ago."

"Perhaps we can help you here."

"No," Carver said. "Doctors have told me this is permanent."

The man smiled. It was an incredibly kind and wise smile. "We don't do faith healing here, sir. I meant perhaps we could help you with your acceptance and your faith."

"Maybe some day," Carver said, making it sound sincere. "Is Reverend Freel available?"

"I'm Jergun Hoyt. Perhaps—"

"I'm afraid only Reverend Freel will do," Carver interrupted.

"And you are?"

"My name is Fred Carver. I'd like to talk to the reverend about a private matter."

Jergun Hoyt studied him with his faded, kindly blue eyes made to seem wiser by the crow's-feet at their corners. "Reverend Freel isn't in today, Mr. Carver. If you could leave a message—"

"Where might I find him?"

The crow's-feet extended and deepened as Jergun Hoyt smiled wider. "Oh, I'm afraid he's unavailable. You must understand that many people walk in here and request an audience with him. Though he'd love to, he simply can't comply with them all. That's why if you were to leave a message, or phone for an appointment, it might be better for you."

"What exactly is your position with the church, Mr. Hoyt?"

"I'm the reverend's assistant. During services I lead the choir, and I tend to the church in Reverend Freel's absence."

"A sort of sinecure?"

Hoyt smiled tolerantly. "A sinecure is paid much to do little, Mr. Carver. I take care of quite a bit of the church's business, much of it of a financial nature, and my work is strictly voluntary.

I retired to Florida five years ago after a long career in the banking industry."

Carver considered asking for Freel's home address just to see if Hoyt would refuse, then decided against it. Hoyt might alert Freel, and Carver had the address in the file Desoto had given him anyway.

"I'll take your advice and phone later," Carver said and thanked Hoyt for his time.

Hoyt stood, stooped and still smiling, watching as Carver limped from the church. Carver thought that if it were possible to smile your way into heaven, Jurgen Hoyt would be high among the angels.

SURPRISINGLY, Reverend Freel's house was rather modest, secluded behind a stone wall and lush foliage but with a shallow front yard. There was an unlocked gate, which Carver opened, at the mouth of the driveway.

Leaving the Olds parked in the street, he walked up the driveway to the house and onto the front porch. At least Freel didn't use his congregation's donations to treat himself to a high lifestyle. Unless he had other property in other cities under other names, not to mention investment portfolios. For some people, life was a game with mirrors.

The house itself was a white clapboard structure, well kept up, with dark blue trim and an aluminum screen door. A radio or TV was on inside; Carver thought it was probably a TV soap opera but couldn't be sure. When he pressed the doorbell button, the incomprehensible dialogue between a man and woman abruptly stopped.

A small woman in a white dress approached behind the dark screen door. She opened it to see Carver more clearly, and revealed herself to his gaze. She was pretty but with coarse features softened by dyed blond hair piled high on her head and combed in wild little wisps around her ears—the cotton-candy blond Desoto had described. Beneath the white dress, her figure was beginning to thicken with middle age. He guessed she was in her late forties.

"Belinda Lee Freel?" he asked.

"I am."

"My name's Fred Carver. I dropped by the Clear Connection to talk with your husband and they told me he could be found here."

She smiled. "Well, this is where he lives." She had a hint of southern accent.

"Then he's home?"

"I surely didn't say that. Just why do you want to talk to him, Mr. Carver?"

"It has to do with the Women's Light bombing in Del Moray."

Her darkly made up eyes narrowed. "Would you be another reporter?"

"No, I wouldn't be," Carver said honestly.

"Police?"

"No."

"What, then?"

"A woman I—a woman carrying our child was injured in the bombing."

She let the screen door shut and backed away a few steps, retreating into shadow. "Are you dangerous, Mr. Carver?" she asked in a tone she might have used to inquire about the weather.

"No. Not to you or your husband, certainly. There are just some questions I need to have answered."

"Are you attempting to prove Mr. Norton guilty?"

"I don't think the authorities need me to do that, Mrs. Freel."

"The authorities are in league with evil, standing in the way of God's work."

"Norton and the rest of the demonstrators were from Operation Alive. I understand your husband organized the demonstration that day."

"My husband has a mandate from God, Mr. Carver. I do think I fear you. I fear for him."

A larger form took shape beyond her, behind the screen. "I don't believe we have anything to fear from Mr. Carver," a resonant male voice said.

"He's an agent of the devil," Belinda Lee said.

"I hardly know the devil," Carver lied.

"I am Reverend Freel," the male voice said. "Meet me around back of the house, Mr. Carver, in the garden. We can have that talk you want. Perhaps I can help you in some way." He sounded as if he sincerely wanted to help, just like Jurgen Hoyt.

The door behind the screen door closed.

Carver left the porch and limped along a stepping-stone walk that led alongside the house and to the backyard. An iridescent green hummingbird hung suspended on the bright blur of its wings before a red feeder mounted on a pole, then whirred away in an abrupt, flat trajectory like a jade bullet. Butterflies flitted about in the flowers bordering the walk.

It was a surprisingly large backyard, and private. The grass smelled as if it had recently been mowed. A tall stockade fence followed the property line except for a space in back that allowed a view of trees and a small lake. Gardenia bushes grew along the fence on both sides of the yard. In a corner formed by the fence in the back of the yard were two concrete benches in the shade of a tree.

"Mr. Carver, how nice to meet you."

Freel had come out a back door and was standing beside Carver. He was a tall man of about fifty, with black hair going gray at the temples. He had a chiseled face and large, bulbous forehead.

His eyes were gray, friendly but calculating, and remotely amused. There was a curved scar near the right corner of his thin lips. Carver had seen scars like that left by broken bottles used as weapons. Freel was wearing gray slacks that draped like expensive cloth, a white shirt with a button-down collar, no tie. On his feet were gleaming black loafers with pointed toes.

"Do come sit," he invited, leading the way to the benches beneath the tree. "I could have Belinda bring us some lemonade," he said over his shoulder. "My wife has received a spate of threatening letters from pro-choice activists lately, so you can understand her suspiciousness."

Carver declined the offer of lemonade.

Freel sat down on one of the benches and rested his hands on his knees. He looked inquisitively at Carver, who sat opposite him on the other bench. He wasn't at all what Carver had expected. This man was genial and a little rough around the edges, though that might have been a pose. He did have a confidence man's air of total trustworthiness, too good to be true except for those who were yearning for someone or something to believe.

"I heard what you said about your wife losing your child in the explosion," he said. "you have my sympathy, Mr. Carver."

"Not my wife. My child, though."

"Horrible," Reverend Freel said, either about Beth's marital status or about the death of the unborn. "But wasn't she going there to . . . ?"

"She was going inside to cancel her appointment," Carver said. "We were planning to have the child."

"I'm sorry, Mr. Carver. Violence has a way of begetting violence."

Obviously Freel was referring to the violence done to the unborn inside the clinic. "I'm told Adam Norton is a member of your congregation as well as of Operation Alive."

"Most Operation Alive members are also members of the congregation."

"Do you believe Norton is guilty?"

Freel rubbed his chin. "I wouldn't anticipate the judicial system, Mr. Carver."

"Why is Operation Alive's attorney defending Norton?"

"Adam Norton is one of my flock who's in dire trouble. Wouldn't you agree he needs the best legal counsel?"

"Yes, but aren't you afraid the presence of Jefferson Brama in the case will make it seem all the more likely that Operation Alive was behind the bombing?"

"It might well look that way, Mr. Carver. But Adam Norton acted alone when and if he planted that bomb." Freel leaned forward, resting his elbows on his knees. "Your friend who lost the child, does she need help?"

"What kind of help?"

"The sort of help the church can provide. Do you yourself need spiritual guidance and comfort, Mr. Carver?"

Carver smiled sadly. "Probably we all do. Did Adam Norton give you any indication at all that he was fanatical enough to plant a bomb?"

"He seemed dedicated, Mr. Carver. Fanatical? I'm not sure. There's a certain line between fanaticism and dedication not so easy to discern. Reasonable people might differ as to whether someone's crossed that line. Was Martin Luther a fanatic?"

"I expect so," Carver said.

"Then maybe Adam Norton is. He believes in the sanctity of unborn life, and he acted on that belief. Improperly, I certainly agree. And if guilty, he should pay the penalty. But before judging Adam Norton outside of court, Mr. Carver, or judging Operation Alive, consider the life that was lost inside that clinic on a daily basis."

"You can't stop that from happening," Carver said. "The other side is as determined as you and Norton and Martin Luther. And the law is with them."

"The law of man doesn't mean much in this instance except as an inconvenience."

"It means the abortionists are acting legally and you're criminals," Carver pointed out.

"Civil disobedience can be a citizen's responsibility, Mr. Carver."

"Is that in the Bible?"

"Oh, of course. I'm speaking of Jesus. But it's not only in the Bible. Thoreau—"

"Thoreau never set off a bomb," Carver interrupted.

"Nor did Jesus. That I would not condone."

"Would you condemn it?"

"Certainly."

"Publicly?"

"I've stated publicly that I do not condone it. Bombs are not a part of Operation Alive."

"Norton had books on bomb making in his home," Carver said. "The police found blasting caps in his car. Did he mention anything about this to you, talk at all about bombs, before he used one on Women's Light?"

"We didn't discuss bombs, only the strategy for that day's demonstration in Del Moray."

"Were you in Del Moray at the time of the bombing?"

"No, I was here in Orlando." Freel straightened up, looked as if he might yawn and stretch, but didn't. "I answered all of these questions when they were posed to me by the authorities. I'll be glad to answer them again for you if it will help to ease the pain of your grief."

Carver stood up and leaned on his cane. "Your wife Belinda, Reverend Freel, is she a true believer?"

Here was a question the authorities hadn't asked. For an instant, surprise, then maybe anger, flashed in Freel's eyes. "My wife is a born-again Christian, Mr. Carver, if that's what you mean by 'true believer.'"

"Adam Norton describes himself as a born-again Christian."

"And so he sees himself."

"Christians don't blow up innocent people with bombs."

"That's certainly true. Not without sin or regret, anyway. And, hopefully, not without redemption." Freel stood up. "May I walk with you to your car, Mr. Carver?"

"No thanks, I'll go it alone. I appreciate you giving me some of your time, Reverend Freel."

"Certainly. And no man or woman has to go it alone in this life."

"Just to my car, though," Carver said, "I don't think it will matter much."

As he made his way along the stepping-stone walk toward the front of the house, Carver heard a door close as Freel went back inside. Though he hadn't been the fire-breathing clergyman Carver had expected to meet, the reverend's determination and self-righteousness fairly shone from him.

Carver disagreed with Desoto's assessment of Freel as a more of a con man than an idealist. The reverend was a fanatic with a mission.

|23|

CARVER STOPPED at PetPitStop, a sort of supermarket of pet supplies just outside Del Moray, and bought a twenty-five-pound sack of Bow-Wow-WOW! low-calorie dog food. After a recent diet of table scraps and premium frankfurters, Al needed something to keep his weight down. Carver was dismayed to find a wide selection of dog pedicure clippers to choose from. He stood before the display for a while and then chose an efficient-looking pair of nail clippers he thought he wouldn't mind too much if he were a dog. Insomuch as he could imagine having paws instead of feet. Why he was willing to buy such expensive clippers he wasn't sure. Maybe he felt guilty for buying the low-calorie dog food, which was the cheapest of an array of choices and probably *not* what he would have selected if he were a dog. Al would eat economy class but have a top-notch pedicure.

As he drove the rest of the way into Del Moray, it occurred to Carver he'd be passing within a few blocks of A. A. Aal Memorial Hospital. He decided to drop in and see if Dr. Galt was available.

It might be a good idea to talk to him without Beth knowing about it, to see what he thought about Beth leaving the cottage so soon and coming in this evening to visit Linda Lapella.

After parking in the lot near the main entrance, he went into the spacious and cool lobby and asked a woman at the information desk if Dr. Galt was in the hospital. She told him the doctor wasn't on duty but would be there to make his evening rounds at about seven o'clock. Carver thanked her and turned to go back outside to his car.

That was when he saw Dr. Benedict sitting on one of the low, soft sofas in the lobby, leaning forward with his elbows on his knees and staring at the floor. His shoulders were hunched and he looked weary.

Carver walked over to him.

"Dr. Benedict?"

Benedict nodded without looking up.

"Taking a break?" Carver asked.

"I'm not seeing patients today," Benedict said. "I came here to see Delores Bravo." Still not looking up at Carver.

"Something wrong?" Carver asked.

Benedict raised his head and stared up at him. His features were set in distress and anger. A vein was pounding like a pulsating blue worm in his temple. "The violent cretins have claimed another victim. Another senseless death for a cause already lost."

"*Delores Bravo?*" Carver asked, feeling a thrust of rage himself at the thought of the spirited young woman's death.

"Officer Lapella," Benedict said.

Carver sat down beside him on the sofa. This wasn't right. The doctors had diagnosed Lapella's injuries and predicted recovery. "But the prognosis—"

"The prognosis was wrong," Benedict said. "They are sometimes. It was the head injury. A kick to the head, who can tell what damage it causes? She'd had a CAT scan and an MRI, and the images hadn't shown the kinds of injuries that would be fatal. But the images are difficult to interpret, even for experts. There was more damage than anticipated. There was unexpected hemorrhaging, pressure, cell degeneration in vital areas. She died a little over an hour ago."

"Murder," Carver muttered. "For nothing but trying to do her job."

Benedict glanced over at him, more defeated now than angry. "Tell me about it," he said bitterly.

Carver knew what he meant. In the past week, Benedict had lost his fellow physician and friend in an act of futile terrorism. Now the people who had perpetrated that act, killing an innocent patient in the process, had directly or indirectly caused another, periphery death. The circle of violence was expanding.

A flurry of motion caught Carver's attention as the lobby doors burst open and McGregor, followed by several grim uniformed officers, stormed into the lobby and strode toward the elevators. McGregor's lanky, coiled body was tense and his prognathous jaw was thrust even more forward than usual as he moved with loping strides across the tile floor. His demeanor, and the look in his tiny blue eyes, caused people to stare at him and step aside.

When he caught sight of Carver and Benedict, the procession suddenly stopped. McGregor motioned curtly for his men to continue without him, swiveled on the heel of one of his giant brown wing-tip shoes, and headed toward Carver.

Neither Carver nor Benedict stood up. Benedict, staring at the floor again, might not have noticed McGregor's approach, although Carver could not imagine anyone failing to pick up the lieutenant's scent of stale sweat and cheap deodorant.

McGregor, looming over them, moved to the side so Benedict was staring directly at the huge brown shoes.

"Dr. Benedict, funny finding you here," he said as Benedict looked up.

"This is a hospital," Benedict said in a somewhat puzzled voice. "I'm a physician."

"Oh, yeah," McGregor said. "What with your clinic blown all to hell, this is the place where you open the oven door and pop 'em out before they're done."

Benedict stood up, his face dark with anger. "I don't like your sense of humor, Lieutenant."

McGregor smiled, gratified. "You should go somewhere else then, Doctor, where maybe you can tune in a 'Gilligan's Island' rerun."

"Don't let him bait you," Carver advised Benedict.

"I'll take no shit at all from you," McGregor told Carver. "We got a cop killing now. One of my men's been killed by these crazies because that asshole Wicker and his feebs can't do their job."

"She was a woman," Carver pointed out.

"A cop's sex don't matter," McGregor said in a sudden burst of political correctness. "She was a uniform under my command. Her death reflects on me."

"On *you?*" Benedict said in disbelief. "Is that what you're so upset about?"

"He's partly responsible," Carver said. "He assigned her to a shit job and then forgot about her."

McGregor's face flushed and his tiny piglike eyes widened until they were almost square. Then he breathed out so hard that spittle flew. "You won't get under my skin, dickhead. To me you're nothing but a mosquito—you can cause an itch every now and then, but that's all."

"Mosquitoes carry yellow fever," Dr. Benedict said, as if calmly informing an intern or curious patient. "They can cause misery and death."

McGregor stared at him, pointing the pink tip of his tongue at him from between his front teeth. Then he laughed. "Well, well, a medical insult." He motioned with a quick jerk of his thumb. "Leave us, now, Doctor. I wanna talk alone to the rat that carries the plague."

Benedict looked over at Carver.

"Never pass up an opportunity to avoid this man," Carver said.

It took Benedict a few seconds to make up his mind, then he gave McGregor a look of disgusted incredulity and walked quickly toward the lobby exit.

McGregor stared after him, grinning. "Probably on his way to play a few rounds of golf. Or maybe drive the Mercedes someplace and have a few martinis. That's what doctors do, drink and play golf. When they're not fucking the nurses."

"Hardly leaves time for billing," Carver said.

"They find time. This murder's in my jurisdiction, and the victim's one of my people. That means it's my case alone, without FBI interference. So I expect complete cooperation from you."

"My guess is that you're trying out your twisted legal theory on me to see if I agree with you. I don't. I would think Lapella's death is legally linked to the clinic bombing. That means FBI involvement in the investigation."

McGregor gave him a level stare. "Was Lapella pregnant? No. Was she at the clinic when it went bang? No. Is her alleged killer connected to the bombing? We don't know that he is. This isn't FBI territory, it's mine. Now that we got that settled, what do you know about Lapella's death?"

"Only what Dr. Benedict just told me."

"Which was?"

"What he would have told you, if you'd asked him nice."

"Or officially. Like I'm asking you."

"Complications set in," Carver said. "It was her head injury;

the doctors can't always tell for sure about them, and they were wrong this time. Lapella's brain started to bleed, there was pressure, damage. She died."

"Because that bastard kicked her when she was lying on the floor."

"We agree on that," Carver said.

"What do you know about him?"

"Probably less than you do. His description, not much else. Other than that he quotes scripture while he's breaking fingers and committing murder."

McGregor ran a plate-size hand down his stained tie, as if smoothing it in preparation for a photograph. "The goddamn media's gonna be all over my ass because of this."

"Send them to Wicker."

"I told you, this is my case, and when I solve it, the same media dorks'll be knocking on my door and calling me and throwing themselves in front of me with their recorders and cameras. Meantime, I'll just have to put up with 'em and tell plenty of lies."

"They'll probably want to talk to me, too," Carver said. "Certainly they'll want to interview Beth."

McGregor's eyes flared for a moment in sudden alarm. Here was a vulnerability he hadn't anticipated. "I'm gonna be out to your place to talk to your dark-meat friend, Carver. Get her official statement. And whatever she says either to me or to the media jerk-offs better fit with the facts. She witnessed this murder, and she's got a legal responsibility."

"And ethics."

"Don't be so sure. Ethics are for naive assholes like you. Only reason she's sleeping with you is so she can take advantage of you some way. You just haven't figured it out yet. Probably won't until it's too late."

Carver simply stared at McGregor, refusing to be provoked.

"I can tell you ethics aren't gonna stop *me* from setting this thing right," McGregor said. "Neither are dumb fucks like you and Wicker. Nobody makes a media patsy outa me. This religious nut that killed my officer, he just *thinks* he knows about being crucified! I'm gonna nail him to the cross like he never dreamed of, in or out of church!"

"I hope you're right," Carver said. "If anybody can make the biblical Romans seem like nice guys, it's you."

McGregor ignored the compliment as he stalked away toward the elevators.

Humble, maybe.

24

WHEN CARVER entered the cottage, the sack of dog food slung beneath one arm, the other straining with the cane, he saw Wicker sitting on one of the stools at the breakfast counter, sipping from a glass of ice water.

Beth, who'd been seated in a chair facing Wicker, stood up and came over to Carver, taking the dog food from him.

"Heavy," she said. "Did you remember the nail clippers?"

"In my pocket," he said as he nodded to Wicker.

Wicker remained on his stool and leaned back, propped with his elbows on the counter behind him. The posture caused his pot belly to protrude and made him look particularly unkempt. A trace of stubble showed on his chin. He even needed a haircut, something you couldn't often say about an FBI agent.

"I don't know about this kind of dog food," Beth said, leaning the sack against the wall by the door. "It doesn't look very tasty."

"The guy at the store said dogs love it," Carver improvised. He pulled the nail clippers from his pocket and laid them on a table near the sofa. He had to poke the lining back into his pocket before sitting down. The clippers had shifted as he walked and poked a small hole in the pocket, maybe even in the material outside the lining. Chalk up a pair of pants to Al. Then it hit Carver: *where was Al?*

"Why didn't Al bark when I drove up?"

"He's out," Beth said in a tone of voice suggesting that Al was a doctor not presently in his office. The watchdog is out.

"For a guard dog," Carver said, "he spends a lot of time away from the person and place he's supposed to protect."

"He's new to the job."

Carver suspected Al was visiting Agent Anderson again for another impromptu meal.

"You having a guard dog here," Wicker said, "that's a good idea."

"For the dog," Carver said.

Wicker removed one elbow from the counter to take a sip of ice water. "I understand you've been in Orlando. What did you think of Reverend Freel?"

"He's a true believer."

"Could be."

"I'm not so sure about his wife, though."

Wicker appeared interested. "Oh? She struck me as just as fanatical as her husband. The ideal helpmate in the service of hubby and heaven."

Carver shrugged. "Maybe I'm wrong. Just an impression. As for Freel and Operation Alive, I can see the organization being behind the clinic bombing. Apparently Norton was an involved member and a regular demonstrator."

"Thing to remember," Wicker said, "is that a lot of Freel's congregation aren't Operation Alive members, and not all Operation Alive members endorse bombing the abortion clinics they picket."

"What I've read about them," Beth said, "describes an extremist organization."

"Being an extremist and advocating murder are two different things."

Beth looked at Carver. "Could this be an FBI agent who's undergone sensitivity training?"

Wicker smiled. "You'd be surprised. We're not the stiff-backed, stereotypical outfit of Hoover's era."

Carver tried to imagine Wicker as a cross-dresser but couldn't. But then Hoover was a stretch, too.

No one said anything while Beth went into the kitchen, then returned with a cold can of Budweiser and handed it to Carver.

"She seems to be feeling better," Wicker said, nodding in Beth's direction.

Beth sat down beside Carver. She had on a yellow blouse, faded Levi's, and black sandals. Her hair was combed back and braided and she was wearing makeup and gold hoop earrings and a matching gold bangle bracelet. She thought that in an hour or so she'd be leaving to visit Lapella.

Carver hated to tell her the reason why she wasn't going. Even more, he hated the idea of someone else telling her. He wished the lump in his throat were in someone else's and that it were someone else's heart taking on an irregular rhythm and growing heavier by the second.

"I stopped by the hospital on the way here," he said. "Linda Lapella died from her head injury."

He heard Beth's sharp intake of breath, almost a sob.

Wicker removed his elbows from the counter and sat up straighter on the stool. "When did this happen?"

"She died just before I arrived, maybe two hours ago." Carver put his arm around Beth. Her back and shoulders were trembling with each breath. "McGregor came into the hospital when I was there talking to Dr. Benedict."

"So we've got another murderer."

"McGregor considers it his murderer to catch. He doesn't seem to think the link with the bombing is strong enough to involve the FBI."

"McGregor's wrong," Wicker said. "Lapella was killed while guarding a victim of the clinic bomber."

Beth slipped from beneath Carver's arm, stood up, then went over to the window that looked out on the ocean. "I don't care who catches him," she said, "but I want the bastard caught."

"I talked to Desoto when I was in Orlando," Carver said. "He doesn't have a line on the WASP either." He glanced at Wicker. "Lieutenant Desoto's an old friend. He mentioned the bureau had talked to him."

"We know about him," Wicker said. "And we know all about the history you two share."

Carver felt a twinge of uneasiness. The positioning of Anderson to watch the cottage might not be nearly the extent of the bureau's covert intrusion in his and Beth's lives. Maybe Wicker was more like Hoover than he was saying.

There was noise out on the porch.

"Al coming back," Beth said, turning away from the window.

Wicker downed some more ice water. "Not unless he's wearing shoes with leather soles."

"I wouldn't be surprised," Carver said.

There were obvious footfalls on the plank porch then, and a solid knock on the door.

"Not Al," Beth said, opening the door.

Al walked in.

"The way he was acting," a male voice said, "I figured he had to be your dog."

"He is," Beth said, and stepped back to admit a tall man with angular features and a full head of gray hair. He was a nice-looking guy and had a little brush mustache and reminded Carver of an older Douglas Fairbanks, Jr.

When he saw Wicker, he smiled. "Evening, Agent Wicker."

Wicker returned the smile and slid down off his stool. "Mr. Duvalier and I have met," he said to Carver.

"I'm Gil Duvalier," the man said. From a pocket in his brown-and-cream-checked sport jacket he drew a white business card and handed it to Beth. "That's sure a nice dog. He looks as if he has eyebrows."

"Future Rock Fidelity," Beth read.

"That's an insurance company," Wicker said. "It has nothing to do with popular music." A beeper on his belt shrilled and Al trotted over to within ten feet of him and sat staring. Wicker opened his coat, pressed a button on the beeper, then tucked in his chin and squinted down so he could read the return phone number to call.

"Phone's right behind you on the counter," Beth said.

Wicker shook his head. "I'll call from my car. I imagine the latest murder was finally brought to our attention."

"Latest murder?" Duvalier repeated, looking confused.

"Officer Linda Lapella," Beth said.

"Isn't that the woman who was attacked at the hospital?"

"I'm afraid so," Wicker said, detouring around the watchful Al and moving toward the door. "I think you're going to have the same conversation with Mr. Duvalier I had this morning," he said to Carver. He waved a hand as he went out. "Evening, all."

Carver looked at Duvalier. "What conversation is that?"

"About Nate Posey," Duvalier said. "My company's making preliminary inquiries."

"I can't tell you much about him, other than that he tried to hire me to find out more about the clinic bombing. I refused the case, didn't want to take the kid's money for something I was going to do anyway."

Duvalier looked interested.

"Maybe you can tell us more about Posey than we can tell you," Beth said, saying what Carver was thinking.

"Two months ago," Duvalier said, "Posey's fiancée Wanda

Creighton made him the beneficiary of her hundred-thousand-dollar life insurance policy."

Carver remembered his conversation with Posey. "So he wasn't kidding when he said he could afford to hire me."

"He could hire you twenty times over," Duvalier said. "The policy provides for double indemnity."

Carver remembered the old movie of the same title, Fred Mac-Murray murdering Barbara Stanwyck's husband and faking an accident, making it look as if the husband had fallen from the back of a moving train. The insurance company didn't want to believe it was an accident but considered the possibility that the husband had committed suicide. Keys, the brilliant claims investigator played by Edward G. Robinson, had scoffed at the notion and asked his and MacMurray's dense boss if he knew the actuarial odds of a man committing suicide by leaping from the back of a train.

Duvalier had seen the movie, too. He smiled at Carver and said, "What are the odds of a heavily insured woman being blown up in an abortion clinic bombing?"

Al stretched, yawned, and noticed the sack of Bow-Wow-WOW! leaning against the wall.

He ambled over to it and lifted a leg.

25

CARVER LEFT Beth at the cottage the next morning, in the care of Al and the stealthy and continual presence of Anderson.

He hadn't checked for Anderson's presence yet without finding the FBI agent on duty in or near his government-issue blue Dodge. Carver never revealed himself and talked to Anderson, though he was sure Wicker had informed him that Carver knew of his presence. But he made it a point to make sure Anderson saw him leave the cottage, so he'd know Beth was alone except for the questionable company of Al. Beth had come to believe more and more in Al's abilities as a protector, while Carver had developed some doubts.

Beth was itching to leave the cottage and to become more involved in trying to prove or disprove Norton's guilt and whether he'd acted alone in the clinic bombing. Duvalier's revelation that Nate Posey was the beneficiary of Wanda Creighton's life insurance policy had prompted Beth to voice the theory that Posey had been the bomber, using Norton as the fall guy and the Operation

Alive demonstration as a cover and a possible motivator of Norton. Carver had differed with her, but he knew she might be right.

The answering machine in his office was aglow with the news that he had seven messages. He sat down at his desk and wondered at a world where callers could nail you with messages and obligations even if you didn't happen to be home or in your office. Alexander Graham Bell might have decided not to invent the phone if he'd anticipated that. But then someone selling vacation time shares would surely have figured it out.

One of the messages was a sales pitch not for time shares but for municipal bonds to help repair damage from a recent hurricane on the Gulf Coast. One was a wrong number. Four were from McGregor, cursing at Carver and taunting him, and finally telling him to call him at police headquarters. Wicker must have talked to McGregor about easing up on Carver, and straightened him out as to who had jurisdiction in the Lapella murder. Carver decided not to return those calls. The last call was from Beth, telling Carver that Al was refusing to eat the Bow-Wow-WOW! and suggesting that on the way back to the cottage he stop and buy some cans of beef broth to pour over what the Bow-Wow-WOW! label called "delectable nuggets of pure deliciousness."

Broth! Carver thought in disbelief. Did other dogs convince their owners to pour messy beef broth over dry dog food? He doubted it. What he should do is stop on his way back and buy a cat, see what Al made of that. He was finding it possible to work up a dislike of Al.

He was erasing his messages when he heard someone enter the anteroom. The office door was open, so he sat and waited for whoever it was to appear.

She peeked shyly around the doorjamb, gave a smile a try, then gave up on it.

As if fighting an invisible magnetic force, she made herself step completely into the doorway so she was framed in total view. Her obviously painful self-consciousness brought to mind the term *frontal nudity* even though she was fully dressed. Carver guessed her age as about thirty, but it was difficult to know for sure. She was a child-woman redhead who might have been twenty or forty, her gauntness emphasized by one of those silky, loose-fitting dresses that were given shape only by an elastic clip in back at the waist. The dress's straps lay crookedly on her bony shoulders, and its low neckline revealed little other than countless freckles. She had prominent cheekbones that seemed about to protrude through her pale, freckled flesh. Her eyes were large and innocent and blue, and her mouth, sans lipstick, was stretched over even but protruding teeth. She was attractive but looked like she needed food, clothes, and consolation. Carver knew he was a sucker for such women and warned himself.

"Mr. Fred Carver?" she asked. Her accent was very southern. Kentucky, Carver guessed. It made him think of thoroughbred horses and split-rail fences and fried chicken and a woman he knew in Paducah.

He acknowledged that he was indeed himself sitting in his office and she seemed pleased.

"I don't want to be here," she said. Another nervous attempt at a smile.

He returned the smile quickly, before hers disappeared. "Neither do I, a lot of the time."

"Oh!" she said abruptly, as if remembering a missing letter in a spelling bee. "I forgot to introduce myself. I'm Carrie Norton."

Carver tried to recall the first name in police or news reports.

"Adam Norton's wife," she said, helping him out. "I guess you never expected I'd show up here."

"No, but I'm not sorry you did. Why don't you come in all the way? Sit down and we can talk about whatever it is you came for."

She entered slowly, moving tentatively, and sat down in the

chair facing his desk. She rested her hands in her lap and pressed her knees tightly together beneath the material of her dress. The dress had a muted flower design on it, distorted where her thighs creased it in a tight valley. On her left ring finger was a simple gold wedding band. That was her only jewelry.

"I heard about you going around asking people questions regarding the Women's Light bombing," she said. "Known for a couple of days you were investigating the crime."

As he listened to her soft, lilting voice, he wondered if she were here to try to hire him, like Nate Posey.

"I don't know if this'll do much good," she said, "but it gnawed away on me that I should try, because maybe you'd pay at least some attention and have an open mind. Not like the police and those FBI folks. Why I came here, Mr. Carver, is to convince you my husband is innocent."

"I can't promise you that will be easy," he said honestly.

"Oh, I don't need that promise. Not much has been easy in my life nor in Adam's. We got married five years ago where I grew up in Faircrest, Kentucky, because that's where Adam finally found himself a job after drifting around the country. We met in church."

Carver could have guessed.

"I knew Adam was a good man when first I laid eyes on him. Five years of marriage and a criminal charge hasn't changed that. Oh, I know you and the police and FBI have got your evidence and clues and statements. But I got something none of you has, and that's long-true knowledge of what's in my husband's heart."

Carver spoke softly, in the manner of a man trying not to frighten a small animal and make it bolt. "Did Jefferson Brama advise you to come here, Mrs. Norton?"

She met his eyes directly; he saw bluegrass and blue skies. "No, he did not. Mr. Brama is my husband's lawyer only and doesn't advise nor control me in my personal actions."

Carver sighed and stared out the window at the patch of ocean visible between two buildings on the other side of Magellan. The sun was shooting silver sparks off the shimmering water, making the sight beautiful but so brilliant as to be an assault on the eyes. "Let's look at this objectively, Mrs. Norton."

"That's all I ask. It's surely not what's been happening."

"Adam was seen running from behind the clinic, where he was in violation of the law, moments before the bomb exploded. Bomb-making literature and material was found in a search of your home. There are witnesses who will testify that he was experimenting with bombs, and blasting caps were found beneath the seat of his car. In a journal he kept, he described himself as someone chosen to be the lightning, arm, and sword of the Lord. Or words to that effect."

Carrie Norton's jaw tightened as she listened to Carver. Then she said, "He did not confess to the crime. There are no words to *that* effect."

Carver raised his hands, then let them drop back onto the desk. "But what about all the evidence, Mrs. Norton?"

"Circumstantial, every bit of it."

"There will be testimony by eyewitnesses," he reminded her.

"They only saw him where he wasn't supposed to be. They did not actually see Adam throw nor plant the bomb."

True enough, Carver had to concede.

"And those blasting caps, they're like the ones in our garage, maybe even come from there, but Adam never carried them in the car, so they had to have been planted there to help convict him. As for the so-called bombs the police say my husband exploded, those weren't bombs at all, merely blasting caps. He was just experimenting, so he could be sure the timing mechanisms he was making would work like he planned and set off a real bomb."

"Then he did intend to explode a bomb at the clinic."

"Well, of course, eventually. But not necessarily *that* clinic. And yes, he did write in his journal that he was the terrible swift sword of the Lord. You gotta understand, Mr. Carver, my husband thinks it's his duty to strike the heretics dead even if it means sacrificing himself. But the fact is, he never had time to act. He never harmed nobody at all, any time or any place, much less that Women's Light Clinic."

"You're saying he really did simply go behind the building to wave his sign at the windows."

"Of course that was all he did."

Carver looked into her guileless, unblinking blue eyes. "Let's suppose what you say is true. If your husband were to be acquitted of the Women's Light bombing, he'd soon commit a similar crime somewhere else."

"Sooner or later, I suppose he would."

"How do you feel about that? Didn't you try to talk him out of experimenting with timers and blasting caps and planning something that might kill innocent people?"

She sat forward in her chair, clasping her hands in her lap. "Be clear on this. I believe in whatever it is my husband wants to do, Mr. Carver. If he says it's his duty to slay the heretics who are themselves slaying thousands every day, I won't stand in his way nor interfere in any fashion. I believe as he does and support him in his plan to learn how to build and use bombs to destroy abortion clinics and stop the killing of the unborn. But the point is, he hasn't done anything yet. He's pure innocent."

"If he were freed and continued with his plan, you'd soon lose him again."

"When the *Lord*, and *not* the government, says it's time!"

"Might the Lord be working through the government?"

She sat back stiffly in her chair, seemingly offended by his suggestion. "That," she said, "is highly unlikely. But if the Lord might, so might the devil."

She had him. Carver should have known better than to argue religion with her.

"What do you want me to do, Mrs. Norton?"

"I can't afford to pay for your hire," she said. "But you aren't one of the government people and might be impartial and fair to Adam. That means much to me. All I ask of you is to keep an open mind, and if you find evidence that Adam is innocent or that someone else is the bomber, promise me that you'll be an honorable man and see that the truth comes to light. I would sleep better knowing that was the case."

Carver thought about it. Wasn't that what he wanted, too, seeing that the truth came to light?

"I can promise you that."

As soon as he'd let fly the words, he remembered that promises hastily made had been the cause of most of his problems in life.

26

JUST BEFORE NOON, so he could beat the lunch crowd, Carver drove to Poco's Tacos for lunch. It was a cloudless and balmy day, and many of the pleasure boats usually docked at the marina were out to sea. Carver sat at a table in the shade of its umbrella, took a crunchy bite of taco, and watched sailboats, cabin cruisers, outboard runabouts, and a guy on a Sea-Jeep frolicking in the ocean. The peril-fraught sea of Columbus and Magellan had become a playground.

As he was sipping soda through a straw, he happened to glance toward the street and notice a big black Buick parked at the curb near the marina entrance. The man behind the wheel was watching him through the windshield, which reflected the sun so that Carver couldn't quite make out his features. Then either the man shifted position or a cloud passed over the sun, blocking or changing the angle of reflection, and for a second it looked as if the driver was a large man wearing black horn-rimmed glasses.

Carver gripped his cane and stood up, ducking his head to

avoid bumping it on the umbrella. Carrying his cup of soda in his free hand, he walked toward the Buick.

The car's door opened and the driver got out and stood tall. He was a broad-shouldered man wearing a dark blue suit, white shirt, and red tie. He had a blond crew cut and was indeed wearing black horn-rimmed glasses. They made him look studious but didn't keep him from looking dangerous. *The WASP.* He crossed his arms, leaned back against the car, and put on a waiting smile.

Carver limped toward him faster, feeling fear mixed with elation, weighing the odds. This was a well-traveled street in broad daylight. It was unlikely that the WASP would display a gun or knife. Whatever physical was going to happen would be fast. Fast was fine with Carver. Fast was what he was about, even if he lacked lower-body mobility. He had quickness and reaction time. And he had his cane for a weapon.

When he was a hundred feet from the WASP, he tossed aside his soda cup, litterbug ready for action. More than ready. Carver's blood was up. The WASP liked to break fingers, let him see if he could break Carver's.

When Carver was fifty feet away, the WASP unhurriedly climbed back into the Buick.

The engine was idling, but the car didn't move. He knows I can't get there in time with the cane, Carver thought. The bastard's toying with me, reminding me I'm a cripple.

He let Carver limp to within ten feet of the car before driving away. He didn't wave, didn't even bother to glance at Carver. It was a nondisplay and it plainly showed disdain, demonstrating who had control.

Carver hadn't even been able to make out a license plate number. The plate was in a chrome holder with a plastic cover that was conveniently discolored from the sun.

Carver walked back to where he'd flung aside his soda cup and whacked it with his cane, scattering cracked ice. Then he retrieved the mangled cup and dropped it and his half-eaten lunch into a trash receptacle. He was still in fight-or-flight mode, and he'd chosen fight; his blood was racing and his heart continued hammering with anticipation, pumping adrenaline. His mind knew the crisis had passed but his body, processing older and essential signals that urged survival instead of death, hadn't caught up. It was an effort for him to calm down.

As he looked out again at the day sailors and pleasure yachts and the man on the Sea-Jeep, the ocean didn't look so blue and innocent. Florida off and on shore wasn't the playground pictured in glossy chamber of commerce brochures and travel agency ads. Mickey Mouse and Goofy were here. So were sharks and alligators.

Thinking about the direction the black Buick had taken, he decided to drive to the cottage to be with Beth.

BEFORE TURNING from the coast highway onto the road leading to the cottage, he parked the Olds and walked to the spot from which he could usually see Anderson's parked car. This time Carver couldn't find the usual patches of blue metal visible through the thick foliage. Either Anderson wasn't on duty or he'd decided to observe the cottage from another position.

Lowering himself into the Olds, Carver put the car in drive, eased back onto the highway, and drove toward the turnoff and home.

Beth's car was parked in its usual spot in the shade. At least she hadn't decided to go somewhere on her own, making Anderson work harder for his bureau salary. Or maybe it would have been better if she *had* left the cottage, with or without Anderson following.

Carver parked the Olds next to her car and got out.

He'd taken a few steps toward the cottage when a loud bark made him stop and stand still.

Al shoved open the screen door and ran toward him, fangs

bared, ears so flat against his head they were invisible. Another deafening bark. Carver stood dumbfounded. Was this really Al?

Al didn't slow down. His rear paws kicked up puffs of dust as they dug at the sun-baked ground for traction. The barking became a low, menacing growl. Carver felt a chill of fear and raised his cane.

"Halt, Al!"

Beth's voice.

Al skidded to a stop, staring at Carver. Then one of his ears shot erect and he cocked his head, seeming to recognize his master, the guy who'd saved him from the pound.

"It's all right, Al," Beth said. She was standing on the porch, holding the screen door open behind her, looking tall and coolly beautiful in a long white dress flowing in the sea breeze.

Suddenly she seemed to realize she was letting in mosquitoes. She released the wooden door and it slammed shut with a reverberating noise like an echoing gunshot.

Al trotted over to Carver, who resisted the temptation to crown him with the cane and instead leaned down and ruffled the fur between his ears. Wasn't this why he'd adopted Al, to guard against intruders and protect Beth?

Sure, but . . .

"C'mon in, boys," Beth said, opening the door and hip-switching back inside.

Carver and the other boy followed.

Beth had settled down on the sofa. The TV was on and she was watching CNN. An attractive and serious female news anchor Carver hadn't seen before was talking about where interest rates would be heading and what that would mean for the housing market. Trying to guess where mortgage rates were going was like trying to forecast the weather, she said. So much ambiguity in the world, Carver thought. The weather, interest rates, murder . . .

He sat in the chair at a right angle to the sofa and leaned his cane against its upholstered arm. He decided that Beth didn't have to know he'd seen the WASP near Poco's Tacos and been taunted by him. She'd worry. Besides, she'd always warned him that Poco's was a dangerous place to dine.

"Everything all right here?" he asked.

She looked at him curiously. "Of course. I've got Al."

Al was enthusiastically devouring what looked like bits of meat and gravy stuck to the bottom of his bowl. He raised an eyebrow and glanced with concern from the corner of his eye, as if any second Carver might throw himself to the floor and try to usurp his place at the bowl. His canine expression suggested that Carver had done such a thing before and wasn't above suspicion. Al was enjoying Bow-Wow-WOW! nuggets, no doubt, covered with rich broth from a can Beth must have found in the back of a cabinet. Carver thought the animal might be putting on weight.

"Dr. Galt called," Beth said. "I have an appointment this afternoon to go into the hospital and have my remaining stitches removed. He'll examine me then, tell me I'm up to par."

"Do you feel up to par?"

"Feel like an eagle on every hole, Fred."

Al choked, recovered, continued eating.

The news anchor on CNN was talking about the abortion clinic bombing in Del Moray. Carver and Beth watched as a tape of the boarded-up clinic was shown. Mug shots, front and profile, of Adam Norton came on the screen. Norton didn't look contrite and was in fact smiling with an infuriating smugness. The scene cut to a local newsman interviewing Reverend Freel in front of the Clear Connection. ". . . of course Operation Alive doesn't endorse violence," Freel was saying into the microphone thrust toward him. "It's the violence happening inside those clinics that we object to and cannot—will not—accept. Violence is precisely what we abhor and are demonstrating against."

"But don't you think the inflammatory rhetoric of you and your group might lead to more violence?" the newsman asked. He was young, had a mass of wavy hair, and kept a neutral tone and a strict poker face, as if his cheeks had been shot full of Novocain.

"What's being done to our unborn citizens is what's creating an atmosphere of violence," Freel said. "If the government continues to try to justify this kind of mass murder, I'd say it's almost inevitable that violence will occur."

"You deny any responsibility for the bombing, but Adam Norton is a member of your congregation as well as Operation Alive."

"So is Betty Charles."

"Who?"

"Betty Charles. I use her as an example of someone the media and the public have never heard of because she would never plant a bomb or harm any human being and is a member of both my congregation here at the Clear Connection and of Operation Alive. We simply can't be responsible for the actions of all our members. If indeed Adam Norton committed this crime, the truth will certainly emerge and society will deal with it."

"Then you don't think your previous incendiary remarks—"

"The fire of the Lord ignites weak tissue even as it comforts and heals. If his message is misinterpreted by some, that is as it has always been. In Deuteronomy, God requires burnt sacrifices. We are locked in a battle for the way of the Lord here. Much of what occurs is tragic, of course, but misguided and innocent people have always suffered in the struggle for truth. That is the human tragedy and the human glory and the shining path to redemption."

"He reminds me of the preacher man who seduced and abandoned my aunt," Beth said.

"Is Operation Alive going to continue demonstrating and picketing outside abortion clinics?" the newsman asked Freel.

"Certainly. We'll go wherever the butchers are and make sure they are aware of their sins. *And* that the way to their salvation and our sick and festering society's is for them to stop killing our unborn children."

"Are you afraid of more violence, sir?"

"Yes, I am. If you're trying to get me to denounce violence, I'm doing so now. I don't want violence. Operation Alive doesn't want violence. We abhor violence both inside and outside abortion mills."

Freel's image faded from the screen, as did the newsman's. But the newsman instantly reappeared, standing in front of a low stone wall with a view of palm trees and the ocean beyond it. A split second in time but miles in distance away from the Clear Connection in landlocked Orlando. Technology making the world smaller but more deceptive. No wonder people like Freel could seize and mold confused minds and emotions.

"We attempted to interview Dr. Louis Benedict," the newsman said. "Dr. Benedict is the other physician who performed abortions at the Women's Light Clinic. But he refused to be interviewed, for obvious reasons of safety. However, he did tell us he's continuing to perform abortions and that he's received numerous death threats since the Women's Light bombing. Back to you, Julie."

Julie, the newscaster Carver didn't recognize, was on screen again seated at the CNN anchor desk. "Thanks, Earl," she said. "When we come back, we'll show you how a squirrel can delay a major-league ball game for almost an hour while players and unhappy fans—"

Beth used the remote to switch off the set. "Hypocritical bastard."

"Reverend Freel or Julie?" Carver asked.

"Why are you playing it so light and loose, Fred? Are you getting afraid of what's happening and where it might lead?"

"That's close," Carver said. He couldn't hide from her even in the farthest corners of his mind.

She came over and kissed his bald pate. "You're no hypocrite, anyway. Want some lunch?"

"Had some."

"I'm going to eat a sandwich, then drive in to the hospital to keep my appointment. Want to come along?"

"I'll drive you."

She smiled and opened the refrigerator. "Okay, but that will be the end of it."

"It?"

"You treating me like a delicate invalid."

He knew she was anything but delicate. Actually, he'd already decided to go with her to the hospital because Dr. Benedict was probably there, and he wanted to talk to him about the threats the doctor had continued to receive. But he didn't tell Beth that. He let her think his motive for accompanying her was solely concern for her condition.

Hypocritical of him, maybe, but probably somewhere in the Old Testament he was covered, at least in the Reverend Martin Freel's interpretation.

27

DR. GALT WASN'T immediately available but had left instructions for Beth. Carver went with her to the hospital's third floor, followed a nurse's directions, and they were met by a ponytailed male intern wearing a medical-emblem earring, whose name tag read HALEY, outside an unmarked door. Haley asked Carver if he wanted to have a seat in a small waiting area off the hall, but Carver opted to be in the room with Beth.

He watched while carefully, deftly, Haley removed the stitches from Beth's healing cuts. While the stitches were plucked from the cut on the right side of her neck, her expression remained stony.

Haley had to smile. "I know I'm good at my work, Miss Jackson, but you seem impervious to pain."

"Nobody's that," Beth said as he dabbed antiseptic on her face.

"We need to examine your right hip," Haley said, glancing at Carver, who was familiar with Beth's right hip and saw no reason to take the hint and leave.

There was a knock on the door and it opened slightly. Dr. Galt stuck his head in, smiled, then opened the door all the way. "How we doing, Beth?"

"Fine." She nodded as if in affirmation of what she'd just heard herself say. "Doing fine."

"Let's take a look at you," he said, and came all the way into the room. Dr. Galt glanced meaningfully at Carver. "Mind waiting outside?"

Carver couldn't remember being so disinvited. He moved around Dr. Galt and out into the hall, closing the door.

Leaning with his back against the opposite wall, he watched the cross-traffic at the end of the hall: a stern, bustling nurse rolling a gurney; a shuffling woman in a white robe; a man with a dark beard being pushed in his wheelchair by an attendant, an IV tube coiling down to his arm from a packet hung on a metal rod that jutted from the chair like a thick, inflexible antenna; Wicker pushing Delores Bravo in a wheelchair.

Huh?

Carver clutched his cane and made his way down to the end of the hall as fast as he could, but Wicker and Bravo were already almost out of sight. He thought about calling to them; he wouldn't have minded talking to Wicker. There was no mistaking the way Wicker was leaning forward and seeming to whisper in Bravo's ear as he pushed, a stupid grin on his face even from this distance.

Well, why not? Love could strike unexpectedly anywhere and smite the most unlikely people.

Moving slower, a little winded, Carver returned to where he'd been standing outside the door of the room where Dr. Galt was in talking with Beth. He took up position against the wall again, glancing down the hall to see if maybe Wicker and Bravo would pass going the opposite direction. But they didn't. A man in a robe, using an aluminum walker, went by. Then a shapely, long-legged blond nurse with a clipboard under her arm strode past at about sixty miles an hour.

Five minutes passed before Dr. Galt emerged from the room. Carver noticed that the doctor needed a haircut; the long strands of hair combed across the top of his head curved upward on the side of his head opposite their roots. He moved down the hall a few yards, motioning for Carver, to follow, so they wouldn't be heard inside the room.

"How is she really doing on a day-by-day basis at home?" Dr. Galt asked.

"I think she's okay," Carver said. "She's tough."

"Physically, you mean?"

"Yes. And mentally."

"I'll vouch for the physical part. She's a fast healer. The bruising is beginning to disappear on her right side, and her superficial cuts are all closed and knitted perfectly. Does she talk about the baby she lost?"

We lost, Carver thought. "Sometimes. Not as often as she did just after the bombing. Beth isn't the type to talk things out of her system." *Neither am I.*

"She still thinks about it a lot," Dr. Galt said. "Believe me. She doesn't like to show pain or weakness. If she were a man we'd call it machismo."

"It comes from survival," Carver said, "whatever your sex."

"Be gentle with her when discussing the subject of the baby."

"I have been. Always will be."

Dr. Galt studied him. "How are *you* coping with the loss of the child?"

Well, well, the father had been remembered. As Dr. Galt rose in his estimation, Carver thought about the question. "I don't talk about it as much as just after the bombing."

"If you need counseling," Dr. Galt said, "either of you, it's available here at the hospital."

"We're both survivors."

Dr. Galt gave a hopeless little chuckle, but if he was amused, it didn't show on his face. "You don't have to hurt as much as possible in order to survive."

"Sometimes you have to develop contempt for the pain."

Dr. Galt glanced down at Carver's cane and bad leg. "Possibly. I suppose contempt can be a curative. But it might leave long-lasting and undesirable aftereffects. Watch Beth, and don't try to dissuade her if she wants to come back here for help. In fact, encourage her."

"I promise to do that," Carver said.

"So did she," Dr. Galt said, "when I asked her not to dissuade you from coming here." He nodded, smiling at Carver, and started down the hall.

"Do you know if Dr. Benedict is in the hospital this afternoon?" Carver asked, stopping Dr. Galt after three steps.

The doctor turned around and shrugged. "I don't know any Dr. Benedict."

"He's from Women's Light Clinic. He switched his practice here temporarily after the bombing."

Dr. Galt shook his head. "Sorry, can't help you. I've never seen Dr. Benedict, don't know what he looks like." He smiled again at Carver and continued his walk down the long corridor. From behind he looked small and tired.

Carver watched him until he reached the intersecting hall and turned right, in the direction taken by the long-legged blond nurse. He remembered what McGregor had said about doctors and nurses and was briefly ashamed. McGregor could make a kindergarten birthday party seem a riot of sin. That was simply the way he thought. The man's moral compass had no needle.

"Dr. Galt leave?"

Beth was beside him. She looked fine except for the small bandage on the right side of her neck.

"He had other patients waiting," Carver said. "Was it decided that you're healing okay?"

"Sure. I'm in better condition than before I was blown up. Might do it to myself from time to time. Want to grab an early supper downstairs in the cafeteria?"

"While we're here, I'd like to talk with Dr. Benedict."

"I'll go with you," she said. "It's too early for supper anyway."

He couldn't think of a reason to refuse her.

Seldom could.

THIS TIME Dr. Benedict was easy enough to find. Carver and Beth wound up in the cafeteria anyway, after a nurse on two had informed them that Dr. Benedict was there relaxing between appointments.

Carver saw him immediately, sitting alone in a booth on the far wall. A paper plate and white plastic fork or spoon were before him on the table, and Dr. Benedict was staring into his foam cup of coffee. Carver and Beth got cups of self-service coffee, paid for them, and carried them over to Benedict's booth.

As they approached, he noticed them and managed a tight, determined smile. He was obviously not glad to see them. Carver formally introduced Beth to the doctor.

"Mind if we join you?" Beth asked.

"As if you were coming apart," Carver said in the face of the doctor's relentless, humorless smile. "Sorry. It's an old Groucho Marx joke, though I'm sure I don't have it exactly right."

Dr. Benedict's smile stayed glued to his face. He was a gamer. Carver and Beth slid into the booth to sit opposite him. Carver saw that the plate in front of Benedict contained crumbs from a piece of pie. The white implement was a plastic fork.

"Is the pie any good here?" he asked.

"Better than the coffee," Benedict said. "What brings you two here?"

"I had the stitches removed from where they plucked broken glass out of me," Beth said.

An expression of compassion passed over Benedict's face. "Good. From what I heard, you had a close call. If you'd gone into the clinic a few seconds sooner, you might have been killed."

"How is the nurse who was injured in the clinic?"

"Delores? I saw her this morning. She'll be sent home soon. She lost her right foot, you know."

"I thought I saw Sam Wicker with her a little while ago, pushing her along in a wheelchair."

"Wicker? Ah, the FBI guy. Yes, they seem to be spending more time together than is officially necessary. That kind of thing is good for Delores. It'll give her some hope. What happened to her, just doing her job and then suddenly . . ." He looked into his coffee cup again and shook his head. "Those bastards! How can they possibly think they're doing God's work?"

"Martin Freel would explain it to you," Carver said.

"I've seen him on television, heard him denounce violence. While all the time he's inciting his misguided flock to terrorize innocent women and menace physicians acting within the law."

"I understand you've received more threats," Carver said.

Benedict didn't look up. Something fascinating about that coffee. "Yes. Death threats. They're coming with increasing frequency. Crudely printed notes the police can't trace. Phone calls in the middle of the night. I try to answer them, but sometimes my wife picks up. She's brave, but she's scared."

"Why don't you get an unlisted number?" Beth asked.

"It doesn't do any good. Of course I've had it changed three times. You must not realize the deviousness and evil of the people doing this sort of thing to doctors who perform abortions."

"Do you have any idea who's making the threats?"

Benedict looked at him unbelievingly. "You must be joking again. It's Martin Freel and his Operation Alive fanatics. Don't tell me you believe his public statements about abhorring violence? He's stepped up his attack on me so the police will think the bomber's still out there. Some of the notes actually claimed whoever wrote them planted the bomb at Women's Light. That's the whole idea behind the continuing threats—to make Norton look innocent by giving the impression that the real bomber's still at large."

"Are the threats getting to you?" Beth asked.

"I won't pretend they don't have some effect. But I'm not going to be frightened away from my work." He finally looked up from his cup and his gaze traveled back and forth between them. "I believe in what I'm doing just as strongly as the people trying to stop me believe in what they're doing. A physician who performs abortions *has* to feel that way. There aren't that many of us left. If we're all scared out of business, women will have to return to back-alley butchers, knitting needles, and wire hangers."

"Maybe the French abortion pill will solve the problem," Beth said, "make abortion a private matter known only by the woman and her doctor."

"Well, God speed the pill!" Dr. Benedict said.

Carver wondered if he really meant it. The expression on his face when he'd pledged to continue his good fight was similar to the one Carver had seen on Freel's face in Orlando. Sometimes the struggle could take on more importance than the cause.

Carver knew. He'd been called obsessive often enough to wonder from time to time if it might be true.

. . .

THAT NIGHT in the cottage, he and Beth made love for the first time since the explosion. He was as gentle as possible, and so was she. Which was unlike her. He remembered her once losing herself so in her passion that she'd lashed out with a long leg and knocked over a motel lamp, not realizing it until later.

Now she lay beside him on her back, her right leg slung over his left. They were both nude and on top of the sheets. Carver felt the breeze pushing through the open window play coolly over his perspiring body.

"The room smells like sex and the sea," Beth said. "I like that."

He smiled.

She unhooked her leg, then sat up and swiveled to a sitting position on the mattress. "Thirsty, Fred?"

"Some."

She stood up and walked across the sleeping area, switching on the TV near the foot of the bed as she passed it. He raised his head so he could watch the elegant magic of her walk. She moved like a flame in the flickering light from the TV screen.

He heard her cluttering around in the kitchen, and a few minutes later she returned carrying a can of Budweiser.

"Here," she said, handing him the can. "I'm finished with it." She settled back down on the bed beside him, then reached for the remote and turned up the TV's volume. Carver could no longer hear the whisper of the surf from down on the beach. He took a long sip of cold beer and rested the icy can on his bare chest, peering over it at the TV screen.

Beth ran through the channels until she came to the local news. An anchorman named Bart something, flawlessly coiffed and tailored but ruggedly handsome enough to be in a Land's End catalog, was finishing sentences for a blond anchorwoman named Christine seated beside him. Carver liked Christine. She seemed to be playing the news anchor game with barely disguised disdain. She might even be a journalist.

Bart and Christine said that a four-year-old boy had drowned in a swimming pool in East Del Moray. Carver knew the address, a wealthy area not far from the beach. There was a shot of an expensive home and an interview with a distraught neighbor. The newsman holding the microphone saw the dead boy's mother near the gate to the house's driveway and immediately cornered her, expressing sorrow and asking if she knew how the boy had drowned. The mother couldn't unlock the gate and get inside fast enough. She melted down and began to sob. The camera zoomed in close so as not to miss a falling tear.

"Vampires," Beth said.

"You're a member of the fourth estate yourself," Carver reminded her.

"Not like that."

The image of the grieving mother faded and gave way to a tape of fire trucks and other emergency vehicles parked around a small burning building.

"On Vernon Road, just outside Del Moray," Bart and Christine said, "a bomb exploded earlier this evening at Coast Medical Services, a women's health facility that performs abortions. Reports are that the bomb went off in a storage building behind the actual clinic, which sustained only minor damage. Thankfully, no one was injured and the fire is now under control. Police won't speculate on whether this bombing is connected to the Women's Light Clinic bombing a week ago here in Del Moray."

Staring at the TV screen, Carver knew that anyone nearby would have been killed or injured when the bomb exploded. He hoped the firefighters wouldn't run across a charred body in the debris.

After a few seconds more of the camera fixed on the flames shooting into the night, Bart and Christine reappeared. They looked serious for a moment, then smiled broadly. "Old man weather is acting up, which means rain might be closing in on us," they said. "Hey, not that we can't use it! After these messages, Gail Tropical will tell us what to expect—"

Beth aimed the remote and switched off the TV. They were in darkness again, and Carver could hear the surf working away at the beach.

After awhile he said, "Another attempt by the Christian soldiers to divert suspicion away from Adam Norton?"

"I never was certain that Norton's the clinic bomber," Beth said. "I told you after we learned about Wanda Creighton's insurance policy, I kind of like Nate Posey for the deed. People are just as fanatical about money as they are about Christianity."

"They're both religions," Carver said, lying motionless in the dark and still seeing the flames of the burning abortion clinic.

Remembering what Reverend Freel had said about burned sacrifices in his TV interview.

28

BETH SAT ON the beach, as she sometimes did, to watch Carver during his morning swim. She occasionally swam in the ocean, but never with him in the morning. She knew his solitary daily swims had become as much a time for meditation as for physical therapy.

He didn't go far from shore, wanting to keep her in sight where she lounged on a beach towel with Al sitting on his haunches beside her. Al held his nose high as he sniffed the ocean breeze. Carver had risen before Beth and was already in the water when she appeared on shore, and they hadn't talked more about the abortion clinic bombing on last night's news.

The morning wasn't yet hot, but the direct sun bearing down and then glinting off the water was searing Carver's shoulders, the back of his neck, and his head. He rode the swells, treading water for a few more minutes, then leveled out into a fast crawl stroke and made for shore.

As he was swimming toward the beach, he glanced landward and saw Beth's tall form striding toward the cabin, her beach towel slung over one shoulder, Al loping along at her heel. Al looked thinner in silhouette, trailing Beth's lean outline. A couple of gaunt wolves.

While Carver showered, she prepared breakfast. He'd ground coffee beans and switched on the Braun brewer before leaving for his swim, and when he was dressed, he and Beth had a breakfast of coffee, eggs, and toast as they sat diagonally across from each other at the narrow counter. She was still wearing the shorts and faded Florida State University T-shirt she'd put on to walk down to the beach, and her bare feet had trailed sand on the kitchen floor.

"I've slept on it," she said, "and I still think Nate Posey might be the clinic bomber."

"Could be," Carver said, spreading butter liberally on his toast. The hell with calories and cholesterol.

She sipped coffee and lowered her cup. "You don't seem to endorse my view, Fred."

She was right. He didn't agree with her. "Maybe last night's bombing was exactly what Dr. Benedict was talking about yesterday at the hospital: an attempt by Operation Alive to mislead police and the public into thinking the real bomber's still out there and Norton's innocent."

"And I think it's possible Posey bombed the clinic last night so people will assume that what Benedict says is true."

"Uh-huh. Wheels within wheels."

"That's what life is, Fred, a great big mechanism with lots of meshed, turning gears that have teeth missing."

That was a strange way to look at life, Carver thought, but it might be fairly accurate.

He said, "I'd figure if Posey bombed Women's Light as a cover to kill his fiancée and collect her insurance, he'd sit tight and let Norton take the blame and the fall."

"But you don't figure like a man who'd blow up his fiancée for money—like Posey. He had the motive, and as far as we know, the opportunity."

"So find out from Wicker where Posey was at the time of the bombing."

"I already did that," Beth said. "Talked to him yesterday. Posey was working at his job at Second Sailor, a place that refurbishes yachts, when the bomb blew at Women's Light. His boss and fellow employees confirm that."

Carver finished chewing a bite of toast, then washed it down with coffee. "You think he planted the Women's Light bomb earlier, with a timing device?"

"Exactly. He doesn't have an alibi for the night before the bombing, claims he was alone in his apartment. And Wicker said a few pieces of clockwork were found in the debris near the point of detonation."

Gears with missing teeth, Carver thought. "They might have found what's left of a timing device that allowed Norton half a minute to get clear. It might have nothing to do with Posey."

Beth spread strawberry jelly on a slice of toast she'd already coated with butter, not looking at him, apparently not worrying about calories or cholesterol, either. Culinary daredevils.

"World's full of mights, Fred. I think Posey's worth watching. Folks at Second Sailor say he's using vacation time and he'll be off work for another week. If I drive into Del Moray, I should be able to find him and tail him." She put down her knife and bit into the toast. "Don't worry, I won't approach him," she said as she chewed. Eating fast. She was revved up about this, eager to rejoin the world after declaring herself healed. He remembered what Dr. Galt had said and hoped she really was healed.

"What do you expect to learn by following him?" Carver asked.

"I'm not sure. It's possible he has more than money as a motive. In fact, I wouldn't be at all surprised if there's another woman in his life."

"This kid acted like he was grieving and still in love with his dead fiancée. I can't imagine another woman in his life."

"We've run across a lot of convincing actors, haven't we?"

Carver couldn't deny it.

"I thought you were the great cynic, Fred. Here you are believing everything 'this kid' told you."

He knew he wouldn't be able to talk Beth out of this. And maybe he shouldn't try. If she was thinking about Nate Posey, she wouldn't be thinking about what she'd lost. Also, while she was watching Posey, Anderson would be watching her.

"Why don't you take Al with you," he suggested.

She laughed. "Al's trained in protection and attack, not in surveillance."

"Al's trained in ingratiating himself and in mooching."

Al, who'd been sprawled as if dead in a corner, rotated his one erect ear as he gazed from the corner of his eye at Carver without moving his head.

"If you won't take the dog," Carver said, "take the gun."

"I won't need a gun."

"Take it anyway," he urged. "Join everyone else in Florida. It's a social thing. There's jelly on your chin."

She used a napkin to wipe her chin clean, then finally agreed to take the gun and not the dog. She got dressed and fed Al a large bowl of Bow-Wow-WOW! nuggets that had been marinated in beef broth, then she drove away in her LeBaron.

Carver was worried about her, but it made him feel good to watch her enthusiasm. She had the car's top down, taking advantage of the healing sun while the morning was still bearable, if not cool.

Al continued to eat, glaring up at Carver as if suspecting an imminent raid on his bowl.

Carver poured himself a second cup of coffee and decided to drink it on the porch, then drive into Del Moray and talk to Benedict either at the hospital or the doctor's home. It might be interesting to get Benedict's slant on last night's bombing, and to see if he was taking his recent spate of death threats more seriously.

The phone rang as he was moving toward the porch. He turned around, hobbled quickly to it, and answered it on the third ring.

It was Wicker.

"Beth's gone into Del Moray to tail Nate Posey," Carver told him. "She thinks he's good for the clinic bombings."

"Plural, huh?" Wicker said. "Then you already heard about the Coast Medical Services bombing last night."

"Saw the tape on TV. What do you know about it?"

"Not much yet. But it appears dynamite was the explosive. Same as in the Women's Light bombing."

"Could have been the same bomber."

"We haven't ruled anything out," Wicker said.

Carver told him about his conversation with Dr. Benedict yesterday, and Benedict's belief that Operation Alive was mailing and phoning threats to him to make Norton seem innocent.

"We already talked to Benedict about that. He might be right, but there are a lot of crackpots out there who'd get a charge out of shaking him up so soon after the Women's Light bombing. I don't see Posey as much of a danger, though, so if Beth has to follow anyone, he's a good choice."

"That's the way I look at it," Carver said. "But I'm still glad Anderson's watching over her."

"That's the main reason I called you," Wicker said after a pause. "Because of the bombing last night, I had to pull Anderson and use him in the field investigation. Beth's on her own."

Carver didn't say anything. He felt flushed with worry and fear, and a sense of betrayal he knew wasn't justified. He'd known all along that Anderson wouldn't be around the entire time until the WASP was apprehended.

"She'll be fine," Wicker said, interpreting Carver's silence correctly. "We've checked Posey's background and he's pure. And he has no connection with Norton or Operation Alive. There's no reason to be following Posey, so no one will even know that's where Beth is and what she's doing."

"I hope you're right," Carver said.

"What about that dog you got her, the one looks like he's got eyebrows . . . what's his name?"

"Al." At the mention of his name, Al stopped licking the bottom of his bowl long enough to curl a lip and glare at Carver. "She wouldn't take him with her. He's here with me."

"Well, no matter. She's in a backwater of the investigation and will be safe." Wicker laughed. "Anderson sure likes that dog. He told me to let you know if you ever want to get rid of Al, he'd be glad to take him off your hands."

"Don't let anything happen to Anderson," Carver said, and hung up.

He hadn't told Wicker about the gun in Beth's purse.

29

THE HOSPITAL had informed Carver that Dr. Benedict wasn't seeing his first patient that day until two o'clock. Carver didn't phone Benedict to see if he was home. Better to surprise the doctor than to reveal the day's prognosis.

As he turned the corner and drove down Macon Avenue toward the Benedict house, he saw about a dozen pickets in front of the driveway, another half dozen or so across the street. He pulled over to the curb half a block away and studied them. They were ordinary enough looking people, many of them women. They were dressed for casual comfort in the heat, wearing short-sleeved shirts or pullovers, shorts, and athletic shoes or sandals. A few of them wore plastic water bottles slung around their necks, the kind with thin plastic tubes protruding from their caps, like athletes use when they want to tilt back their heads and squirt water into their mouths as if it were wine from a goat bladder. One of the women, blond, heavyset, in her twenties, carried an infant in a sling so that the child sat facing her ample chest. Carver saw that several other women carried infants as well, and there were two girls of about twelve among the pickets. One of the preteen girls carried a sign showing the universal circle-and-slash "No" signal superimposed over what looked like an enlarged photo of a bloody fetus. Some of the other demonstrators carried the familiar white wooden crosses, resting them on their shoulders military fashion at a forty-five-degree angle, as if they were the rifles of troops on the march. Christian soldiers.

Carver gripped his cane and climbed out of the Olds, locking it behind him. As he approached the demonstrators, they stared at him. He squinted against the sun and stared back, trying to place faces, but he couldn't remember if any of these people had been at the Women's Light Clinic the morning of the bombing.

The sign the young girl was carrying did indeed depict a dead fetus. There was no lettering on the sign. Other signs read KILLER LIVES HERE, DOCTOR MURDER, and BABY KILLER.

A tall, skinny man on the other side of the street lifted a bullhorn to his mouth, danced around in a tight circle to gather energy and attention, and screamed, "Stop slaughtering the unborn!" He screamed it again, louder. Then over and over at a pitch of high emotion.

The demonstrators repeated the appeal after him, and the pace of those who were walking back and forth with signs and wooden crosses picked up. They repeated the "stop slaughtering" chant three or four times, apparently prompted by Carver's arrival. For all they knew, he was from the press. The rest of the block was as bustling as a sunny ghost town. Who could blame anyone for staying inside? The demonstrators were intimidating the Benedicts' neighbors.

Finally the skinny man stopped gyrating and shouting, lowered the bullhorn and placed it on the ground, and the knot of demonstrators fell silent.

Up close they looked sweaty, miserable, and determined.

"Are you with Operation Alive?" Carver asked no one in particular as he approached the mouth of the driveway.

A shirtless, middle-aged man wearing khaki shorts and an NRA baseball cap with an oversize bill glared at him and yelled, "Stop the slaughter!" again and again. The woman behind him joined in the mantra, now that the guy across the street with the bullhorn had run out of breath. She was wearing a faded T-shirt lettered THE QUICKEST WAY TO A MAN'S HEART IS THROUGH HIS CHEST. The young girl with the bloody fetus sign was sporting a Grateful Dead shirt. Back at the cottage, Carver had a Jerry Garcia designer tie in his closet. Things sure were getting mixed up.

No one touched Carver or tried to block his way as he turned into the driveway and walked toward the low brick house with the wide tinted windows. He thought he saw movement behind one of the windows but couldn't be sure. Mostly what he saw in the windows were reflections. Behind him, the guy with the megaphone was at it again, maybe with another slogan, but from even this short distance, it was difficult to make out what he was saying or what the demonstrators were shouting in response.

Carver stepped up onto the porch and used the tip of his cane to press the doorbell button.

Almost immediately Leona Benedict opened the door.

"I was watching you approach," she said, "in case somebody out there did anything to you."

"They're loud," Carver said, "but they don't seem to be building up to action. Maybe it's too hot."

"I hope so. I hope it gets even hotter for them."

Leona stepped back and Carver entered the house for the second time.

"Is your husband home?" he asked.

"No. You just missed him. I don't know where he went." A

whiff of gin fumes carried to him as she spoke. In Carver's experience, the drug of choice for lonely women.

He noticed a folded blue garment bag with red trim lying on the floor near the door.

"I was packing," Leona said, seeing his gaze fall on the bag. She was slurring her words slightly now. The control she'd exercised to answer the door and appear sober was slipping. He stood silently, and when she saw he wasn't going to comment or leave, she said, "You gotta excuse me while I finish. A cab's on the way to pick me up."

"Where are you going?" Carver asked, leaving the elegantly furnished living room and following her down the hall to a bedroom, as if she'd invited him to watch her finish packing.

"Away from this place." She resumed transferring lingerie from a dresser drawer to a hard-sided blue suitcase open on the bed.

"To get away from the demonstrators?"

"To get away from my husband," she said, throwing a bra into the suitcase as if for emphasis.

Carver had no idea what to say about that.

She continued with her packing, examining the contents of a small, felt-lined jewelry box she'd removed from the drawer, as if trying to decide which pieces to take with her. She closed the lid and placed the entire box in the suitcase. "Away from his long hours and macho determination to keep working while he plays the hero and expounds on the nobility of his calling. I've had enough of his ego and self-importance, and I'm afraid for my own life." A pair of sweat socks followed the bra and jewelry box into the suitcase. "I'm finally leaving him."

"Finally? As in forever?"

"As in forever," she repeated. "As in for eternity." She pointed toward the front of the house and the chanting demonstrators, barely audible in the bedroom. "I've tried to live with that kind of thing, but I can't. Whatever I try, no matter how hard I attempt to ignore them, it works for a while, but only a while. And then it gets worse than ever before. The pressure, what they do to you, it builds up in you, and eventually they win. They know that. It's why they're out there. They know they can outlast people like me."

"But not your husband?"

"Oh, no. They might think so, but they're mistaken. They won't outlast Saint Benedict!" She slammed down the lid on the suitcase, lifted it slightly for a second to poke a corner of material back inside, then latched it and tried to drag the suitcase off the side of the bed and onto the floor.

It was too heavy for her, and she emitted a frustrated, boozy sigh. Carver walked to the bed and helped her stand the suitcase on the floor. He saw that it had plastic wheels. She unfolded a small handle from it and rolled it into the living room to leave it near the garment bag.

Carver followed. "If you don't mind my saying so," he told her, "you seem too angry to be thinking clearly right now. Maybe you should calm down, then see if you still want to leave."

She stared at him, her lower lip trembling. "Men! You think this is sudden, that the geeks outside are the final straw and I broke. Mister, I've been contemplating this for months. Years!" She walked to a walnut desk and pulled open a large drawer. From the drawer she pulled out a sheaf of newspaper clippings and handed them to Carver. "Look at this—my collection. You'll get some idea what our marriage has been like for the past year, and even before that. You'll understand why I've had my fill and have to get out."

There was a burst of noise from the demonstrators, then the sound of a car in the driveway. A horn gave two curtailed beeps, as if not wanting to further disturb the neighbors.

Leona opened the front door about six inches and peered out. "That's my cab," she said. She opened the door all the way and stood in the doorway.

A few seconds later she backed up a step, and a wizened, gray cab driver appeared and entered the house. He glanced at Carver, then hoisted the garment bag and heavy hard-sided suitcase and lugged them toward his cab, out of sight.

Leona paused for a moment in the doorway, looking at Carver, who was standing with newspapers clippings in each hand.

"If you see my husband," she said in a flat, decisive voice, "tell him I didn't say good-bye to him or this house or this city. Tell him I walked away and didn't look back."

She picked up a large white purse from a nearby chair and stalked out, leaving the door hanging open as she disappeared from sight. For a woman who'd obviously drunk way too much, and on such a hot morning, she moved steadily and in a straight line. Carver guessed she'd been a regular drinker for a long time, and he wondered if Dr. Benedict, busy with his calling and his patients, had noticed.

He heard car doors slam, then the cab drive away. There was another burst of shouting from the mouth of the driveway as the vehicle slowed and made its turn into the street. The man with the bullhorn shouted something Carver couldn't make out.

The demonstrators might not know it yet, but they'd achieved at least a partial victory in their ongoing war. They'd contributed to the breakup of an abortion doctor's marriage.

Carver sat down on the white leather sofa, the mass of newspaper clippings in his lap. In the bright light streaming through the open door, he leafed through the clippings. They covered more than two years and were all from the *Gazette-Dispatch*, articles about protests, threats, demonstrations that had gotten out of hand. There were plenty of photographs. In one, Carver noticed white wooden crosses and what looked like a duplicate of the dead fetus sign the girl outside was carrying, but the sign in the photo was being waved at a terrified-looking young woman by a man with a beard. Another photo was of two groups of people yelling at each other, some of them throwing what appeared to be rocks and bottles, some in the foreground blurred by their motion as they ran toward each other. One group was carrying pro-life signs, the other pro-choice. They appeared equally, angry with tortured faces, their mouths distorted by the insults and challenges they were hurling at each other. At the left edge of the photo, uniformed police were visible, apparently recently arrived on the scene. The photo's caption identified the groups as demonstrators from Operation Alive and angry pro-choicers from a local chapter of the National Alliance of Women.

He was about to put the photo aside when he noticed in the photo's background a tall man looming above those around him, possibly leaning against a car. He caught Carver's eye because he appeared to be smiling. The photo was grainy, and the man wasn't wearing horn-rimmed glasses, but Carver was sure he was looking at a likeness of the WASP. And he didn't figure to be a member of the National Alliance of Women. Or a cop.

Which left Operation Alive.

Carver folded the clipping carefully, so the face of the tall man in the photo wouldn't be creased, and slid it into his shirt pocket.

After quickly thumbing through the other clippings, he got up and replaced them in the desk drawer. He looked around the peaceful, well-furnished house and thought it was a shame two people couldn't find happiness here. Then he went out, setting the latch so the door would lock behind him.

The guy with the bullhorn was quiet, and no one said anything to Carver as he walked from the driveway and made his way to where he'd left the Olds parked. He half expected to find the car vandalized, paint sprayed on it or its tires or the convertible top slashed, but the vehicle sat level and unmarked, and its taut canvas top was unmarred by any new stains or slashes.

As he drove past the Operation Alive demonstrators, they stood motionless and stared at him in the heat with a kind of dull but unmistakable hostility, as if he might be hauling lions to the Colosseum.

At his office, Carver put the photograph of the WASP in an envelope and wrote a short note on the back of one of his business cards to accompany it.

Then he addressed the envelope to Desoto and left to find a mailbox with an early pick-up time.

As he drove along streets so hot that rising vapor danced on them, the screaming voice of the man with the bullhorn echoed around the back of his skull. Along with Leona Benedict's words before climbing into a cab and abandoning her world: "Eventually they win."

30

CARVER FOUND Dr. Benedict at the hospital that afternoon, seated on the sofa in the cool lobby where they'd talked the day of Linda Lapella's death. He was reading a newspaper, but when he saw Carver approach, he glanced up and smiled.

"Our conversation shouldn't be so tragic this time," he said.

It hit Carver with a rush of sadness and dread: Benedict didn't yet know about his wife's departure.

"I was at your house this morning," Carver said, sitting down next to Benedict. He didn't want to tell Benedict about Leona leaving him, but neither did he think he should neglect to mention it. At some point the doctor would find out about the scene with the departing Leona and realize that Carver had known.

"Operation Alive is picketing my home," Benedict said.

"I couldn't help noticing."

"That's part of their strategy, to hound abortion doctors, not allow us any peace at work or at home, put pressure on our families. How's Leona holding up? I told her to ignore them and stay away from the doors and windows. The heat will get to them eventually and they'll go away."

"I'm afraid she's the one who went away," Carver said.

Benedict looked puzzled. "Leona? Really? That wasn't wise. Where was she going?"

"She, er, *left*," Carver said.

"Yes, you told me that."

"I mean . . . left for good. That's what she said."

Benedict set aside the paper he'd been reading. Words were becoming thoughts that were boring in, changing his life. The sports page slid from the sofa onto the lobby floor. Carver felt sorry for him. He looked as stunned as if he'd been struck with a hammer.

"I assumed you meant she left the house. But you meant she left *me?*" He still couldn't quite let the idea into his mind to stay.

"When I got there, she was packing. I'm sure she'd been drinking."

Benedict made a little back-and-forth wiping motion with his hand, as if erasing a scene on a blackboard. "No, no, Leona never drinks."

Carver knew better than to argue with him. Secret alcoholics were among the most devious of marriage partners. "A cab came and picked her up, and she left with her luggage."

"She didn't say why?" Benedict was still hoping.

"She said why," Carver told him. "It's your work. She said she couldn't stand the strain and the threats. Before she walked out, she handed me a stack of newspaper clippings about demonstrations and harassment of abortion doctors. You spend too much time away from her, mentally and physically. That's more or less what she said. She thinks your cause is more important to you than your marriage."

Benedict sat silently for a while. A nurse walked by and said hello to him, but he didn't so much as glance up at her. He was lost in the labyrinth of this, his life's latest tragedy, and possibly contemplating a bleak future alone.

"I thought she understood," he said finally.

You also thought she didn't drink. "She understands that you'll never quit."

"Do you think she'll come back?"

The question surprised Carver. Why should he have any insight into the Benedict marriage? He'd merely happened to be on the scene when Leona walked from the house and took a cab. "I don't know. She seemed sure of what she was doing. She told me it wasn't all of a sudden, that the pressure had built over time and she'd been thinking about it."

"And you're sure she didn't tell you her real reason for leaving?"

Real reason? Benedict was still resisting what had happened; he saw himself as a fighter and a winner and didn't want to be the cause of his marriage's failure.

"What she said seemed real to me," Carver said. "It was the pressure of your work, what it did to your lives. That's what she told me, anyway." It always amazed him how a man like Benedict, who held and nurtured a grand vision, could be blind to what was going on immediately around him.

Benedict sat forward and leaned down, resting his head between his knees. It was what doctors told you to do when you felt faint. When he straightened up several seconds later, he looked sick.

"You going to be all right?" Carver asked.

"I'll have to be," Benedict said in a thin voice. "I have to see a patient in less than an hour." He looked at Carver and tried to smile. "You understand that, don't you, that I *have* to see a patient? You understand how important it is? Not just to me, but to her?"

Carver had gotten the message: he, Carver, understood but

Leona hadn't; every problem in the Benedict marriage stemmed from that and was her responsibility.

"If you're ill," Carver said, "you could cancel. Your patient could come back another day."

"Unfortunately, there are no 'other' days! Too many of us have been run out of business by the radicals who are picketing my house at this moment. And I have Dr. Grimm's patients now, the appointments he'll never be able to keep." He stood up from the sofa, swaying slightly, then steadied himself. Wiping his fingertips lightly across his eyes as if to correct some minor vision problem, he said, "God, what a business, what a world this is!"

"I've thought that, too," Carver said, "in my business, in my world. Nobody has much choice but to keep pushing on."

"That I can do," Benedict said. He stood straighter and buttoned his suit coat. "That I can damned well do!"

He made a good show of walking away toward the elevators, pace steady, shoulders squared. To look at him from behind, you wouldn't guess he had a care or a want.

But Carver knew Benedict had a want.

He was sure that right now the doctor wanted to scream.

AT NINE that evening, Beth returned from following Nate Posey.

Carver, sitting on the sofa and watching the light over the ocean dim beyond the cottage's wide window, turned his head when she came in and thought immediately that she looked tired. He wouldn't say anything to her about that, or about his having to clean up the mess in the cottage because Al had had no way of going outside to relieve himself.

"Why are you staring at me?" she asked as she set her computer case on the counter. She carried the little notebook computer almost everywhere these days.

He decided not to tell her how he thought she might still be too weak to be out shadowing players in a murder investigation. He knew she'd simply brush away his words, or possibly get angry and argue. Like him, she resented being vulnerable and having it pointed out.

"You're a magnet to my eyes," he said.

"Very romantic, Fred." Her tone of voice suggested she didn't believe him.

Looking again at the ocean and darkening sky, he waited silently while she went into the kitchen. The refrigerator door opened, altering the pattern of light and shadow on that side of the cottage, then closed.

"Too dim in here to see much of anything," Beth said a few minutes later, sitting down in a chair opposite him. But she made no move to switch on a lamp or suggest that Carver do so. She had a glass of milk in one hand, a chocolate chip cookie in the other. After kicking off her leather sandals, she wriggled lower into the chair, scooting her rump forward, then stretched her long legs out in front of her and crossed them at the ankles.

"I was watching the ocean and sky," Carver said. "The stars will be out soon." When she didn't reply, he said, "There's been another casualty from the clinic bombing."

"Oh?"

"The Benedicts' marriage. Leona Benedict left the doctor this morning." He related to her what had happened at the Benedict house.

Beth listened silently, chewing bites of cookie and occasionally taking a swig of milk.

When Carver was finished, she wiped away a milk mustache and set her glass on the floor beside the chair. "Maybe Leona can't be blamed," she said. "Pro-life extremist groups like Operation Alive are relentless in badgering and torturing doctors who perform abortions, and the rest of the family's made miserable in the process. Under the kind of pressure an abortion doctor's spouse has to endure, Leona probably wore down to her raw nerve ends, and her ability to resist left her." She brushed crumbs from her fingers almost angrily, probably thinking about Operation Alive. "How'd Benedict take it when you told him she'd left?"

"He seemed shattered. Surprised. He couldn't believe the pressure in their lives had resulted in her leaving. He asked me what her real reason was. I told him again why she left, but he didn't like hearing it or believing it, even though he knew he had no choice. Then he sucked up his pain and walked away to tend to a patient who was coming in. I had to admire that."

"Sure you did, being you. Is he considering quitting?"

"I doubt it. My guess is he's more determined than ever to stay on the job, despite Martin Freel and Operation Alive."

Though moonlight was filtering in from outside, the cottage's interior was becoming too dark to see anything clearly. Carver reached over and switched on a lamp by the sofa. Beth winced at the sudden onslaught of light, looking worse than when she'd walked in.

"What about your day?" he asked. "Learn anything from following Nate Posey?"

Al, who had been awakened from a nap behind the sofa, ambled around and stretched out near Beth's chair. He puffed himself up then let out a long sigh. She leaned down and scratched him behind the ears before answering Carver.

"Posey stayed in his apartment most of the day," Beth said. "Left only to run a few errands. And even though he's on vacation time, he stopped by Second Sailor and talked for a while with some employees who were working on a dry-docked yacht. After picking up supper to go at a McDonald's, he drove home and ate it, then a little while later came out dressed in fresh clothes, looking like a dandy."

Carver's interest stirred. Maybe following Nate Posey might lead somewhere at that. "On his way to meet the other woman you suspect is in his life?"

"No," she said, "I followed him to church. That big one on Shell Avenue with the huge steeple."

Carver knew the church she meant. Despite the fact that it was constructed only a few years ago, it looked like a converted warehouse on which someone had stuck a new roof with a steeple and cross, probably because of the scarcity of windows in its plain brick walls.

"I waited outside," Beth continued, "watching other people go into the church for what a sign said was a prayer meeting to aid world refugees. About an hour later, Posey came out, walking with a slim woman with black hair and a long neck. They went to a pizza place and Posey picked at a small salad and drank beer while she ate a pizza about the size of a saucer."

Carver remembered now the young woman who'd been consoling Posey in the hospital cafeteria the day of the bombing. "Love interfering with appetite?"

"I'd like to think so," Beth said, "but they didn't act that close to each other during dinner. They talked and didn't touch. And there was none of the body language, the unconscious imitation of gestures, you see when people are in love or lust. After dinner, Posey drove her back to the church, where she'd left her car. They didn't embrace or kiss when they said good-bye, and she got out of his car and into hers."

"The night was still young," Carver pointed out.

"Not for Posey. He drove home, and I saw him outside a little later watering his geraniums, wearing shorts and a red net muscle shirt." She leaned over and scratched Al behind the ears again. "That's when I gave it up and came here."

"What about tomorrow?" Carver asked, remembering that Anderson was no longer on the job.

"I'll keep following him. If anyone other than Norton actually did the bombing, I think it's Nate Posey. He's the only one we've got with a motive we know about."

"What about Martin Freel and Operation Alive?"

"They've got a motive to blow up anything and everything they want," Beth said. "All they have to do is find the appropriate verse in the Bible. But they usually confine their activities to picketing and harassing. Slashed tires and midnight phone threats are more their speed. I don't rule them out, but Posey is my favorite."

"Maybe you should take Al with you tomorrow," Carver suggested, wishing Anderson hadn't been reassigned.

"I don't need him."

"He needs you. And if I'm gone all day too, there's nobody to let him in and—more importantly—out."

Beth looked down at Al. Al looked up at Beth. His vote was in his eyes.

"Majority rules," Beth said, laughing and stroking Al's scruffy neck. "Al goes."

For good would be nice, Carver thought, but he knew better than to say it.

|31|

THE NEXT morning, Carver finished his swim in the ocean and limped up the beach toward the cottage, his white beach towel slung over his shoulders like a cape, leaning forward with each step as his cane sank into the warm sand. His swim had invigorated him and he felt wonderful. The sun was warm on his shoulders, and even the sand that had worked into his rubber thongs felt good between his toes.

His mood suddenly soured when he noticed the drab brown Plymouth parked near the cottage. It was the unmarked Del Moray police car McGregor usually drove.

On the porch, Carver tapped his cane against the edges of his thongs to knock sand from them, then opened the door and went inside.

The interior of the cottage felt chilly and the light was dim after the brilliance of the morning outside. It seemed even dimmer because of the looming presence of McGregor slouched on one of the stools at the breakfast bar, his long body twisted around in its baggy brown suit so he could look at Carver as he came through the door. Beth was on the kitchen side of the counter, standing tensely with her back rigid, using both hands to sip from a cup of coffee, as if she needed a prop to give her something to do so she wouldn't appear agitated. McGregor had a cup of coffee on the counter, near his right elbow.

"I'm always amazed when you go out to swim and make it back," McGregor said with his lewd grin. "You'd think a shark'd pick off a gimp like you thrashing around in the water."

"I see you're as cheerful and tactful as usual in the morning," Carver said, slipping his feet from the still-gritty thongs and drying himself some more with the towel so he wouldn't trail water. He wadded the towel, tossed it into the canvas director's chair by the door that didn't mind getting wet, and looked at Beth. "Is he trying to bother you?" He pointed at McGregor with his cane while steadying himself with a hand on the chair.

Beth shrugged. "Actually I think he was waiting for you for someone to really bother."

There was a whining and scratching sound at the door, then a single demanding bark.

"That's Al," Beth said to Carver.

He turned around and opened the door. Al came in. He glanced at Carver then walked past him, stepping on Carver's bare foot and causing considerable pain. Then he trotted over to McGregor, sniffed one of his boat-size brown wingtips, and began wagging his tail. McGregor smiled and absently patted the top of Al's head, something Al wouldn't ordinarily like. People were always patting dogs on the head, which wasn't much to them but was probably like a cranial earthquake to the dog. But Al continued wagging his tail, then wagged everything from the midpoint of his body back.

"This is a nice mutt," McGregor said. "Cute, too. He looks like he's got eyebrows." He stopped patting and straightened up. Al yawned, licked McGregor's dangling hand, then stretched out on the floor at his feet. "He's got good instincts."

"Al and I are going to have a talk," Beth said.

McGregor fixed a tiny, cruel blue eye on Carver. "Speaking of talking, I hear that's what you've been doing, fuckhead, wandering around talking to people about the Women's Light Clinic bombing."

"I'm a detective," Carver reminded him. "That's one of the ways I detect."

"Which brings us to why I'm here. It's time for you to bring me up to date on whatever it is you've detected so I can see if it dovetails with what we in the department have learned. We detect also. You remember, don't you, I'm with the police?"

"You're only sort of with the police," Carver said, walking over to the sofa to sit on its arm. "I've always seen you as working almost exclusively for yourself."

"Well, I'm like you, then. An independent businessman only kind of employed." He grinned fiercely. "And empowered. Something you should take into account. Time's gonna come when this case is in the past and the FBI has gone back to fucking Washington where it belongs, then it's gonna be you and me alone without the feebs to watch over you. And believe me, once they're done here, they won't give a fuck if I make sure you get life imprisonment for a broken taillight."

Al raised his head and looked up at McGregor with seeming approval, then dropped his jaw back to rest on his paws.

"Now," McGregor went on, "what do you know that I should know? Keeping in mind that anything you neglect to mention will almost surely come back to haunt you."

Beth went to the brewer on the sink counter and refilled her cup with coffee, then stayed back where she was. Fading away, Carver figured, so McGregor wouldn't ask her what *she* knew.

That was sensible. McGregor was human waste, but he did have authority and would gladly misuse it.

Carver had played this game before with McGregor and had become good at it. He leaned forward, centering his weight over his cane, and told McGregor only what he had to in order to stay legal, but not enough for McGregor to find terribly useful.

When Carver was finished talking, McGregor leaned back against the counter and rubbed his jutting chin with long fingers. The crescents of dirt beneath his nails were vividly dark against his pale skin. Carver wondered if he'd been changing the oil in his hair.

"I didn't know about the Benedict bitch leaving hubby," McGregor said, "but I'm not surprised. The man spends most of his time looking at other women's private parts."

"I doubt that was the reason," Beth said, biting off the words. Carver hoped she could control her temper.

"Then why'd she go?" McGregor asked Carver, as if genuinely befuddled. "She get the hots for somebody richer or better looking? Some guy better hung?"

"Operation Alive was demonstrating outside her house when I was there the day she left. The pressure they and people like them put on her and her husband finally got to her, made her break and run."

"Hmm. Is that what she told you?"

"More or less."

"My guess is it was just an excuse. Time for the doctor's wife to cash in, drag hubby off the golf course and into court, come away with a nice settlement, the house and the Mercedes. One thing I know, Carver, it's women."

Beth moved forward a step, actually drawing her hand back to fling hot coffee at McGregor. Carver gave her a warning look and she seemed to relax. But only slightly.

"Whatever her reasons," Carver said, "she left him."

"So how's Benedict taking it?"

"He doesn't like it."

"He'll get over it. Doctor making all that loot, some other conniving cunt'll put the spell on him, maybe maneuver him into marriage, and he'll probably go through the same financial wringing-out process. That's how women see guys like Benedict, kinda the way Indians used to look at buffalo, a source for everything they need in life. Only they don't have to shoot them like buffalo, all they gotta do is marry them and then be set for life whether they stay or go."

Beth couldn't remain silent. "Anybody who'd think that has buffalo chips for brains!"

McGregor didn't bother to turn and look at her, only grinned and probed between his front teeth with the pink tip of his tongue, gratified by her anger, not knowing how close he'd come with the hot coffee.

"If you're finished with your prairie philosophy," Carver said, "we were about to have breakfast."

"Oh? You're inviting me to join you?"

"Inviting you to leave."

McGregor got off his stool and stretched his long body. "Okay, I already had breakfast. Couple of guys like you." He ambled toward the door with his lanky, disjointed stride. Then he turned. "Another interesting thing is Adelle Grimm, the late doctor's grieving widow. Turns out she's pregnant."

Carver didn't know what to make of that.

Beth said, "What's she going to do?"

"Do?" McGregor looked puzzled. "Oh, you mean is she going to go ahead and have the kid? She's—how'd she put it?—agonizing over it. Those were her exact words. Now that the doc's dead, maybe she doesn't want this kid or can't afford it, or figures it'll cramp her style in looking for another source of cash with a dick. So she's agonizing like crazy, poor thing." He laughed. "It's ironic, ain't it? Hubby short-circuits rugrats by the dozen every day, then gets killed by some dumb fuck with nothing better to think about or do with his time. Then it turns out the late doc's own widow's got one in the oven." He waved a long arm. "Life's just fucking grand!"

After McGregor had gone, Carver went to the door and opened it.

He let it stand open for a while. Clearing the air.

|32|

IT WAS late afternoon when Desoto called Carver's office. Seated at his desk, Carver had finished billing for the second time a client whose son had joined a paramilitary unit training in the Everglades. Carver had managed to talk the boy into coming home by persuading him that communism was dead or dying and his own government wasn't plotting against him, thus taking away the reason and dignity of training in blackface for combat among the mangroves and making it a child's game. So persuasive had Carver been that within days after returning home, the boy had joined the U.S. Marines. Now the boy's parents, Carver's clients, were refusing to pay him, on the grounds that Carver hadn't recovered their son for them but had merely effected a transfer from one military unit to another. Even the uniforms were similar. Carver had included a threatening letter with their latest itemized bill, but he, and probably they, knew his threats were futile, what with the expense of actually following up with legal action. Official red tape! Sometimes Carver thought it was a government plot against him.

"You've come up with a real pip of a bad guy, amigo," Desoto said as Carver sat back in his desk chair, pressing the cool plastic receiver to his ear. He gazed out the window at the traffic on Magellan baking and glinting in the tropical glare as it waited in the shimmering heat of exhaust fumes for the traffic light at the corner to change. "This photo you sent me was all I needed to get a quick trace. Your thug is one Ezekiel Masterson. He's a former leg breaker for the union."

Carver could hear Spanish guitar music faintly in the background, from the Sony portable stereo in Desoto's office. "Which union?"

"Whichever needed him at the time. Ezekiel seems to be more of a tough guy for hire than a dedicated union man—unless there's a skull smashers union. Thirty-five years old, blond and blue, 230 pounds, he's from Miami originally, got a sheet there featuring three assaults and one attempted murder. Only one conviction, but it was for the attempted murder. Did six years and found religion somewhere in his cell or the weight-lifting room before he was paroled two years ago. That's when he hooked up with Reverend Martin Freel and Operation Alive."

"Hmm, you think he's really found religion?"

"No, I think he's found a new employer."

"Norton's a religious man, even though he killed. Or allegedly killed and is at least willing to do so, judging by what his wife says. She thinks it's admirable to let blood for the Lord, too. Ezekiel Masterson might be the same kind of fanatic. He did spout scripture while he was killing Lapella."

"No, what you just described is not my idea of religion."

"If Ezekiel's connected with Operation Alive, maybe Freel *would* go so far as to kill, and Norton *was* acting on the reverend's orders. And Ezekiel was acting on Freel's orders when he beat up and killed Lapella at the hospital in front of Beth."

"I think it's likely," Desoto said. "But it'll be impossible to get anything on Freel. He was here in Orlando when the deaths occurred in Del Moray."

"Do you think they're set-up alibis?"

"I don't know. We're going to look into them more closely and see if Freel can provide a lead so we can find Masterson. There's a murder warrant out for Masterson now, for Lapella's death. I've notified the FBI and the Del Moray police. He's a cop killer, and we want him in the worst way."

"He won't be easy to find. Lapella's death was in the news, and he knows he's good for a murder charge. He's got to be running hard."

"Whichever direction he's running, it's toward a cop."

Carver knew what Desoto meant. The fraternity of police made justice top priority when one of their own was murdered. And efforts weren't restricted only to the police force to which the victim belonged. When a cop was killed, all police departments became one.

"Something else about Masterson," Desoto said. "About a year ago, he wrote a letter to the Del Moray *Gazette-Dispatch* editorial page criticizing Dr. Harold Grimm. It contained nothing technically libelous or otherwise illegal, which is why he signed his name so the paper'd print his letter. It was part of a letter-writing campaign to discredit Grimm and the Women's Light Clinic. When I talked to Wicker this morning, he said a similar letter was in Grimm's mail postmarked last month, this one unsigned."

Carver looked away from the bright light outside and thought about that one. "Maybe Norton didn't plant the bomb. Maybe Masterson's good for that one, too."

"We'll certainly ask him about it," Desoto said, "and in the harshest possible way."

"If you find him."

"*When* we find him. And until then, you'd be smart to stay out of that particular hunt, try not to meet this guy again. Masterson might have found his version of religion, but the word is that he's psychotic and an extremely volatile combination of steroids and Christian zeal. Probably sees himself as King David slaying the heretics."

Carver was impressed by Desoto's biblical knowledge. He knew Desoto was Catholic but couldn't remember him ever going to church. On the other hand, Carver, an occasional Protestant, wouldn't have seen him there.

"You need to exercise great care, my friend."

"I will," Carver said, "but with Lapella dying, Masterson's probably fled the state."

Desoto laughed softly, a sound as tragic as the music seeping softly from the Sony behind his desk.

"He won't run that far, amigo. Remember, he knows he's right."

AFTER HANGING up on Desoto, Carver finished his paperwork, then drove by the post office and dropped the mail in an outside box for early pickup. He could feel heat emanating from the metal mailbox and wondered if glue would melt and the flaps on his envelopes would come unsealed. Nothing to be done about it now.

He drove up the coast highway toward the cottage, the top down on the Olds, hearing the sighing of the ocean on his right even over the rush of wind and the rumble of the dinosaur-ancient V-8. A pelican kept pace with him for a while, flapping along parallel to the coast and only about a hundred feet away from the car and fifty feet above the ground. It seemed to glance at Carver from its round, inhuman eye. Then the bulky yet graceful bird veered away toward to ocean, looking for fish flashing silver just beneath the sea's surface so it could dive and catch one for its supper. Everyone was trying to catch something for one reason or another. There were food chains and then there were food chains.

Beth wasn't at the cottage. Neither was Al. Beth had left a note saying she was trailing Nate Posey again. Al hadn't left a note, but Carver assumed he was with Beth. Carver was pleased about that. It did seem to him that Al should do something to earn his keep and make the cost of Bow-Wow-WOW!, marinated in beef broth, money well spent.

He sat out on the porch and watched the ocean for a while, trying not to think about Beth and Al and anything happening while she was watching Posey. He was sure Posey was a dead-end suspect despite the life insurance policy on his late fiancée. He'd met him, talked to him, and seen dark and real grief in his eyes, heard it in his voice. Beth was acting only on the dry facts of the case. She hadn't had the opportunity to talk with Posey and feel the force of his despair.

After awhile Carver realized that the feeling in the pit of his stomach was hunger as well as worry. He went inside and put a frozen sirloin steak dinner into the microwave. The carton said the dinner was low in saturated fat and contained only 250 calories. Carver didn't see how that was possible, but he wanted to believe.

When he was finished eating, he understood how it was possible to have steak with a minimum of fat and calories; the key was in eliminating taste.

Back on the porch, his stiff leg propped up on the wooden rail, he watched dusk close in and slowly smoked a Swisher Sweet cigar. His mind gave him no rest. Now he couldn't help thinking about Ezekiel Masterson, about the letters sent to the *Gazette-Dispatch* and to Dr. Harold Grimm.

Then he looked at his wristwatch, barely visible in the gloom. He wanted to talk to Grimm's widow Adelle, and it might be a good time to catch her at home. He doubted that she was eating dinner out these days, other than occasionally buying fast food somewhere and then returning to her house. Grieving widows tended to stay close to home, a tangible piece of their less troubled past.

He scribbled a note for Beth and left it next to the one she'd left him, then got in the Olds and raised the top before driving back into Del Moray.

IN THE DARK, the yellow stucco Grimm house looked white, its droopy green awnings black. Most of the visible windows in the house were glowing; Adelle was home.

Carver was steering the Olds toward the curb across the street when he noticed a vertical bar of light on the front porch—the door opening. He nudged the accelerator with the toe of his moccasin and drove on past, parking half a block down and turning off the Olds's lights. Carefully he adjusted the rearview mirror so he could see the front of the Grimm house.

More light, spilling onto the driveway. A few seconds passed, then a car backed into the street and maneuvered to face the opposite direction the Olds was pointed. The light cast on the driveway dimmed as the automatic opener closed the garage door. Red taillights flared, then dimmed and began to draw closer together as the car drove away.

Carver started the Olds, used a nearby driveway to turn it around, and followed.

When he got close enough, he saw that the car was a black or dark blue Oldsmobile sedan, a younger and sedate cousin of Carver's own car. The perfect vehicle for a doctor.

Or a doctor's widow.

Adelle Grimm was driving and she was alone in the car, he was sure now. She'd left by the front door and opened the garage door from outside with a key or opener from her purse. She was sitting very erect, her head and shoulders, her graceful neck, set and stiff. Even from behind, the squarish symmetry of her features was evident whenever the Olds turned a corner or was driving away at an angle beneath enough light to allow the briefest glimpse of her in profile.

Carver was slightly disappointed. He would rather have seen someone else driving the car, someone who had paid a visit to Adelle and whose destination might prove meaningful. The larger the cast of characters, the greater the possibilities.

She drove fast, intent on her destination. Carver kept watching the back of her head, which remained perfectly steady. She didn't so much as glance at her rearview mirror. Why should she? The thing she feared might catch up with her already had.

He fell back a prudent distance anyway, and when they reached traffic let a few cars get between them.

Adelle stayed exactly two miles an hour over the speed limit, probably using the car's cruise control, and was heading east, maybe going somewhere mundane like a McDonald's or to a liquor store. Maybe she was a secret drinker like Leona Benedict. They'd both been under the same kind of strain the last several years, and Adelle's husband had been killed.

Still, Carver was curious.

When she reached the coast highway and turned north, driving away from Del Moray and putting distance between herself and her home, as Leona Benedict had been so anxious to do, he became even more curious.

33

THE COAST highway carried less traffic than the interstate. Which meant Carver had to fall back well behind Adelle's dark sedan. Not that it caused a problem; she continued to hold her speed steady and gave no sign of taking any of the turnoffs.

They drove that way for a while, following their headlights into the night, the ocean on their left yawning vast and black like the edge of the world. Then, about three miles beyond the Del Moray city limits, the glowing red taillights flared and merged as Adelle braked and made a right turn off the highway.

Carver slowed and pulled the car to the shoulder, listening to the crunch and plunk of gravel as the tires mashed it and slung some of it against the fender wells. From where he was parked, he could see a tall neon sign in the form of a leaping blue dolphin above the letters BLUE DOLPHIN MOTEL. He depressed the accelerator and steered the Olds back onto the highway, then drove to the sign and made a right turn, as Adelle had done a few minutes before.

The motel was a long, low building made of rough tan stone. The office was brightly lit. A separate brick building was built in a *U* around a swimming pool, which was lit and threw a wavering blue glow over the area around it. Two heavyset women in red swimsuits were sprawled in webbed lounge chairs, listlessly watching some preteen kids splashing around in the shallow end.

All of the rooms looked out over the pool, and all of their doors were visible. Carver didn't see Adelle either on the ground floor or on the steel catwalk running outside the second-floor rooms, and he didn't think she'd had enough time to park her car, walk to one of the rooms, and disappear inside.

He tapped the accelerator and drove between rows of parked cars until he saw the dark sedan. It was at the far end of the lot, nestled alongside a white van with Illinois license plates and a chrome ladder up its back to allow access to the mound of plastic-wrapped luggage strapped to its roof. Adelle's car was midnight blue rather than black, he decided, seeing it up close for the first time.

He drove past the late-model Olds and parked his own ancestral Olds at the opposite end of the lot, then walked through the dark evening heat toward the office. He couldn't see or hear the ocean, but he could smell it, and a thick, salty dampness lay oppressively over his exposed skin. Near the motel entrance was a smaller door with a glowing blue neon DEEP WATER LOUNGE sign above it. Deep indeed, Carver thought.

As his hand moved toward the brass push plate of the lounge door, he paused. Better to go into the lobby and approach the Deep Water Lounge through a lobby entrance, if there was one. Assuming she wasn't in one of the rooms, he might push open this door and be face to face with Adelle. He could see into the lighted office and lobby and knew she wasn't there.

As he entered the lobby, he smiled and nodded to the middle-aged woman behind the desk. She smiled back, looked at him expectantly from beneath thick gray bangs for a moment, then went back to something she was working on with a hand-held calculator when she realized he didn't want a room. The lobby spread out far beyond the desk and was carpeted in dark blue. Cream-colored wing chairs were grouped around glass-topped low tables with plastic NO SMOKING signs on them. No one was in the lobby other than an old man in a white pullover shirt, plaid shorts, and startlingly white deck shoes, seated in one of the chairs and reading a *Glamour* magazine. Its glossy cover promised latest beach fashions and the answers to a previous marital sex quiz, and featured one of those interchangeable supermodels in a scanty two-piece swimsuit, standing and posturing with long legs spread wide and elbows thrust behind her as she smiled dazzlingly at whoever might buy the magazine. The old guy was engrossed in the magazine's contents and didn't seem to notice Carver.

There was an entrance from the lobby to the lounge, a stucco archway with lighted Spanish sconces on each side that looked like ships' lanterns.

Carver approached it cautiously yet casually, moved parallel to it, and saw Adelle Grimm seated alone in a booth near the rear of the lounge, facing three-quarters away from him. The lounge was crowded, with most of the patrons at the bar watching a Marlins-Mets game.

There was a shrill giggle behind Carver and he turned and saw four women in business clothes approaching in a tight group. They were talking animatedly and headed for the lounge.

He saw an empty stool where the bar made a right angle, timed his entrance, and used the four gesticulating, noisy women as a diversion and to shield him from view as he made his way to the stool.

Very neat. He congratulated himself. He couldn't see Adelle from where he sat, but he found that if he leaned slightly to the left, he could observe her reflection in the back bar mirror. The bartender, a young dark-haired guy in a blue shirt and red vest, approached and Carver ordered a draft Budweiser.

"They can't beat the friggin' Mets, they oughta take up some other sport," the man on the stool to Carver's right said.

Carver looked at him in the mirror, a very fat man with dark eyebrows that grew together and long, greasy hair, no tie, wearing an unstructured white sport coat that made him look even more immense.

"Football, maybe," Carver said, turning his body slightly away. He hoped the big man was sensitive to body language. He didn't want to talk baseball right now, or any other subject.

"Yeah, football. They kick the ball around a lot anyway," the man said.

Carver didn't answer, glad when the batter singled and a Marlins run scored. There was cheering along the bar, which meant he wouldn't have to make more conversation.

The four women were in a booth directly behind him. One of them said, "When he told me a raise, I didn't think he meant my skirt." The giggler sounded off shrilly again, causing the fat guy in the white jacket to swivel ponderously on his stool and look for the source of the noise.

That was when Carver glanced in the mirror and saw Martin Freel.

At first he didn't believe it. But there was the good reverend, wearing dark slacks and a gray-and-yellow tropical-pattern silk shirt, passing within ten feet of Carver.

When the reflected image passed beyond the shelf of liqueur bottles next to the mirror, Carver leaned forward to make sure he hadn't imagined seeing Freel.

This was getting better by the second. Freel was sitting down opposite Adelle Grimm.

Carver leaned forward as casually as possible so he could see them both. A barmaid walked over and Freel said something to her. Then he and Adelle leaned toward each other over the table, heads close together, and began talking earnestly. The reverend was nodding his head. Adelle seemed to be doing most of the talking.

They paused in their conversation as the barmaid returned with their drinks, a mug of beer for Freel and a fresh whatever-clear-beverage Adelle had been drinking, and took away Adelle's half-empty glass. Then Freel reached across the table and gently clasped Adelle's right hand with both of his, as if it were a delicate bird he didn't want to be injured or fly away.

They sat that way talking for almost fifteen minutes, not touching their drinks, apparently captivated by each other. Now Freel seemed to be guiding the conversation. Carver watched as Adelle's composure disintegrated. Her free hand rose to brush tears from her eyes.

Suddenly she stood up. She was gripping her purse which had been sitting on her side of the table. Freel stood also and touched her shoulder, as if urging her not to leave. But Adelle spun around and strode from the lounge. Freel stared after her with a hopeless, longing expression on his tanned face.

Carver wanted to follow Adelle, but he knew Freel would notice him if he limped away from the bar with his cane. Maybe Freel would run after her and Carver could follow them both, or have his choice.

But Freel stood watching until Adelle had disappeared out the door to the parking lot, then he slumped back down in the booth and sipped his mug of beer.

Ten minutes later, he laid a couple of crumpled bills on the table, stood up, and walked from the lounge, using the exit to the parking lot. Carver left the bar and went through the archway into the lobby. Standing inside the glass front entrance doors, he watched Freel make his way along a row of cars parked to the left.

It was easy to follow the almost luminous yellow pattern of the reverend's silk shirt in the dark, moving and undulating like a bright spirit of the night. Carver's Olds was parked to the right. He slipped out through the door and hurried in that direction.

He was sitting in his car and had just started the engine when Freel drove toward him in a sky blue Cadillac, then steered toward the driveway. The Caddy paused, then smoothly turned and accelerated out onto the highway.

Carver put the Olds in drive and followed.

He stayed behind Freel until the Caddy turned off Highway 1 and sped west on 50 toward Orlando. That was something of a disappointment. The odds were that Freel was simply going home or to the Clear Connection.

Carver lost interest and turned back toward the coast, heading for the cottage, thinking hard all the way to the hum of the engine and the ticking of the tires over seams in warm pavement.

Maybe the Women's Light bombing had nothing at all to do with abortion rights; maybe that was simply a blind. Freel might have set up Norton and used the anti-abortion demonstration as a cover for the murder of Dr. Grimm, and for one of the oldest, most compelling motives in the world: he wanted the man's wife.

Freel himself might have somehow planted the bomb, timed to go off during the demonstration. Or, more likely, he'd used the unknowing Norton, instructing him when and where to plant the bomb, so he could be sure Dr. Grimm would be at the clinic that day and would be near the blast point. Some of the death threats received by Freel's wife Belinda Lee might have been sent by Freel himself. Now he could be setting the stage for *her* murder so he could be free to maintain his reputation and standing with his congregation and pro-life advocates, and at the same time possess forbidden fruit Adelle Grimm.

Hypothesis, Carver warned himself, speeding along A1A with the sharp ocean breeze cutting in through the car's open windows.

He'd gotten into trouble before by hypothesizing and then acting without ascertaining the facts. His theory about Freel and Adelle Grimm might be nothing but speculation. Yet it answered so many questions.

And he'd seen them together in the motel lounge, an obviously furtive and emotional meeting they'd both driven a long way to attend in an attempt at secrecy.

That wasn't speculation. That was fact.

And it had to mean something.

34

THE LIGHTS were on and Beth was awake when Carver entered the cottage. She was wearing a black top and yellow shorts and was barefoot, seated on the sofa with her computer in her lap. There was a dreamy expression on her face and she was busily pecking away at the keyboard, as if she were playing a musical instrument only she could hear.

"Al didn't bark," he said.

She didn't look up. "He knows your step. The cane."

Carver wasn't sure Al was that smart. "What are you working on?" he asked, limping over and settling into a nearby chair.

"Piece on the clinic bombings. Jeff wants something for the next issue." Jeff was Jeff Smith, Beth's often demanding editor at *Burrow*.

Carver heard a crunching sound coming from behind the breakfast bar. He figured Al must be back there, scarfing down a late snack.

"He hasn't had anything to eat since we stopped by a McDonald's and got cheeseburgers and shakes," Beth explained. She continued working away again at her computer, not looking at Carver.

"Here's something *not* for *Burrow*," Carver said, trying not to think about Al eating as well as he, Carver, usually did. He told Beth about Adelle Grimm and Reverend Freel meeting at the Blue Dolphin Motel. After the first few words, she ignored her computer.

"That's quite a ways out of town," Beth said. "They must have wanted to keep their meeting secret."

"My impression is that it wasn't the first time they'd met there." He went on to tell her his theory about Freel using Adam Norton to get rid of Dr. Grimm so he could have Adelle to himself.

"Adelle the Jezebel," Beth said absently.

"Something you and she have in common." Carver made sure he was smiling when he said this.

"What about Freel's wife?" Beth asked. "That nauseating blond with the big mouth and all the makeup. He'd have to get rid of her, too, if he wanted to save his reputation as a family values firebrand and keep TV contributions and local congregation money rolling in."

"That might be the next step."

Beth saved what she had on the computer, then switched it off and lowered its lid. "Could be," she said. "But maybe you're taking something simple and making too much of it."

"Simple?"

"Possibly Adelle Grimm and Freel have been romantically involved with each other, but maybe it has nothing to do with the clinic bombing that killed Dr. Grimm."

"Hell of a coincidence," Carver said dubiously.

Beth smiled. "And you don't believe in coincidence, do you, Fred?"

"I don't like how it affects my work. It gets in the way of the truth."

"And truth is *your* religion."

"Maybe. If it is, I'm more loyal to it than Freel is to his religion."

"And possibly more obsessed." She smiled up at him. "But that's okay, Fred. I like men who are a little mad."

Carver was about to tell her why that might be so, when Al wandered out from behind the breakfast bar, gave him an uninterested glance, then sat leaning against Beth, with his muzzle flat on her bare thigh.

"Aren't you going to ask me about Nate Posey?" Beth asked.

"I assumed he had another early night," Carver said, "or you wouldn't be here ensconced on the sofa with old dog Al."

"He did, but that's not why I'm here instead of watching him. Turns out somebody else is following Posey."

Al arched an eyebrow and glanced up at Beth. Carver wondered if she meant Anderson. He had no idea what Al was wondering.

"That insurance investigator, Gil Duvalier, is tailing Posey. I saw him sitting in his car, thinking he was parked out of sight, so I confronted him. He's known from the beginning I was following Posey."

"He must be thinking along the same lines as you and trying to get evidence of insurance fraud," Carver said. "If that's his game, he won't give up until his company decides to pay the claim on Wanda Creighton's policy."

"I don't see the point in both of us watching Posey," Beth said. "I can spend my time in better ways."

Carver wasn't so sure. He believed now more than ever that Posey had nothing to do with the clinic bombing, and Beth still wasn't completely herself.

"Fred, I—" She stopped talking as they both heard the sound of tires crunching on the gravel drive outside the cottage.

Carver looked at his watch. Almost eleven o'clock. He stood up and went to the window as Beth laid her computer aside on the sofa.

A car was now parked outside. It was too dark to make out what kind, but there appeared to be two people inside it. The driver's side door opened and the dome light came on for a moment, illuminating the car's interior. A woman sat on the passenger side; Carver could see an untucked white blouse, a flowered skirt. In the few seconds before the car's interior went dark again, he recognized the man climbing out of the driver's seat as Special Agent Sam Wicker.

Carver opened the cottage door for Wicker as the FBI agent walked up onto the porch. He looked beyond Wicker at the shadowed form of the woman in the car, but she wasn't moving and was obviously not coming in.

"Surprise," Wicker said with his thin little bureau smile.

As he entered the cottage, he widened his smile and nodded to Beth, who was still on the sofa. Al, who was lying down now, spotted him, struggled to his feet in sections, and ambled over to lick his hand. Wicker patted the top of Al's head. Al's pupils jiggled but he didn't seem to mind.

Carver closed the door, looking more closely at the rumpled FBI agent. There was something even more unbusinesslike than usual about Wicker tonight, not so much in his unkempt appearance—which was normal for him—but in his oddly awkward yet cheerful bearing.

"Ordinarily a visit from the FBI at this hour means somebody's under arrest," Beth said. Al moved back across the room to collapse in sprawling and complete comfort in his previous position at her feet.

"Not in this instance," Wicker assured her. "I had something to tell you two, and we were out driving around, so I figured it wasn't all that late and you might still be awake."

"We?" Carver said.

Again Wicker's thin smile invaded his features despite his obvious effort to remain straight-faced. "Delores and I," he said. "She's been released from the hospital except as an outpatient, and I'm, er . . ."

"Helping her in her recovery," Beth finished for him.

Wicker brightened. "Something like that."

"She should come in," Carver said.

"No, no. She still needs a wheelchair. Soon she'll be fitted for a prosthetic foot, then she'll get around on crutches for a while as she learns to walk again. Believe me, she's got the spirit to do it! The doctors say within a year she might even be playing tennis. She used to love tennis. Still loves tennis, I mean . . ."

Beth stood up from the sofa. "I need to get away from this gibberish. I'm going out and talk with Delores." Al stood up, too.

Both men stood silently until woman and dog had gone out the door into the night.

Carver offered Wicker something to drink, but Wicker declined, saying he had to leave soon. His glance slid toward the door, toward Delores Bravo. Carver walked around the counter and got a Budweiser out of the refrigerator, pulled the tab, then leaned on the counter and waited.

"We've found parts from the Coast Medical Services bomb," Wicker said. "Bits of material from the container, some wire splices and plastic connectors. It looks like the same kind of bomb that went off at the Women's Light Clinic. The bomber's signature's the same."

Carver knew that "signature" was bomb squad talk for the distinctive method each bomber employed to construct his or her deadly packages. He set his beer can on the counter and stared at it, then at Wicker. "You're saying Norton couldn't have been the Women's Light Clinic bomber? That the real bomber's still at large?"

"No. I'm saying someone—maybe Norton—made both bombs. The explosives were sticks of dynamite set off with blasting caps, a battery, and a timer, all contained inside a large hollowed-out Bible."

"Your lab can tell all that?"

"You'd be surprised how much is left of an exploded bomb," Wicker said, "if you know where and how to look. Sometimes we can even lift the bomb maker's fingerprints." He made a helpless gesture with both hands. "Not this time, though, at the site of either clinic."

"You going to keep holding Norton?"

"Sure. He could have been the Women's Light bomber and made both bombs. The Coast Medical clinic explosion might have been the work of another Operation Alive fanatic, taking up where Norton left off."

"Or trying to make Norton look innocent."

"We're taking that possibility into account, too."

"What about Norton's wife, Carrie? Might she be the second bomber?" Carver found it hard to imagine even as he made the suggestion. Frail and shy Carrie Norton, who would look twelve until she was forty.

"Not her. She's been under surveillance since the bureau entered the case."

Carver came out from behind the bar, leaned on his cane, and said, "I've got some information for you, too." He told Wicker about Adelle Grimm's motel meeting with the Reverend Martin Freel.

"Unlikely lovers," Wicker said.

The sound of women's laughter drifted into the cottage on the ocean breeze. Beth and Delores. Carver and Wicker looked in the direction of the melodious laughter. Beautiful, Carver thought; he loved hearing the laughter of women. He'd mentioned that once to Desoto, who had agreed with him. Then

Carver recalled the shrill giggler in the Deep Water Lounge. *Some* women's laughter was beautiful.

"The fact is," Wicker said, "Freel's got a solid alibi for the days before and after the time of the Women's Light bombing. He was with half a dozen people in Orlando at the time of the detonation. And we've investigated him thoroughly and found no indication of an affair with Adelle Grimm."

"They would have been careful," Carver said.

Wicker rubbed his cheek, thinking about it. "She must know Freel might have been behind her husband's death, Carver. Are you saying . . ."

"Maybe they were both behind Dr. Grimm's death. Or maybe Freel acted on his own and Adelle didn't know about it ahead of time. Maybe she doesn't believe now that he had anything to do with the bombing. Freel could easily convince her that Norton acted alone."

"There's still Freel's alibi," Wicker said. He shifted his weight from one foot to the other, suddenly restless. He wanted to leave, to get back to Delores. "I think you'd better tell McGregor about this, Carver, stay on the legal side of the line."

"I will, but tomorrow's good enough."

Wicker grinned. "Okay, but do it first thing in the morning. I'll wait until tomorrow afternoon to notify him. Give him a chance to act smug."

"Smugness is one of the few things about him that isn't an act."

Carver reconsidered waiting until tomorrow to phone McGregor. Maybe he should call him tonight, possibly waking him up. Hadn't he insisted on information as soon as possible?

He went with Wicker out to the blue FBI sedan. It looked like the one Anderson had parked in to watch the cottage. Its engine was off and was ticking in the heat; or maybe that was Wicker.

Carver said hello to Delores Bravo, who flashed a white smile and looked much better than she had in the hospital. Her long dark hair was combed back, flowing over her shoulders, and her brown eyes gave back the moonlight.

Beth came around from the passenger side, where she'd been talking with Delores through the window. Wicker gave his guilty little smile again as he got in the car and started the engine.

Beth moved closer and stood next to Carver, and they watched the blue official car drive away. Al took a few steps in the direction it had gone, as if considering chasing it, then trotted back and sat on his haunches next to Beth.

"Surprise, surprise," Carver said as the taillights disappeared in the darkness around a curve in the road to the coast highway.

Beth looked over at him. "You mean you didn't see that coming?"

"Sure, but not to such a feverish degree until the investigation was ended. Wicker's a pro. An open and obvious affair with a crime victim isn't very professional."

Beth laughed and shook her head. "Come off it, Fred. Poor love-struck guy didn't have any choice. It happened *to* him, maybe in an unguarded instant. One day everything's normal, next thing he knows, he has no appetite and his sleep is disturbed."

She was right, Carver knew. He shouldn't have been surprised. Maybe not even by Adelle Grimm and Martin Freel.

Beth leaned over and kissed his perspiring cheek. "Sometimes love even disturbs *your* sleep, Fred."

They walked back toward the cottage.

"Before it does tonight," he told her, "I'm going to finish this can of beer. Then I'm going to phone McGregor and disturb his sleep."

"Then?" she asked.

"Then I'm going to disturb your sleep. Or at least delay it."

She veered toward him and let her bare arm brush his. "Sounds like a good night's work."

As they opened the cottage door, Al barked loudly.

"I think he's still hungry," Beth said.

"No," Carver said, "I recognize that bark. He's trying to tell us he wants to spend the night on the porch."

And he nudged Al outside with his cane and shut the door.

|35|

THERE WAS a message on Carver's office answering machine the next morning from Norton's attorney, Jefferson Brama. In a smooth but booming voice, Brama informed Carver that he was in Del Moray and would like to see him later that day. He left a phone number for the Surfside, an ocean-view hotel on Cortez Way, a finger of land jutting out to sea, then crooking south at the first knuckle to run parallel to shore. It featured the best beach in the area and was a magnet for tourists with too much time and money. When the attraction waned and they departed, they still had too much time.

Carver called the number, asked for Brama's extension, and as soon as the phone on the other end of the connection was answered, he hung up. Brama was in his room, which was what Carver wanted to know. The Surfside was only fifteen minutes away.

He gripped his cane and stood up, slipped his gray sport coat on over his black polo shirt, then left the office and crossed the already-baking parking lot to where the Olds sat in partial shade. He'd take the initiative by determining the time and place of his meeting with Brama, and by making an incursion into Brama's territory.

Something about what he knew of the man, and the voice on the answering machine, made him think his best strategy was offense.

THE SURFSIDE was a twenty-story building that looked like a stack of blue-and-white ice cube trays. It was one of half a dozen luxury hotels lined side by side on the most expensive real estate in Del Moray. The spacious lobby, all tile and glass and polished stainless steel, added to the icy impression and seemed as cold as the inside of a refrigerator. All of the buildings on Cortez Way were air-conditioned almost to the point of frost. The wealthy clientele seemed to require it. Carver had seen women wearing bikinis, high heels, and mink jackets cruising the exclusive shops on the palm-lined avenue. They seemed one with the blue herons and flamingos roaming the immaculately tended grounds of the hotels, exotic and not at all out of place.

Carver had no trouble getting Brama's room number from the desk clerk. He didn't phone upstairs before riding the elevator to the nineteenth floor. It got colder the higher he went.

When he knocked on the door to Brama's room, it opened almost immediately.

A sixtyish, potbellied man with steel gray hair combed straight back without a part looked out at Carver with bright blue eyes. He was medium height, wore pleated, pin-striped gray dress pants, a white shirt, and broad paisley suspenders. He smelled strongly of cologne. The scent wasn't offensive, like McGregor's bargain brands. Brama smelled clean and expensive. His sleeves were rolled up neatly and he was holding a white towel, still absently going through the motions of drying his hands.

"I thought you were room service," he said. His blue gaze flicked up and down Carver, hesitating only a moment as it took in the cane. Brama smiled. "Please do come in, Mr. Carver."

Brama had a corner suite. The cream-colored drapes on the wide, right-angled window were open to reveal a vast view of sea and shore. A tiny palm-top computer sat next to the phone on a table by the cream leather sofa, a coiled black wire connecting it to the base unit.

As soon as Brama closed the door, there was another knock. "Excuse me," he said to Carver, and reopened the door.

This time it really was room service. Brama instructed the bellhop to carry the covered tray out to the balcony.

"Help yourself to something from the service bar," he said to Carver, pointing to the wood-paneled door of a small refrigerator set in a credenza near a desk. "There's enough on the tray for two, I'm sure."

Carver got a bottle of Perrier water from the refrigerator and walked toward the sliding doors that led to the balcony, the tip of his cane leaving deep, round impressions the size of quarters in the plush blue carpet.

There was a sweeping view from the balcony. The white hulls of boats from the marina dotted the ocean, and far out to sea an oil tanker and a cruise ship were visible, squatting on the horizon like islands. A gull soared past, lower than Carver, and seemed to glance up at him with amused disdain; what was a human with a cane to a creature with wings?

The bellhop placed the tray on a white, decorative iron table and whipped the white cloth napkin from it to reveal a squat silver tea or coffee pot, a wicker basket of assorted pastries, and two plates whose contents were concealed beneath silver covers.

Brama held the room service check steady in the breeze and signed it with a flourish, poked his gold pen back in his shirt pocket, then tipped the bellhop with a five-dollar bill.

As the bellhop left, Brama smiled and motioned for Carver to sit opposite him in one of the matching wrought iron chairs. Carver did. Brama waited until he was seated before sitting down himself. He had a beaming, friendly smile. Carver knew that behind it, Brama was assessing him.

"There's enough tea here for both of us," Brama said, "if you'd prefer that to bottled water. And do help yourself to a roll."

Carver declined the tea but chose a small cheese Danish. Brama tucked a large white napkin into his collar and removed a silver cover from a plate of bacon and eggs, another cover from over a grapefruit half that had a maraschino cherry perched in its center like an exposed secret heart. He began eating with obvious enjoyment, saying nothing, playing the good host but putting Carver slightly ill at ease, waiting for him to fill time with words and possibly say something unwise. Carver knew the game. He sipped Perrier water and enjoyed the view.

Finally Brama lifted his napkin for a moment to dab delicately at his lips, which were curved in a faint smile. "I'm going to subpoena your friend Beth Jackson," he said. "And possibly you." He gave his tea bag a final few dips in his cup of water, then lifted it by its tabbed string and placed it on a saucer. "I'm sorry about having to do that, but you're both eye witnesses to the Women's Light bombing."

Carver showed no reaction. "Is that why you wanted to talk?"

"Not entirely. Do you feel uncomfortable speaking with me without legal counsel present, Mr. Carver?"

"No. I have no reason to feel uncomfortable."

"That's a fine, forthright answer, even if some, quite wrongly, would deem it a foolish one. I wouldn't think the highest of a man who would voluntarily sit across from an attorney in a conversation that might involve a homicide if he felt uncomfortable doing so."

"I didn't see much that morning. And nothing that would help your client's case."

"I prefer witnesses who didn't see much, but remember what they *did* see."

"When the bomb went off, I was sitting in my car half a block away."

"That gives you distance, objectivity. I like that in a witness."

Carver felt like someone being blocked whenever he moved a checker.

"Your friend Miss Jackson is another story," Brama said.

"She is," Carver said. "She was closer."

"Yes. I'm truly sorry about that." Brama sipped his tea. "I'm not so much interested in what you saw the day of the bombing, Mr. Carver, as I am in what you've seen since. I understand you've been investigating, plying your trade—as well you should—and that she is working on a series of articles for *Burrow*."

"She's plying her trade, too," Carver said.

Brama waved a strip of bacon he'd been about to bite into. "Of course, of course. As she should be, working to ease the shock and memory of her experience. Do believe I'm not trying to pump you for information, Mr. Carver."

"Of course."

"I've learned that true and useful information is a shy creature that most often comes unbidden in its own time and place. And I understand perfectly well that your personal interests lie with the prosecution in this case." Brama took a generous bite of scrambled egg, then a sip of tea. "But before we get into legalities, I thought we might speak off the record."

"Are you going to try to convince me Norton's innocent?"

"No, we won't get into that."

"I'm not sure he's guilty," Carver said.

Brama sat back and smiled at him. His right eye picked up the blue of the sea and glinted in the sun like a diamond. "Oh? Why not?"

"There's been another clinic bombing, and your client's in jail and obviously couldn't be the perpetrator."

Brama smiled wide, winked, and shook his head. "It doesn't suit you to play dumb, Mr. Carver."

"I don't consider myself overly smart."

"Well, that's fine. That's sensible. A man who sees himself as uncommonly intelligent probably isn't." Brama leaned forward. There was a dark droplet of tea on his chin. "But forget intelligence. What about instincts? Do you have good instincts, Mr. Carver?"

"Sometimes."

"Ah! So much more important than intelligence, especially in your line of endeavor." The drop of tea plummeted and made a vertical streak on the white napkin tucked into the neck of Brama's shirt.

"What about your other client?" Carver asked.

Brama stared at him across the table, letting his eggs cool in the breeze. "What other client?"

"Reverend Martin Freel."

"Oh! He truly isn't connected with the Norton case except in the most peripheral manner. The FBI, your friend Wicker, will attest to that."

"Sometimes a man like Freel uses the Bible as a shield to guard and conceal his true self," Carver said.

"That certainly is a bare, undeniable fact about some people." Brama tasted a bite of egg, decided it was cold, and lowered his fork. "But it isn't true of Reverend Freel. I know the mind and soul of the man."

"What do you know about his marriage?"

Brama slowed his hand almost to a stop as he lifted his tea cup.

"I know for sure it's a sound and joyous union. Reverend Freel and Belinda Lee are in love in the best and most wholesome sense of the word."

"Have you ever seen the reverend with Adelle Grimm?"

"Adelle who?"

"Grimm. She's the widow of one of the murder victims."

"Ah, Dr. Grimm the late abortionist. Why would Reverend Freel be with his widow?"

"Perhaps because of love not in the best and most wholesome sense of the word."

Brama sat motionless, then let his jaw drop as if he were momentarily speechless. If he was feigning shock, he was good at it. Carver couldn't decide if he was acting or was honestly surprised.

"Do tell me you're joking, Mr. Carver."

"Can't do that," Carver said.

Brama laughed loudly, incredulously, as if he thought a romance between Freel and Adelle Grimm was as likely as one between a plant and an animal. The laugh sounded genuine. "Well, I do admire someone who doesn't joke about such things, Mr. Carver. But I can assure you, on or off the record, there is nothing to the notion of any sort of, er . . . romantic involvement between Reverend Freel and Adelle Grimm."

"People lead secret lives," Carver told him.

"Oh, *everyone* does. But Reverend Freel is my client. I know his secrets."

Carver decided he should be the one to end the conversation, to keep Brama off balance—if he actually was off balance. If he'd ever been off balance in his life. "There are secrets and then there are deep, dark secrets," he said.

"And how did you come by what you consider to be knowledge of Reverend Freel's deep, dark secret?"

"Since I'm going to be subpoenaed anyway," Carver said, "I prefer to save that answer for when I'm under oath."

"Well, ordinarily that would be wise of you, only I don't intend to enter into that area of inquiry."

"Maybe the prosecution will."

"Oh, I do doubt that," Brama said. "It's not a thing to be taken lightly, spreading tales when the facts aren't known and proof isn't forthcoming."

"The longer we talk, the more you sound like an attorney."

Brama poured hot water into his cup and dropped in a fresh tea bag. "Mine's a twenty-four-hour-a-day occupation, I'm afraid. Like yours, Mr. Carver."

Carver pushed back his chair, scraping its iron legs over the balcony's concrete floor, and stood up.

Brama didn't try to stop him from leaving, which meant he'd accomplished his purpose. He'd wanted to talk with Carver to determine what he knew about Freel and Adelle Grimm, and to warn him, however subtly, about a libel suit if he continued to defame the reverend. It didn't shock Carver that Brama had somehow found out about him following Adelle and seeing her meet Freel at the Blue Dolphin Motel. An attorney of his stature and with his connections would have informants, but not necessarily ones who knew all the facts. Or maybe Freel or Adelle had noticed Carver observing them and informed Brama. Either way, Brama had to be aware that he might not know everything pertinent about his clients. It had to be a worry.

Carver smiled down at him. "Don't interrupt your breakfast. I'll show myself out."

"We should talk again," Brama said. "I enjoyed it."

Carver nodded, leaned his weight over his cane, and turned to walk back inside the room.

Brama unconcernedly resumed eating his scrambled eggs with obvious appetite and enjoyment.

But Carver knew they were cold.

|36|

BACK AT his office, Carver turned up the air-conditioning, then called Desoto in Orlando and told him about his conversation with Jefferson Brama.

"The man has a point," Desoto said. "Operation Alive has Brama on retainer, and if you go around slandering Freel, you might find yourself slapped with a defamation of character suit. A con man with a congregation can't have a devil like you threatening the bottom line."

"You're suggesting I should ignore his secret meeting with Adelle Grimm at a motel outside of town?"

"Maybe it was innocent."

"You know better. How many reasons are there for a widow to meet her late husband's possible killer?"

"I wouldn't hazard to guess," Desoto said, "and neither should you. Listen, amigo, I'm a sympathetic ear, but you should stop talking about this until maybe someday in court. I've come around to your way of thinking that Freel and Operation Alive planned the Women's Light bombing and Norton was acting as their agent. The Coast Medical Services bombing, with clues left all over the place that it was the work of the same bomber, doesn't mean to me that Norton's innocent and both bombings were the work of somebody other than Operation Alive. That's like when Hitler burned down the Bundesbank and blamed his enemies."

"Wasn't it the Reichstag Building Hitler burned down?"

"Whichever it was, it only worked for a while. And Hitler eventually wound up being the one who got burned."

Desoto was quiet for a moment while Carver considered this shorthand interpretation of history. Spanish guitar played softly in the background like Muzak.

"I wonder if Dr. Grimm knew about his wife sneaking around behind his back with somebody like Freel," Desoto said.

"I doubt it. People like Grimm are dedicated and pretty much blind to what's going on in their personal lives." Carver thought about Leona Benedict climbing into the taxi that would take her away from her life of pressure and fear. She had decided she'd had enough, and her choice had become simple. Cab fare was cheaper than the price of marriage to a man with a mission. Adelle Grimm had endured the same ugliness and threats, existed under the same kind of terrible and destructive pressure.

"Perhaps Dr. Grimm stopped paying attention to his wife in the essential ways," Desoto said.

Carver knew he didn't mean sex alone.

"There are rumors here in Orlando," Desoto said, "that Belinda Lee Freel has the same sort of problem with her husband. His cause has consumed him and left nothing for her."

"Except money," Carver said.

"It's not a question of either-or, my friend. She and the good reverend have shared more than the same toothbrush through the years. Belinda Lee's name is on most of the corporate papers. The

Freels' business interests are entwined in ways that will guarantee her at least half their worldly goods. And if she gets a good divorce lawyer, Reverend Freel might walk out of court with only other-worldly goods."

"That means if Freel killed Dr. Grimm, maybe Belinda Lee is next."

"God would frown," Desoto said.

"Possibly somewhere along the line Freel changed gods, and now he worships money. The dead presidents on money never frown."

"But those presidents are stern. Money can be a harsh god, amigo. And unlike the other God, it's unforgiving."

"Wicker says Freel's alibi for the time of the bombing is tight."

"It is. I double-checked it personally. He was chairing a church council meeting at the Clear Connection at the time the Women's Light Clinic blew up. At least that's the story of the other six council members who attended."

"You sound dubious."

"Freel might be a confidence man," Desoto said, "but his followers are fanatics. They'd lie for him if he asked. To them, the pro-life movement is a holy crusade. They'd be lying so he could commit murder to save lives. *He'd* lie so he could commit murder to have Adelle Grimm and his unsullied reputation and all of his money. Both gods would approve."

Carver wasn't as sure as Desoto that Freel was completely a confidence man. He remembered the note in Freel's voice and the pure bright light in his eyes. Might he not worship two gods and still be a true believer? The loudest singers in the church choir on Sundays sometimes manipulated stock or juggled the books through the rest of the week.

"Why would Freel have to be in Del Moray to plant the bomb himself?" Carver asked. "Why wouldn't he simply use Norton?"

"He couldn't be sure that way, because Norton wouldn't know the real purpose of the bomb. Even though Freel planned the bombing for when Grimm was in the clinic, he had to know the bomb would be close enough to his victim to prove fatal when it went off. My guess is he planted it in the clinic well before the demonstration and set it off unseen from nearby, or activated the timer for when he knew Grimm would be conducting an abortion, leaving himself plenty of time to get clear of the area. Norton was a bomb nut and made such an obvious patsy, he might have even given Freel the idea."

"Have you offered your theory to the FBI?" Carver asked.

"Sure. They didn't buy into it. They still like Norton because they've got him, and with plenty of evidence. As they see it, Operation Alive is involved only because it unknowingly—or at least unprovably—provided motivation. Suggesting a conspiracy and a different actual suspect makes the investigation messy. The feebs like to get in and out in a hurry without losing any skin." Desoto paused. Carver heard him draw a deep breath on the other end of the line. "There is one bit of information on our friend Ezekiel Masterson, by the way. You know a woman named Mildred Otten?"

"I've talked to her," Carver said. "She has a bitter and biblical view of the world."

"We've talked to her, too. It turns out Ezekiel is her son from her first of many marriages. Not that she knows where he is. Not that she'd tell us anyway. She says they're estranged and the only time she sees him is at services at the Clear Connection, and he hasn't attended for weeks."

Mildred's son. Carver thought about it. "I guess it figures. Spouting scripture might be an inherited trait."

"It seems so in some families, especially these days and with families involved with the good Reverend Freel."

There was a flurry of unintelligible voices on the other end of the connection. Voices speaking in English, though, and not coming from Desoto's stereo.

"Crime marches on," Desoto said into the phone, "and it just marched into my office. I've gotta go to work here."

"So you're saying Freel's alibi only *looks* good?" Carver said. He valued Desoto's judgment on such things and wanted to be sure of what he thought.

"Freel is a guy who's claimed out-of-body experiences," Desoto said. "He can go anywhere he wants anytime, and with an alibi. Believe me, he could have been in Del Moray the morning the Women's Light Clinic went up. And in solid enough form to have detonated a bomb."

Desoto hung up to join in battle with the forces of crime before Carver could thank him.

Carver let the receiver clatter back into its cradle, then sat back and looked at the closed office drapes, glowing with light and heat filtering through them to make the air-conditioning work its hardest. Natural heat was always in a battle with artificial cold in Florida. It was unrelenting and implacable. It knew that eventually it would win.

People like Martin Freel felt that way, too, whatever their delusion. Sooner or later they would win, if not in this world, in the next. Carver himself was usually reassured in time of doubt by the knowledge that he could outlast if not outsmart any adversary. When the people hanging by their fingertips finally let go, he'd still be there hanging by his finger*nails*. He would do what was necessary for as long as necessary. He knew that about himself. It was his religion.

Now he was beginning to recognize the same characteristic in Freel. And maybe Freel, with *his* religion underpinning his self-righteousness and will, was even more obstinate and persevering than Carver. More obsessive.

Carver didn't like to think of himself as obsessive; he preferred to be regarded as dedicated rather than obsessive. But he knew that in different fashions, he and Freel might have the same relationship with truth, might carry the same burden.

So there the two of them were.

Obsessive.

|37|

AFTER LUNCH, Carver drove into Orlando. He parked near the reverend's house on Selma Road for a while but saw no one arrive or leave.

Starting the engine and running the air conditioner from time to time wasn't enough to make the car's interior bearable. The sun glared through the windows and radiated with thermonuclear might through the canvas top, and everything metal became hot enough to fry food on.

Finally Carver gave up and drove to the urban oasis of a shopping mall, where he had a Diet Pepsi and sat on a bench and cooled off, watching the roaming consumers: retirees in walking shoes, simultaneously exercising and escaping the heat; idle teenagers seeking each other's support and trying not to "fall into the Gap"; expensively dressed plastic-possessed women from East Del Moray, cruising the more exclusive shops. Malls were as American as Sunday barbecues and Charles Keating.

It was late afternoon, and a few degrees cooler, when he staked out the Clear Connection. He sat in the Olds, watching sunlight glint off the wide areas of glass and make the building seem a delicate crystal creation meant to be a temporary thing of beauty, as ephemeral as life itself. Excessive, for sure, but he had to admit it was appropriate architecture for a church.

Within an hour, Freel's sky blue Cadillac pulled from the front drive and jounced over the slight incline to the street. Freel was alone in the car and appeared to be smiling.

Carver started the Olds and followed, staying well back, occasionally even using parallel streets as a precaution against being seen. Freel would have talked with Jefferson Brama by now and would be on his guard.

They drove out the Orange Blossom Trail until Carver noticed a parked police car and a crowd of people carrying signs. They were dressed casually to withstand the heat and seemed to be milling in a general circular motion. The Caddy braked, veering right, and parked behind the police cruiser. Carver made a left turn into a restaurant parking lot and found a slot where he could see what was going on across the street without being noticed.

The crowd was picketing a low white building with a door simply stenciled TRAIL CLINIC in blue block letters. White wooden crosses as well as signs were being carried, and Carver recognized some of the pickets. There was the skinny guy with the bullhorn who'd been yelling outside the Benedicts' house, shirtless and wearing baggy plaid shorts. He was dancing around and yelling through the bullhorn now, whipping up the demonstrators for Freel, but Carver couldn't understand what he was saying. Cars driving by were slowing, their drivers swiveling their heads to read the pickets' signs and see what was going on. A few of the drivers honked their horns, either in derision or support. One man shouted something and made an obscene gesture as he drove past.

Carver saw Freel standing on the sidewalk with one of the uniformed cops from the cruiser. Both men had their fists propped on their hips and seemed to be talking calmly. The cop removed his cap for a moment and wiped perspiration from his forehead with a handkerchief.

After awhile, Freel walked over to one of the demonstrators, a middle-aged man wearing a blue muscle shirt, and said something. A young woman carrying a bloody-fetus sign joined them and they moved away from the other demonstrators and talked for a few minutes. Then they hugged each other good-bye and Freel returned to the Caddy. As he started the engine, he smiled and waved to the cop he'd been talking to earlier, who was still standing fists on hips and somberly observing the demonstrators.

Freel drove back toward Orlando.

This time Carver followed him to a cable TV station. Freel went inside and was there for more than an hour, probably taping his weekly sermon for Sunday.

When he came out, a woman was with him. Carver, who by now was sweating and impatient in the hot confines of the car, perked up.

Freel had his arm strapped around the woman's shoulder. She was wearing a long blue dress and high heels. She might have been attractive, but Carver couldn't be sure. She had on oversize sunglasses, and he was parked too far away to make out her features. He noticed the color of her dress matched the Caddy as she got in. Freel walked sprightly around to the driver's side.

"Maybe we've got something going here," Carver said aloud to himself as he waited for the Caddy to pass, then fell in behind it.

The Caddy made its way to downtown Orlando, wove through the crowded streets for a few minutes, then parked in front of a restaurant on Amelia.

When Freel walked around the car and opened the driver's side door like a gentleman, and the woman in the blue dress climbed out, smoothed her skirt with her hands, and stood up straight, she removed her tinted glasses. Belinda Lee Freel. As they walked away from the Cadillac, the reverend seemed to glance toward where Carver was parked, for only an instant, and he might have smiled. It was the same smile he'd given the uniformed cop just before driving away from the demonstration on the Orange Blossom Trail.

Carver swallowed his frustration and let out a long breath. He saw no reason to sit outside the restaurant in the stifling car. The Freels would doubtless linger over dinner in cool and pleasant surroundings, then drive home.

He decided to do that himself.

IT WAS DARK when he parked beside Beth's car outside the cottage. He had stopped for chili and a beer, and his stomach was in minor rebellion. The evening had cooled and he'd driven with the top down, smoking a Swisher Sweet cigar. He could still taste chili and tobacco as he raised the top.

The weather forecast he'd heard on the car radio had hinted hopefully at rain. Probably it was only another futile prediction and the storm clouds that blew in periodically from the Gulf would soar over Florida to vent their moisture in the Atlantic, but Carver didn't want to take a chance on getting the old car's interior soaked. Though it seemed impossible now, sooner or later it would rain again in sun-punished central Florida; what was summer without steam?

It took him awhile to get the top fastened down and the windows cranked up. The sky had become darker and the breeze was rattling the palm fronds. Maybe tonight was the night. He was acting wisely here, battening down the hatches on the rusty old land yacht.

Beth wasn't in the cottage. Neither was Al.

Carver opened a can of Budweiser, then went out onto the porch and stood leaning on the wooden railing, looking toward the ocean. Lightning fractured the sky far out at sea, the promise of an off-shore storm, and he was sure he saw the forms of Beth and the dog walking along the beach.

He wiped moisture from the beer can off his fingers onto his shirt, got a firm grip on the crook of his cane, and went to join them.

Beth smiled at him through wind-whipped strands of hair when he approached. She didn't have to adjust her pace to his as he fell in beside her; she was already walking slowly. Al ignored Carver and ran through the surf, picked up something in his mouth, then dropped it as a wave broke late and bowled him over.

"He likes the surf," Carver noted. The breeze grabbed his voice and tried to whisk it away, but he was sure Beth had heard him.

She looked over at Al as he leaped into an oncoming wall of foam. "He even likes to swim," she said. "Maybe he'll go out with you some morning."

Carver wasn't sure what he thought of that idea. He stared at the damp sand, careful about where he placed the tip of his cane. "I talked with Jefferson Brama today." He had to raise his voice above the breeze and surf.

"He assure you of Norton's innocence?"

"Not so much Norton's as Freel's. In his lawyerly way, he warned me not to delve any further into a possible romance between Freel and Adelle Grimm."

Beth paused, picked up a lumpy piece of driftwood, then hurled it into the sea for Al to retrieve. "He might be right about Freel's innocence," she said, "but not about Adelle's."

Here was something new. Carver stood next to her and watched Al fling himself into the surf and search fruitlessly for the chunk of driftwood.

"I had Adelle's house staked out as usual tonight and I saw a man enter," Beth said. "He approached the house on foot and was inside almost before I knew he was there."

Carver continued watching the dog. "Freel?"

"I don't know. I think so. But he seemed larger than Freel."

"Was he let in?"

"Yes, I'm sure of that. He was inside so fast, he wouldn't have had time to use a key. A light came on in the rear of the house, and I saw that the drapes weren't closed all the way in one of the windows. I got out of the car and moved onto the property, sure I could sneak a peek inside." She started walking slowly again along the surf line, keeping her bare feet on the firm, wet sand. "Then Al barked."

"Barked at what?"

"I don't know, a squirrel or something. Maybe the breeze blowing a leaf. Or maybe something else. I thought I heard somebody moving in the bushes, saw someone's shadow, but I can't be sure. I know I was spooked. I ran. We ran. Back to the car. When I was halfway there, I heard an engine and turned around and saw that big black car of Adelle's come roaring out of the garage and tear away down the street. I'm sure there were two people in it, and a man was driving. There was no time to follow. They were out of sight even before the automatic garage door lowered, and I saw that all the lights in the house were off."

"Blue," Carver said.

"What?"

"Adelle's car is dark blue."

Al was barking now, standing and staring out at the ocean, angry that it had appropriated his driftwood. Lightning made the sky glow yellow again out over the sea, and thunder rolled softly like low celestial laughter, nature putting on quite a show to taunt the simmering land.

"What did you mean about Freel being innocent and Adelle guilty?" Carver asked.

"I've been making contact with people, asking about Adelle Grimm. Her maiden name was Neehaus. She came from a wealthy family in Philadelphia who more or less disowned her after she stole some money and was thrown out of Vassar. She went through half a dozen jobs before she married Harold Grimm, who was already practicing medicine at the time, and regained financial solvency."

"How did you find out about this?"

"By modem."

Carver, who was barely computer literate, must have looked puzzled.

"Using the Internet. Someone even faxed me a copy of the fourteen-year-old newspaper item about the embezzlement from the university. Adelle claimed she stole the money out of love for one of her professors. He was a married man and denied any involvement. She was convicted and given probation. Even after that, she came close to going to prison because she continued her claims on the professor and almost destroyed his marriage."

"Fourteen years is a long time ago," Carver said.

"Maybe, but it provides some insight into Adelle. She can be a possessive woman. I think it's possible she killed her husband to be with Freel, and Freel might know nothing about it. Now she's emotionally distraught and financially strapped again, but she isn't opting for an abortion because it's Freel's child she's carrying and not her dead husband's."

"Which would give her considerable leverage over Freel."

"It would if she needed it."

"If she was from such a wealthy family, why would she have to embezzle money when she was in college?"

"She was on a meager allowance, and her parents were strict disciplinarians determined not to let their daughter be spoiled by wealth. Adelle didn't adhere to their philosophy. She'd had trouble before with money."

"I doubt if she's poor now. Grimm was doing okay financially, and he probably had life insurance."

"He did, for two hundred thousand dollars. But that isn't much to a woman who has roots in obscene wealth and might want to recapture it. Reverend Freel has major-league wealth, and she might be pregnant with his child."

They reached the rocky area of beach and turned around to walk back the way they'd come. "That's a lot of conjecture," Carver said. "You might be making it all too complicated. Seems more likely to me that Freel wanted Adelle and used his band of pro-life fanatics and Norton to kill Grimm and cover his true motive."

"What about his alibi?"

"Desoto isn't as sure as Wicker that it's solid."

"Adelle had access to the clinic. She could have planted the bomb there anytime, possibly days before it went off."

"How could she know she's carrying Freel's baby and not Grimm's?"

"The point is, how could *Freel* know?"

Carver realized Beth had given this hypothesis considerable thought. It was amazing what a labyrinth had to be negotiated to reach the truth. It was so difficult to be sure of anything.

Al trotted up to them and shook his entire body violently, spraying water over Carver and Beth. Carver was irritated, but Beth leaned down and hugged the still-soaked dog, then kissed the top of his nose. What could Carver say. She'd lost a child and gained a pet. It was the sort of trade that wasn't really a trade, that made him want to cry.

When she straightened up, Carver hugged her to him, then kissed her on the lips. She smiled at him, sad in the faint light, and leaned back away from him, staring at him with her dark eyes.

"You okay?" he asked.

"I'm getting okay, Fred. Isn't that what life's all about, getting over things, all the way if you're lucky, before something else happens?"

"Seems that way," he said.

She stared out at the lightning-illuminated clouds on the horizon. "We've all got to learn to do that. Otherwise the past will pull us under."

He kissed her again. "Not you," he said.

"No, not me."

WHEN THEY returned to the cottage, the phone was chirping. Beth answered it, looked puzzled and concerned, then said simply, "Yes," and held the receiver out for Carver.

He pressed it to his ear and said hello.

"This is Archie Anderson," a man's voice said.

It took Carver a few seconds to realize who was speaking.

"FBI Agent Archie Anderson," the voice said before Carver could reply. "The agent who had your cottage under surveillance." Anderson sounded more than tense, almost enraged, as if barely holding himself in check. "You might want to drive out here, Mr. Carver. Oliphant Road, about five miles out of town, a big orange grove with a white rail fence running alongside it."

"I know where it is," Carver said. "What's wrong?"

"Wicker's here," Anderson said. "McGregor's here, too. You'd better come." Emotion had a grip on Anderson's throat, choking off his words. Not at all like someone connected with the bureau; lawyers and accountants with guns.

Carver said he'd be there in less than twenty minutes and hung up.

When he told Beth about the conversation, she insisted on going with him.

"All right," he said reluctantly, already moving toward the door. "But leave the dog. I don't know what this is."

38

THEY TOOK Carver's car and were on Oliphant Road in less than fifteen minutes. Beth had been quiet during the drive, and Carver had said nothing to interrupt her thoughts. The Olds's windows were down and the air rushing into the interior made the taut cloth top slap against its steel struts while the pressure of the wind whistled and drummed.

The flat, paved road narrowed and ran between acres of orange and grapefruit trees. The trees were all of uniform size and aligned in neat rows that seemed to run together just before they disappeared in the night, like an art class study in diminishing perspective. They must have been recently irrigated. The wind caroming about the inside of the car carried a fresh, fertile smell of damp leaves and rich earth.

A white wooden fence appeared on the right, running alongside the road. It was made of thick posts about ten feet apart, to which were nailed two rows of parallel horizontal boards, one about a foot above the ground, the other a foot lower than the tops of the posts. Except for the occasional orange and yellow dots of citrus fruit among the clumped, shadowy branches of the trees, the white fence was the only bright object on a bleak landscape.

Then Carver saw flashing red-and-blue lights ahead and tapped his foot on the brake pedal, leaning forward to peer through the windshield.

Several cars were parked on the gravel shoulder, along with what appeared to be an ambulance. Carver braked harder as he saw a Del Moray police cruiser parked sideways in the middle of the road. A uniform was standing by its front fender, prepared to stop and divert any traffic on the little-traveled alternate route between two state highways.

The uniform walked toward the Olds as soon as it stopped.

A young blond patrolman without a cap leaned down to peer into the driver's side window. His gaze flicked to Beth, back to Carver. "You'll have to turn around, sir, or proceed slowly and carefully on the left shoulder."

"Anderson sent for me," Carver said. "Name's Fred Carver."

The uniform didn't move for a long moment, as if weighing what Carver had said. Finally he nodded, then walked toward a knot of people visible beyond the cars parked on the right shoulder. The ambulance's rear doors were open and a white-uniformed paramedic and a man in civilian clothes were dragging a collapsible wheeled gurney out. Alternating blue and red light glinted off its steel frame, then its spoked wheels as they dropped down and locked into place. The uniform who'd stopped Carver walked back out into the road and waved his arm, signaling him to drive forward and park on the right shoulder.

"You'd better stay here," Carver told Beth when he'd braked the Olds to a halt and turned off the engine.

"Think again, Fred." She already had the door open and was climbing out of the car.

But she did lag behind as Carver limped along the shoulder to-

ward the shadowy forms huddled around a section of the white
fence, the tip of his cane occasionally flicking pieces of gravel.
When they were about a hundred feet away, the tallest figure de-
tached itself from the knot of people and came toward them.

McGregor.

"What the fuck are you two doing here?" he demanded.

"I called Carver," Anderson said. He'd been a yard or two behind McGregor, blocked from Carver's vision by the tall, loose-
jointed man with his flapping suit coat.

McGregor turned sideways and waited for Anderson to catch
up. He started to say something, then clamped his lips together as
if he'd changed his mind. Something about Anderson's eyes had
stopped him. Was still stopping him. McGregor slid his hands into
his pockets and silently walked away.

Anderson looked from Carver to Beth but didn't comment on
her presence. "C'mon," he said, and began walking back toward
whatever was going on by the fence. The gurney was there now,
sitting off to the side at a slight downhill angle.

Bodies parted as they approached, and Carver saw the object of
everyone's attention. His stomach lurched with fury and disbelief.
"Christ!"

"I think that's the idea," Anderson said softly.

Wicker was on his knees with his back to a fence post, his lower
legs extended to the other side of the fence beneath the bottom
rail. His head lolled and his arms were spread wide to the top rail,
his wrists bound to the thick white boards with bailing wire. And
something else. Long, thick nails had been driven through his
palms, pinning his hands to the fence board. Wicker's face was
bruised, bleeding from a cut above his right eye. There was blood
in his tousled hair. His eyes were closed and oddly peaceful considering the expression of horror and pain on the rest of his face. His
mouth was contorted, a string of saliva dangling from his lips.

Carver could see Wicker breathing and hoped Wicker was unconscious.

"We got a call saying we'd find him here," Anderson said.

The paramedics were bending over Wicker now, studying the situation, figuring out the best way to remove the nails. One of them was working to loosen the bailing wire, which had cut off the circulation so that Wicker's impaled hands were pale as bone in the moonlight.

"The caller identify himself?" Carver asked.

"He didn't have to."

Wicker opened his eyes. They rolled around, found Carver, and fixed on him. "Masterson," Wicker said in a dry, thin voice. "He did this to me, told me I might find redemption here."

"We'll find *him*," Anderson promised.

Beth moved forward as if to comfort Wicker, but one of the paramedics extended an arm and waved for her to back away. She stood next to Carver. He could hear her breathing, soft, airy whimpers of rage and horror.

"He mentioned your name," Wicker said to Carver. "Told me you were a sinner just like me in the service of Beelzebub."

While he was driving nails through a man's palms, Carver thought.

Anderson pulled him aside and they walked a few feet away, letting the paramedics do their work. Beth followed, staying close to Carver.

"Ezekiel Masterson," Anderson said. "We'll find him."

"Lieutenant Desoto in Orlando might be able to help," Carver suggested. "He's the one who ID'd Masterson for us from a photo I sent him. Reverend Freel might know something, too, but he probably won't talk."

"He will if we don't ask him nice," Anderson said.

"That might have been you nailed to that fence," Beth said.

Anderson's jaw muscles flexed. "Any one of us."

Carver remembered Beth thinking there might have been someone in the bushes outside Adelle Grimm's house earlier that evening when Al barked. He told Anderson about it, and about his conversation with Jefferson Brama at the Surfside Hotel.

Anderson listened closely, staring at the ground. The red-and-blue glow from the emergency vehicles bathed his face with a shifting, harsh illumination that took away highlight and shadow and made his features a flat, tragic mask. The pulsating glare lent the scene even more of a sense of urgency, setting it to a wild rhythm and making the landscape surreal. Somehow a nightmare had found its way into Wicker's time awake.

"We'll get more from Wicker when he's patched up and has some medication for the pain," Anderson said when Carver was finished talking.

But they both knew there was little more to get. Ezekiel Masterson had acted out his fanaticism again, then disappeared, and no one who knew anything would talk. Nothing much had changed except that Wicker had been brutally beaten, then crucified with sixteen-penny construction nails.

"You wanted us to see this to make an impression on us, didn't you?" Beth said. "That's why you called."

"Partly," Anderson admitted. "I feel an obligation to be sure you know what kind of people we're dealing with. And I thought if I got you out here, you might be more likely to tell me anything pertinent."

"Did we?" Carver asked.

"No way to know yet."

Anderson told them good night and turned to walk back to where the paramedics were removing his supervisor and fellow agent from the fence. The strobelike effect of the flashing lights made his movements seem abrupt and intermittent.

He paused and turned. "Stay available, you two. And stay safe."

"You'd better notify Delores Bravo about this," Beth said, "but not yet."

"Do it right," Carver added.

"If only you could tell me how," Anderson said, leaving them in the somber dance of the flashing lights.

39

CARVER WAS quiet for a long time during the drive back to the cottage. Anderson's strategy of calling them to the scene of Wicker's agony had worked. Not that Carver and Beth had had any doubts about Masterson's viciousness after what he'd done to Linda Lapella. But that was a simple, brutal beating that resulted in murder. What had been done to Wicker was different; it was torture in the name of God and as ancient as man, and behind its mask, it was worse than indifferent to the pain it inflicted.

As they were rocketing along the highway, the wind pounding again in the car's interior, Beth said, "I still think Adelle is behind the bombing, and I think she might have hired Ezekiel Masterson. He might have been the man I saw driving away with her from her house earlier tonight."

"Or the man lurking outside her house who might have done to you what was done to Wicker."

She smiled. "You afraid, Fred?"

"Oh, I am most of the time on some level. For me and for you."

"And you still believe Norton acted on Freel's orders."

"Or was set up to take the fall for the bombing. Freel had to know Norton was a nut case who was working away on assembling bombs in his home workshop. What better dupe could he find to take the high-minded blame for what really was a squalid murder for the two most frequent motives in the world—love and money?"

"It sounds good when you say it fast," Beth admitted, "but Adelle's still my choice."

Carver watched the dark road. "Freel will be doubly on guard now that he knows his affair with Adelle is known."

"Still, they'll meet again."

"Lovers always find a way," Carver agreed, trying not to sound like a song title. "Someone else needs to be there when they do. It makes the most sense to put a watch on Adelle and wait for her to go to Freel."

"We'll alternate watching her."

"No," Carver said. "Are you forgetting what we just saw back there nailed to the fence?" He hadn't forgotten and never would. The terrible vision of Wicker's crucifixion, only minutes behind them, remained in his mind with clarity and horror. He knew it would be vivid in his dreams. "I'll shadow Adelle," he said. "You stay at the cottage with the gun and with Al."

"I think not, Fred."

Lord, this woman was stubborn!

"And I think we should buy another gun."

Carver shook his head no. He had never liked guns, and he liked them even less after being shot in the leg. One gun floating around in his life was more than enough.

"You're being stubborn about the gun, Fred."

He seethed.

Finally they agreed that he would be the one to watch Adelle in the evening if she could work the day shift. With the gun and with

Al in the car. She would use her car, with a cellular phone which she could use to check in with Carver or to call for help.

Carver didn't like the idea, but he knew he had no choice but to agree. He did so tersely, letting her know he didn't approve.She smiled in the wind.

The next day, they began their loose watch on Adelle Grimm.

She behaved normally, probably aware that someone might be observing her. That evening, she went out for dinner alone at a neighborhood restaurant in a strip mall, then rented a movie from Mr. Video and returned home.

It went that way day after day, but Carver or Beth stayed close to her. Wicker, hands bandaged in what looked like thick white mittens, was back on the job as agent in charge. The FBI had intensified its search for Ezekiel Masterson, which comforted Carver as it made it more likely that Masterson had gone underground and wouldn't make an appearance for a while. But while the search for Masterson was still going strong, the investigatory phase of the Women's Light bombing had slacked off. The authorities seemed content to let Norton play the martyr. It made everything fit neatly into bureaucratic cubbyholes real and mental, and it made a neat, uncomplicated moral tale for the media. Norton had been arraigned and would stand trial for murder.

It wasn't until the third week, when Carver was convinced that Adelle was asleep inside her darkened house and was about to drive to the cottage and get some sleep himself, that her overhead garage door went up at one in the morning.

Carver, in a weary state of alertness, sat up straight as he heard the faint hum of the opener and noticed the visible corner of the garage door moving. What interested him was that for the first time since he'd been watching the house, the light inside the garage didn't automatically come on when the door rose. Maybe it was burned out. Or maybe Adelle had removed it.

The deep blue Olds backed down the driveway to the street, its headlights dark, and the garage door lowered. Still without lights, the big Olds stopped, straightened out, and began to recede down Phosphorus Lane, its fleeting form blending with the black shadows between streetlights.

Carver left the headlights of his own car off as he followed Adelle through the dark, nearly deserted side streets.

It wasn't until they were near Shell Boulevard, where there was still sparse traffic despite the desolate hour, that she switched on her car's lights so that she wouldn't draw possible police attention. He did the same.

She made several turns, as if trying to make sure she wasn't being followed, then drove west, away from the ocean and toward the less affluent side of town.

Carver stayed well back and used every technique he knew in order not to be seen by her. But such caution might not have been necessary. She had no idea how to shake a persistent tail and wasn't really as careful or elusive as she assumed.

Finally she drove across an intersection with four-way stop signs, then parked her car on Widmar Avenue, in a neighborhood of small shops and apartment buildings.

Carver pulled over to the curb half a block away, on the other side of the intersection, his car's headlights already off. He scooted low in the seat behind the steering wheel. His car might have been parked there when Adelle drove up, simply the last in a row of parked cars.

She got out of her car and walked toward him. She was dressed down, wearing jeans, a dark T-shirt, and what looked like white jogging shoes. From this distance and in the faint light, she might have been a young woman in her twenties, with a spirited walk that suggested she had no cares. He was afraid she was going to keep coming and would recognize his car, then notice him slumped down behind the wheel. But at the intersection, she turned and entered the second building from the corner, moving quickly yet taking the time to glance up and down the street before disappearing inside.

It was one of several run-down four-story apartment buildings. Carver looked at his watch: 1:30 A.M. Most of the tenants should be asleep.

He saw that most of them probably were, as there were lights on in only one unit, on the third floor. Blinds were down on all of the apartment's windows and he couldn't see inside.

After waiting a few minutes, he grabbed his cane, climbed out of the Olds, and crossed the intersection toward the building. A three-legged stray dog, some kind of terrier, standing near the mouth of an alley, watched Carver as if thinking maybe it could use one of those cane things.

He entered the lobby carefully, not letting the street door make noise that might be heard upstairs. The lobby had a cracked and dirty tile floor and smelled like stale bacon grease. The walls were painted a dull green with some kind of sand finish that didn't do much to conceal old cracks and patches.

Carver moved quietly in his moccasins. It was an old building, cheaply constructed, and even small sounds from upstairs were seeping down to him: a window fan humming away and ticking metal against metal; the faint, ratchety noise of someone snoring behind a door at the top of the first flight of wooden stairs. Felt-tip graffiti on the wall next to a door that probably led to a storage room listed things that a woman named Betty would do. Carver read the list and didn't believe half of it. He examined the bank of tarnished brass mailboxes. The name slot above one of the boxes for an apartment on the third floor, 3-F, was blank.

He looked around, noting that the fire stairs were inside the building and there would be no exterior steel fire escape. Then he began climbing the stairs, staying to one side so they wouldn't creak so loudly, placing the tip of his cane carefully on the split rubber treads that were nailed to the steps and curled up at the edges.

The third-floor hall was narrow and dim, painted with the same rough-finish green paint that was in the lobby. A wide black stripe ran horizontally four feet above the floor, but it was badly painted and had dripped onto the green and run down the edges of some of the dark wood door jambs. Carver stood in the stifling heat and calculated which of the doors led to the apartment whose lights were still glowing. A sliver of light along a threshold confirmed his guess.

He limped to the door quietly, still breathing a little hard from climbing the stairs, and smiled. 3-F was stenciled in black on the old, darkly varnished door.

A soft sound wafted from the other side of the door. Then again, slightly louder.

A woman moaning.

Carver moved closer, leaning on his cane and bowing his head, his ear close to the door. Again he heard the moaning. And something else. Faint but urgent movement. An ancient and unmistakable rhythm.

A couple was making love in the apartment.

Adelle, Adelle! Carver thought.

What now? He could kick open the door, rush in, and catch them in the act. If he had a camera, he could pin them to the legal mat with the incontrovertible evidence of photographs. If he hadn't left the gun with Beth, he could wave it at them and freeze them in immoral passion, undeniable guilt, and complicity while he phoned for Wicker and the police.

Instead of any of those things, he raised his cane and knocked gently on the door.

The rhythmic sounds ceased.

He heard a frantic female voice, then a soothing male voice.

There were faint footsteps, the soft creaking of a wood floor, and the metallic click of a lock being released.

The door opened about six inches, and Dr. Benedict peered out.

As Carver was staring in astonishment, something slammed into his shoulder and he bounced off a wall and found himself lying on the thin, coarse green carpet on the hall floor.

Ezekiel Masterson was looming above him, smiling and moving toward him with the look of a predator confident that dinner had been disabled.

40

MASTERSON WAS clean-shaven and neatly dressed, as usual, but not wearing his blue business suit. He had on creased black slacks and a gray silk shirt with a bold sunrise pattern printed across its chest. A brimmed straw hat with a rainbow-colored band was perched squarely on his head. The shirt's top buttons were undone, and a thick gold chain glinted among dark chest hairs just above where the sun was rising. With his getup and black horn-rimmed glasses, he looked like a bean counter on vacation, trying to pretend he was casual and relaxed. It was difficult to believe he was a self-righteous homicidal maniac.

Carver believed. Struggling to stand up, he lashed out with his cane and struck Masterson in the shin bone, then raised the cane and just missed his head with the backswing, sending the jaunty straw hat sailing. The big man blinked in pain and backed away a step. Then he used his forefinger to adjust his horn-rimmed glasses, as if to see Carver more clearly, and came at him again.

Carver, halfway to his feet and leaning against the wall, jabbed at Masterson's face with the cane, but Masterson snatched the cane away and tossed it aside. He threw a powerful punch toward Carver's midsection, but Carver scooted along the wall and took much of the blow's force on his hip, which ignited with pain, then went numb.

Missing full impact with his punch threw Masterson off balance, and he stumbled a few steps. The sudden motion had caused a heavy gold cross on his thick neck chain to work out from beneath his silk shirt and dangle on his chest.

He found himself standing next to Carver's cane, propped at an angle against the wall where he'd flung it. Masterson smiled, drew back a gigantic foot, then stomped hard on the middle of the cane and broke it. He studied the two pieces of the cane, then bent low and scooped up the broken half that had the sharpest point. Holding the cane up with both hands in front of his face, he declared, "The arm and the terrible swift sword of the Lord!"

"Poetic," Carver said, "but it's only my cane."

Masterson moved in on him more slowly now, and with great caution.

When he was a few feet away, he made a move as if to swing at Carver's head with the cane, then with amazing quickness and dexterity he stooped in a momentary squat with one bent knee and kicked Carver's good leg out from under him.

Carver landed hard on the carpet. He rolled over to avoid the kick Masterson aimed at him. The big man knew how to fight and was deadly with his feet. Carver couldn't avoid the second kick, which caught him in the side. He was sure he heard a rib crack. Breath shot out of him and he tried to curl his body into the fetal position for protection.

Masterson would have none of that. He bent low and punched Carver in the forehead, causing a pain as if his skull had been cleaved. Carver fought off dizziness and nausea as he felt himself being forced onto his back.

"The Lord saith, 'Expel the wicked from your company!'" Masterson pronounced, straddling Carver's chest. His weight settled on Carver like a building. He must have recently eaten Chinese; his breath was hot and reeked of soy sauce. He raised the cane high, its pointed end directly above Carver's exposed throat, then grinned wide, the eyes behind his thick glasses like black wells. "Judgment day!" he shouted, and brought the cane down.

Carver clutched Masterson's wrist with both hands. He felt the point of the cane bite at his throat. Then he dug his heels hard into the thin carpet, pushing up with every fiber of strength in his arms and body, and managed to force the cane upward a few inches.

He knew he was only buying seconds. Masterson was as powerful as fate, and the downward pressure of the cane was tremendous. Carver couldn't last long. Every breath was agony. He knew that soon the pointed end of the hard walnut cane would penetrate his throat. When his victim's strength ebbed, Masterson would bring to bear all of his weight and power down on the cane. The sharp wooden point might make it all the way out the back of Carver's neck.

It was probably his last struggle, and Carver knew it. He held nothing back. As he strained to keep the point of the cane away from his throat, his vision blurred. He was aware of Adelle standing near the apartment door, a white sheet draped gracefully over her body like a toga. Benedict was beside her, nude and staring at what was happening before him on the hall floor.

"Not this!" Benedict was repeating in a horrified voice. "Not this!"

One of Carver's perspiring hands lost its grip on Masterson's wrist, then closed on the cross and the heavy gold chain dangling from the big man's thick neck. Carver gripped the cross and deftly wrapped the chain around his hand, twisting, twisting. He saw Masterson's broad face redden as the chain tightened around his neck and dug into his throat, but the downward force on the broken cane remained constant.

That's how they were, Carver trying to strangle Masterson with the gold chain, Masterson inches away from thrusting the pointed end of the broken cane into Carver's throat, when Carver was aware of the naked figure of Benedict standing over them, holding a large orange object in his right hand.

Benedict was shouting again for them to stop struggling. An impersonal bombing was one thing, but the hands-on killing he was about to witness was too much for the idealistic physician to endure. Carver wrestled with Masterson while Benedict wrestled with his Hippocratic oath.

The neck chain broke and fell away to dangle from Carver's hand. Masterson grunted and shifted his body forward, leaning over Carver. The sharp point of the cane was again at Carver's throat. It had already penetrated flesh and he could feel warm blood trickling down the side of his neck.

He was going to die. It was impossible to comprehend, but it was true. He heard a high voice from his childhood, long-ago hide-and-seek . . . *Ready or not! . . . Ready or not! . . .*

There was a shower of ceramic pieces as Benedict brought the heavy orange lamp down on Masterson's head.

The pressure on the cane lessened.

It disappeared altogether as Benedict raised what was left of the lamp base again and hit Masterson behind the ear. This time it was heavy brass that struck thick skull, making a sound like a melon being thumped.

The crushing weight on Carver's chest shifted as Masterson slumped unconscious.

Smelling soy sauce, Carver shoved the huge body away, rolled onto his side, then managed to scoot to a wall and sit up, his back pressed hard against the rough plaster.

"I couldn't let him kill you," Benedict was saying, his eyes wide.

"Useless, senseless death. There's been enough of it." He looked as if he might break and sob. Adelle, in a kind of trance, drifted over to him like a spirit in her flowing white sheet and stood next to him.

Carver's injured side caught fire with each gasp for oxygen. He was aware of footsteps clattering up the stairs. One of the tenants must have heard the fight and called the police.

Two uniformed cops were suddenly in the hall, filling it with blue. One of them was wielding his nightstick, the other had his nine-millimeter handgun drawn and was holding it low and pressed to his thigh, pointed at the floor.

"What've we got here?" the taller of the two asked, trying to be firm and in control but sounding afraid.

Carver attempted to tell him but couldn't get the words out. When he tried to speak, the pain in his side erupted, cutting his breath short. He was afraid the pain, with the exhaustion and lack of oxygen, would cause him to lose consciousness. He tilted back his head. Maybe it would be easier to breathe that way. The hall had become dim, as if curtains had been drawn over the single window at the far end of the corridor. He heard sirens outside now, very close, down in the street.

Then the other cop was standing nearby at an angle and had his walkie-talkie close to his mouth. He was saying something about an ambulance. Carver couldn't understand him or the garbled words coming out of the walkie-talkie. It sounded as if the cop might be underwater. Carver wondered if that could be the problem.

It was possible.

Just as possible as that Red Sea thing in the Bible. Water and miracles seemed to have a lot to do with each other. Wine into water . . .

The hall ceiling tilted and rose up and up, and the pain floated Carver away.

41

"EVERYBODY'S TALKING all at once and about each other," Wicker said to Carver and Beth the next morning on the cottage porch, "and here's how it was." The sea was shooting silver sparks of sunlight in the background and gulls were crying above the rushing whisper of the surf. Wicker leaned with his buttocks against the porch rail, the ocean at his back. Only the palms and backs of his hands were bandaged now, and he was regaining mobility in his fingers. "Dr. Benedict and Adelle Grimm had been having an affair for more than a year. Adelle discovered after her husband's death that she was pregnant."

"With Benedict's child?" Beth asked.

"She had no way of knowing for sure. Benedict was pressuring her to have an abortion. At the same time, she was beginning to suspect to her horror—that's the way she put it—that Benedict might have had some connection with the clinic bombing. Wracked with grief and guilt, in emotional turmoil over Benedict and whether to carry the child to term, she went to Martin Freel to hear from his own lips his denial that Operation Alive was responsible for the bombing. She wanted to try to get a glimpse of the truth, and perhaps to try to find her way to a decision through religion."

"That's when I saw them meet at the Blue Dolphin Motel," Carver said, remembering the intensity of their conversation and how he'd mistaken it for romantic attachment.

"That's right," Wicker said, "and she didn't find the understanding and solace she was seeking. Now we get to Benedict: Adelle had refused to leave her husband for him, and he decided the only way to possess her was to kill Dr. Grimm. Additional incentive was the decreasing profitability of the Women's Light Clinic due to Operation Alive's demonstrations and terror tactics. And Benedict was convinced that soon abortions would be effected through pills, in private, and the clinic would become obsolete. The explosion and ensuing insurance settlement seemed the only way out of the downward financial spiral and would also clear the way for Benedict to be with Adelle. It was Benedict who sent some of the threatening letters to Grimm and to himself, who fired the late-night shot into the clinic, who used Norton as the fall guy. And Benedict hired Ezekiel Masterson to plant the blasting caps in Norton's car and try to scare you off the case so even more blame and suspicion would be focused on Operation Alive. It was Benedict who planted the bomb in Coast Medical Services, in the storage shed so it wouldn't harm anyone, to make it appear that Operation Alive was trying to avert suspicion from Norton."

"So he wasn't the idealist his wife imagined," Carver said, remembering how Benedict had harbored no suspicion that his wife drank. The secrets people kept from each other.

"He was an idealist in love and afraid of how his world was changing," Wicker said. "He's expressed a lot of grief over the death of the patient and the maiming of Delores Bravo at Women's Light, said he only wanted to kill Dr. Grimm but he wasn't knowledgeable enough about explosives and the bomb was more powerful than he intended."

Carver watched a gull soaring in narrowing, ascending circles above the surf. "Then Adelle wasn't involved in the bombing and knew nothing about it."

"That's right," Wicker said. "Dr. Benedict alone planted the bomb in the clinic. He's been charged with the murders of Dr. Grimm and Wanda Creighton. Masterson's been charged with Lapella's murder."

"Is Norton free?"

"Released from custody this morning." Wicker stared down at his bandaged hands and seemed to shiver slightly in the sun. "I talked to his wife. She said Norton was going to plant a bomb in the clinic during the demonstration. That's why he went around behind the building. Then Benedict's bomb exploded, and for a moment Norton thought his own bomb had gone off prematurely and he was going to die. He ran away in a daze, and he and his wife managed to hide the bomb he'd intended to plant."

"Why would she tell you that?" Carver asked.

"It was off the record and without witnesses, so she can always deny the conversation. It's the way these people think. She was boasting."

"He'll try it again," Beth said.

Wicker smiled sadly. "That's what his wife told me. He'll try it again someplace else. I believe her. She seemed proud of him."

Wicker jammed his hands deep into his pockets, tugging his pants low enough for his belt to slide beneath his protruding stomach.

"Now come the lawyers," he said.

"They'll keep coming and take over the world," Carver said.

Wicker smiled and shrugged. "We already have. I meant it was the prosecutors' turn now."

Lawyers and accountants with guns.

Carver and Beth watched Wicker trudge through the fierce sunlight back to his car, his heels dragging on his pants cuffs. Carver was amazed, as he often was, at how the truth had finally spun out. Though it had become a cause célèbre, the clinic bombing and the issue of legal abortion actually had nothing to do with each other.

"It won't be that simple," Beth said.

He looked over at her. "What won't be?"

"The whole abortion rights issue. It's far too complicated to be settled by demonstrations or a bomb, or even a pill that ensures privacy."

Carver figured she was right, thinking of Norton, of what his wife had told Wicker: *He'll try it again someplace else.*

Proud of him.

42

CARVER WAS lying alongside Beth on the big beach towel with the flamingo design on it that afternoon. They'd both been swimming, and he'd gone back to the cottage and returned with sun blocker for Beth and two cans of cold Budweiser. He lay now on his stomach on the towel, listening to the sea and feeling the hot sun on his back while beside him Beth applied the sun blocker to her arms and shoulders. His head was sideways and resting on his arms, but still he saw the shadow on the sand.

He raised his head and tilted it far back, as if he were a turtle. Adelle Grimm was standing over them. She was wearing green slacks and a loose white blouse and holding a white sandal in each hand. She didn't yet look pregnant.

"You're surprised to see me," she said. The sun was behind her, turning her hair into a halo and making it difficult to make out the expression on her face.

"I suppose so," Beth said.

Adelle seemed to be looking at Carver. "I came for . . . I don't really know. Absolution, maybe."

"I'd give it to you if I could," Carver said. What had she done?

Stepped out on her husband. It wasn't an uncommon transgression. She'd had no idea it would mean his death.

But it had. He was dead and now maybe she was pregnant with his child. Somebody's child. Either the husband she'd cheated on or the man who'd murdered him.

"I guess that's really why I went that day to see Martin Freel. For understanding and absolution."

"Maybe you should see him again."

"Are you going to have the baby?" asked Beth, the woman who, because of Adelle's lover, *wasn't* going to have a baby.

"I don't know. I can't decide." The pain in her voice was more burning than the sun.

"You came here for advice," Beth said. "We can't give you any." Carver was surprised by the hardness in her tone, almost a cruelty. "It's your decision. Yours alone. People like Martin Freel don't know it yet, but that's the way it has to be. It's that way for every woman."

Adelle backed up a step, her bare toes digging into the hot sand. She didn't seem to mind the heat, as if the burning of her feet might be some sort of benediction.

"What are you going to do?" Carver asked in a tone kinder than Beth's.

Adelle waited a moment before answering, staring out beyond him at whatever held her eye on the sea. "I'm not sure," she said at last, "but I have to make up my mind soon. I have to get this settled."

She turned and walked away. Carver lay watching her still-slim figure as she climbed the wooden steps from the beach. She bent gracefully to slip her shoes back on, then passed from sight. Beyond her he could see distant storm clouds stacking up for miles in the western sky, blowing in from the Gulf.

He dropped his head and rested it again on his arms. His wristwatch was a hard lump at his temple. Through his ear, through the bones around his ear, he could hear it ticking away time.

F LUTZ

8/96

Lutz, John,

Lightning

9719529

LUDINGTON PUBLIC LIBRARY
BRYN MAWR & LANCASTER AVENUES
BRYN MAWR, PA 19010-3471